Bear Claws

THE IRON HORSE CHRONICLES,
BOOK TWO

BEAR CLAWS

ROBERT LEE MURPHY

FIVE STAR
A part of Gale, Cengage Learning

Farmington Hills, Mich • San Francisco • New York • Waterville, Maine
Meriden, Conn • Mason, Ohio • Chicago

Historical notes can be found at the back of the book.
Five Star™ Publishing, a part of Cengage Learning, Inc.

LIBRARY OF CONGRESS CATALOGING-IN-PUBLICATION DATA

Murphy, Robert Lee.
Bear claws / Robert Lee Murphy. — First edition.
pages ; cm — (The Iron Horse Chronicles ; Book 2)
ISBN 978-1-4328-3048-9 (hardcover) — ISBN 1-4328-3048-1 (hardcover) — ISBN 978-1-4328-3044-1 (ebook) — ISBN 1-4328-3044-9 (ebook)
1. Orphans—Fiction. 2. Union Pacific Railroad Company—Fiction. 3. West (U.S.)—History—19th century—Fiction. I. Title.
PS3613.U7543B43 2015
813'.6—dc23 2015022034

First Edition. First Printing: November 2015
Find us on Facebook– https://www.facebook.com/FiveStarCengage
Visit our website– http://www.gale.cengage.com/fivestar/
Contact Five Star™ Publishing at FiveStar@cengage.com

Printed in the United States of America
1 2 3 4 5 6 7 19 18 17 16 15

Bear Claws

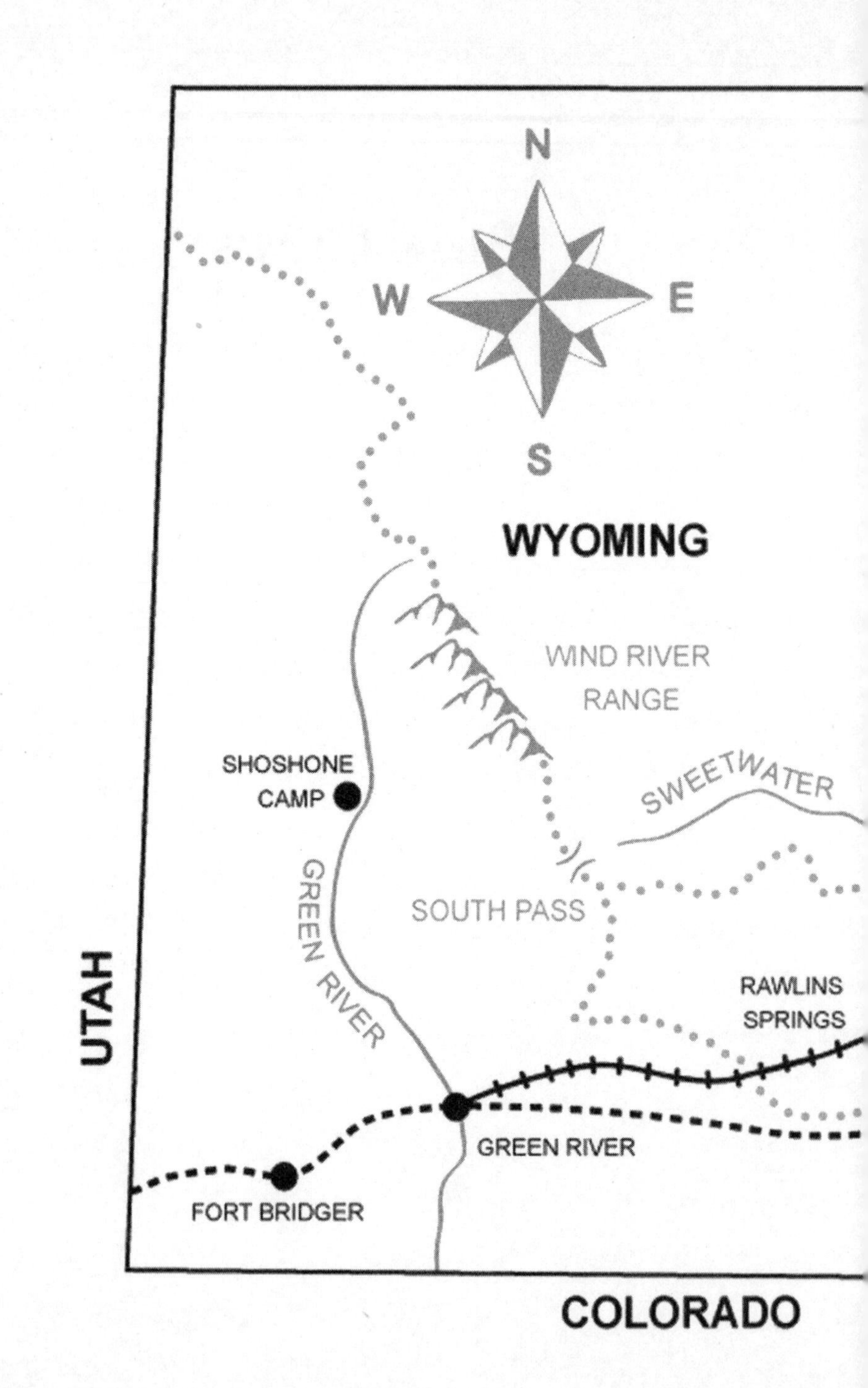
N
W
E
S
WYOMING
WIND RIVER RANGE
SHOSHONE CAMP
SWEETWATER
GREEN RIVER
SOUTH PASS
RAWLINS SPRINGS
UTAH
GREEN RIVER
FORT BRIDGER
COLORADO

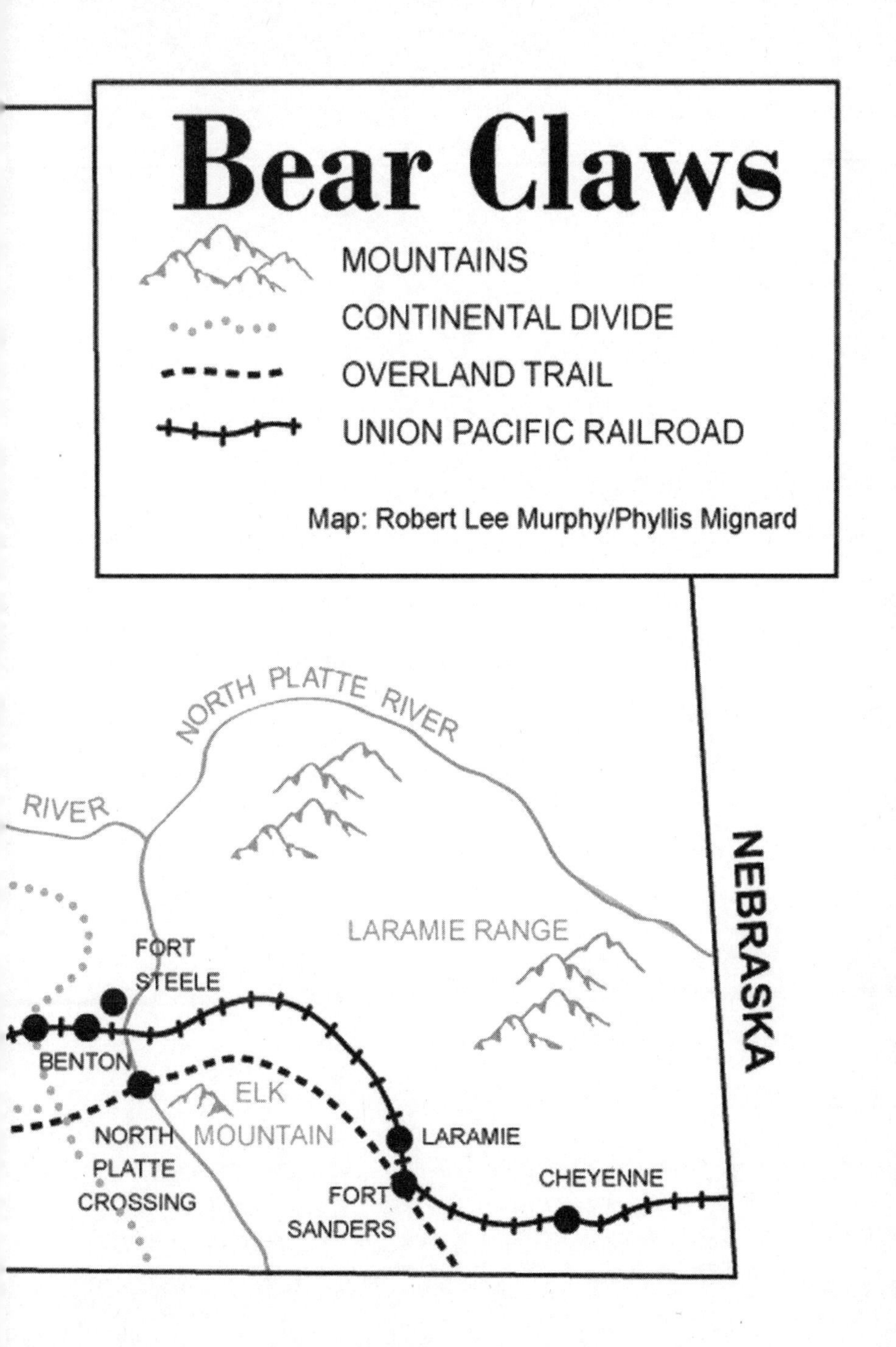

Bear Claws
MOUNTAINS
CONTINENTAL DIVIDE
OVERLAND TRAIL
UNION PACIFIC RAILROAD
Map: Robert Lee Murphy/Phyllis Mignard
NORTH PLATTE RIVER
RIVER
LARAMIE RANGE
NEBRASKA
FORT STEELE
BENTON
ELK MOUNTAIN
NORTH PLATTE CROSSING
LARAMIE
FORT SANDERS
CHEYENNE

For Lauren Elizabeth Murphy and Shauna Anastasia Tiller

ACKNOWLEDGMENTS

I sincerely appreciate the constructive criticisms offered by fellow members of SCBWI Word Worms and Sun City Anthem Authors. The enthusiastic support from both critique groups kept me writing, and their suggestions for improvement and clarification resulted in a better story. I'm especially grateful to Word Worms' member Phyllis Mignard for taking my rough sketches and turning them into publishable maps. Thanks again to the staff of the Henderson, Nevada, Public Library system for obtaining books through interlibrary loan that facilitated my research. Hazel Rumney, Editorial Evaluation and Developmental Coordinator at Five Star Publishing, provided her usual expert advice throughout the editorial process. Marcia LaBrenz provided the copyedit of the book. Thanks to Mary Ann Unger, current president of Anthem Authors, for taking the photo of me that is used on the dust jacket. The staff at the California State Railroad Museum answered my questions about cabooses—they were not in use by the Central Pacific during the time period covered by this book. Lastly, I thank my wife, Barbara, for granting me the freedom to leave her at home on various occasions while I explored the Central Pacific's portion of the first transcontinental railroad between Sacramento, California, and Promontory Summit, Utah. Those journeys, coupled with an earlier trip she made with me over the Union Pacific's route from Council Bluffs, Iowa, to Promontory Summit, plus additional travel by myself across Wyoming, enabled me to place Will Braddock and the characters of *Bear Claws* in realistic settings. I walked the ground where they walk in the book.

Chapter 1

"Why hasn't he come back?" Will Braddock held the flap of the tent open and peered out into the snow, which continued to fall into its seventh day. In his almost fifteen years, Will couldn't remember such an extended period of nonstop snowing.

The shadowy figures of their horses and Ruby the mule, sheltering beneath the overhanging cliff bank, were all that broke the whiteout expanse before him. Buck's coal-black coat made the Morgan stand out more than the other animals.

"Your Uncle Sean will get here as soon as he can." Homer Garcon coughed harshly. The middle-aged Negro had recovered from the worst effects of the strange illness that'd struck the members of Sean Corcoran's survey inspection team a week earlier, but his raspy voice indicated he was not completely well.

"Homer, when he left, he said he'd be back in two days . . . three at the most. That was a week ago."

"We just has to give him more time. Now close the flap, Will. You'se letting out what heat we got in this flimsy tent."

Will dropped the flap and looked at Homer, who sat with his head in his hands near the back of the Army wall tent. The team members preferred to sleep under the stars—but they were fortunate their leader had insisted they carry the tent. The canvas walls gave some protection against the unseasonably late snowstorm that assailed them. Tall enough for a man to stand in the center, the tent's sides rose only waist high. Its narrow interior provided enough sleeping space for the five team members.

Otto Hirsch and Joe Quinn lay wrapped in their blankets along opposite sides of the tent. Normally, they were robust surveyors, with boundless energy, trekking across the wild country through which the transcontinental railroad was being built. Otto and Joe were the chainmen, moving ahead of his Uncle Sean's transit to mark and measure the distance and elevation as the team surveyed a route. Homer served as the team's cook and Will was officially his helper—with the added duty of hunting to provide fresh meat. Will had earned his spot on the team the year before because he'd proven to be a crack shot.

Homer dragged himself outside twice a day, morning and evening, to brew a pot of coffee and prepare a meager meal under a fly attached to the side of the tent. Will would scrounge the only available firewood from scrawny bushes that grew in the vicinity of the small spring that emerged from the cliff face. He'd feed the smaller, leafless twigs to the animals and kindle a cook fire from the larger branches, using his flint and steel. But, now they were running out of food.

"Homer, look at them." Will gestured to the sick men, one on each side of the tent. "They're not going to get well on what we have left to feed them. Even as good a cook as you can't make decent soup out of jerky and hardtack. We need meat . . . and bone marrow."

Homer raised his head and stared at Will with vacant eyes. "Maybe we has to kill one of the horses . . . or Ruby."

"No!" Will shook his head. "We can't do that. We'll need all of the horses to get out of here when the storm lets up. And no way will I butcher your mule."

Only Will had recovered from the illness that'd floored everyone except his uncle. Whatever the ailment was, they'd probably contracted it from a sickly band of Ute Indians who'd wandered into their camp several days ago begging for food. Will had felt sorry for the women and children, their noses red and swollen, but the team didn't have much food left and had sent them away with only scraps.

After seeing the destitute Utes, Will had wondered if his mixed-blood friend Lone Eagle, and the band of Cheyenne to which he belonged, had managed to slaughter enough buffalo to feed themselves through the winter. Will had saved the son of old mountain man Bullfrog Charlie Munro from drowning in quicksand last summer and, in appreciation, Lone Eagle had given Will two eagle talons from his personal amulet. Later, one of those talons had deflected an arrow that could have ended Will's life. He now bore a nasty scar in his left arm where the arrow had passed through the bicep. The wound ached in this bone-chilling weather.

Will wore one of the talons on a horsehair thong around his neck. Whenever he felt it scratch against his chest he thought about Jenny McNabb, the feisty young lady who'd captured his fancy the year before. He'd given her one of the talons, in the hopes it would bring her luck. When her family's wagon had been attacked by the Cheyenne, Lone Eagle had recognized the talon and spared her life.

But where was Jenny now? When he'd ridden out of Fort Sanders on the Laramie River last fall, Will had promised her they'd meet again this spring. Did she still work at Wells Fargo's Big Laramie Station?

Will had spent the closing months of 1867 helping his uncle's team perform surveys in western Wyoming, until cold weather had forced them to hole up at Fort Bridger. It'd been boring waiting through the winter in the small outpost near the Utah border. His uncle had been anxious to get his team back in the field and in early March 1868 he'd decided to start.

Since then, the team had worked its way east, across central Wyoming, heading for Fort Sanders at the base of the Laramie Mountains, where they hoped to receive their next assignment from General Grenville Dodge, the Union Pacific's chief engineer. But now, here they were snowbound at Rawlins Springs, a couple of miles east of the Continental Divide.

Last fall, his uncle's team, accompanied by General Dodge and General John Rawlins, had discovered this vital spring. Rawlins had pronounced the water so refreshing that he'd told Dodge if any spot were to bear his name, he'd want it to be this. Dodge obliged him and wrote Rawlins Springs on the map. When Rawlins returned to his duties as Ulysses S. Grant's chief of staff in Washington, D.C., he'd given his horse, Bucephalus, to Will. Everyone called the big, black Morgan "Buck."

When the snowstorm hit, the team had been a few miles west of the eastern rim of the Continental Divide, which surprisingly occurs twice in central Wyoming. Parallel divides enclose the Red Desert, one hundred miles wide between its eastern ridge and its western one. From the eastern divide waters flow to the Atlantic Ocean. From the western one they flow to the Pacific. In between, the desert is devoid of trees and home to little wildlife. What water flows into the center of the Great Basin either evaporates or sinks into the earth.

Then the illness struck. One by one the men complained of aches and fevers while they struggled through the snow. The horses could no longer wade through the deepening drifts bearing riders, and Otto, Joe, and Homer had trouble stumbling along on foot. They'd finally managed to reach the sheltering ledge at Rawlins Springs.

His Uncle Sean was the only one who'd escaped the fevers and chills. He helped the team set up camp and left Will, the least sick, to tend the others. His uncle had ridden south to intersect the Overland Trail at Bridger's Pass Station, fifteen miles away. There, he hoped to buy food, and perhaps medicine, at the Wells Fargo stage station.

"Homer," Will said. "We have to have food. Something's happened to Uncle Sean. I just know it. He's stuck out there in this storm and can't get back. I have to get us an antelope . . . or maybe an elk."

"I don't think that's such a good idea, Will. What'll your uncle think if he shows up and you'se gone?"

"That's just it. *If* Uncle Sean shows up." Will looked again at Otto and Joe. "I'm going out to hunt."

Chapter 2

"Now how's you gonna know where you're going in this snow?" Homer asked.

"Following the survey stakes. They'll lead me to the North Platte. The river's only fifteen miles east of here."

"Why not go south to the Overland Trail, like your uncle done? Stagecoach comes through there regular like."

"No stagecoach is going to get through this storm. Besides, it's barren country between here and Bridger's Pass. There's no water that direction. The North Platte is where I'll find game. Antelope and elk need water. They'll stay close to the river . . . especially in the winter. So that's where I'm going."

Otto sat up and leaned against the side of the tent. His blanket slipped off his shoulders. "Will," he croaked. He coughed hard to clear his throat. "If you're set on going out in this storm, take these snowshoes."

He held out two strange-looking contraptions. Each slender, wooden bow curved tightly back upon itself in a large oblong arc with the ends lashed together in a tail. The lopsided circle formed by the wood was interlaced with a webbing of leather thongs.

"I've never used them before," Will said.

"We used snowshoes in the old country all the time," Otto said. "I've used them a few times out here. I've even seen the Indians use them."

"Why didn't Uncle Sean take them?"

"When he left, he could still ride a horse through the light snowfall. That's not going to be possible now. Snowshoes are a little hard to walk in at first, but you'll be able to travel pretty fast through the drifts once you get the hang of it."

"I'll try them." Will wanted all the speed he could muster to get to the river and return with his kill. The men's lives might depend on it.

Otto lay back and pulled his blanket up beneath his chin. His face looked flushed and he shivered constantly.

"Homer," Will said. "If it's all right, I'll take Ruby. She's taller than any of the horses. Her longer legs will let her plow through the snow better . . . and she's used to doing pack duty."

"Sure thing."

"Along the river, I'll gather some brush to bring to the horses. They haven't eaten much in days."

"That'd be good. And, if you find a willow bush, peel some bark off and bring it back for the fellows to chew on. Might help lower their fevers."

"Good idea."

Will checked the loads in the six chambers of his Colt revolver, reseated the percussion caps, returned the pistol to his holster, and snapped the flap closed. He raised the flaps on the two belt pouches he wore to be sure he had extra percussion caps and additional revolver bullets. He checked the magazine in the butt of his Spencer carbine and confirmed it was fully loaded with seven shells, but didn't chamber a round. He rolled the carbine and a spare magazine in his blanket and tied the bundle with a cord.

"Don't you want to take more carbine ammo?" Homer asked.

"I've got fourteen shots with the carbine. If I can't hit something with fourteen, I'm not qualified to be the hunter for this team."

"What if you run into Injuns?"

"There won't be any Indians out in this weather."

Will turned the collar up on his heavy coat, buttoned it around his neck, and draped a pair of mittens secured with a leather thong around his shoulders. He pulled on his old, black slouch hat, which had once belonged to his father, and draped a bandana atop the hat's crown, pulling it down over his ears and tying the cloth beneath his chin.

He gathered up the blanket roll and the snowshoes, then paused. "I won't be gone long, Homer. I expect to make the river by nightfall, bag an antelope or elk, and be back by sundown tomorrow."

He stepped through the flap entrance, dropped it back into place, and waded through the knee-deep snow to the horses and the mule. Here, where they'd pitched the tent and tied the animals beneath an overhanging cliff, the snow drifting had been minimal. The wind whistling off the top of the bank blew most of the snow straight overhead and beyond their camp.

The black Morgan gelding whickered. Will rubbed the large white star blazed on the horse's forehead. "No, Buck, you can't come this trip." The horse whinnied and shook his head, dislodging snow from his mane.

Will brushed the snow off Buck's back and tightened the strap that held the saddle blanket in place. He kept a blanket on each of the animals to provide them some warmth and protection.

"Ruby, you, on the other hand, are coming with me." He shoved the snow off the big mule. "I'm not going to ride you. You'll need to conserve your strength for later."

Hee-haw. Ruby brayed a protest.

"Sorry. Homer gave his permission."

Will dropped the snowshoes and the blanket roll beside Ruby. He lifted the mule's packsaddle onto her back. "No load to tote now." He tightened the cinch. "But on the way back, I expect to have you heavily burdened."

Will lashed the blanket roll containing the carbine and extra magazine onto the packsaddle. He stepped into the center of one of the snowshoes, knelt, and fastened the straps around his boot. He fastened the other snowshoe, rose, and untied the mule from her picket pin.

He gathered up Ruby's halter rope, but when he turned to lead her away he stepped on the left snowshoe with the right one and fell facedown in the snow.

Hee-haw. Ruby stood over Will and laughed.

"Not funny, mule."

Chapter 3

Will stepped on one snowshoe with the other a couple of times until he figured out he had to keep his feet farther apart. Otto was right. It was awkward and took some practice, but he could walk on the surface of the snow without sinking deep into the powder. Ruby, on the other hand, was almost up to her belly in the drifts. The mule snorted and blew, struggling to lift a leg and move it forward.

Ruby wasn't going to last much longer through the deep snow. The railroad survey stakes followed the course of Sugar Creek from Rawlins Springs for about five miles. When the creek took a turn to the north, the stakes continued due east along a ridgeline. The drifts weren't as deep on this elevated ground as they'd been along the creek. Here Ruby only sank to her hocks.

About midafternoon the snow stopped falling. The temperature had stayed well below freezing for days. Maybe the storm was finally playing out. Sunbeams streaked through gaps in an overcast sky. The warm rays caressing his shoulders felt good. The ache from the old arrow wound diminished.

He estimated he was making two miles an hour trudging on the snowshoes. His normal walk could cover solid ground at three to four miles an hour. But his slogging through the snow, plus Ruby's struggling, made for harder going. With each breath he took he dragged ice-cold air into his lungs. White mist appeared in the air before him with each exhalation. Still, he perspired in his heavy coat. He unfastened the top two buttons.

A couple of hours later, Ruby nudged him in the back of the arm with her muzzle and snorted. Will could hear her labored breathing and, when he looked back, a cloud of steam obscured her nostrils.

"Yeah, I agree. We've been doing this for a long time."

The sun was well down over his back now. They'd been walking since early morning, and even at his slow two-mile-an-hour pace, he thought they should be nearing the North Platte River.

"Come on, girl. Just a little farther." He pulled on the halter rope, and the mule fell in behind him.

A couple hundred steps later he stopped. There it was. Stretched out before him, the tops of a line of cottonwood trees poked above the white expanse. Their leafless limbs exhibited a dirty brown line across the horizon.

"We're here, Ruby."

From where Will stood, the North Platte flowed far to the north in a hundred-and-fifty-mile loop, before swinging southeast to hook up with the South Platte in western Nebraska.

After a few more paces, Will stood looking down at the river. Cottonwoods lined the banks on both sides, the fifty-foot trees extending their barren limbs above the level of the plain on either side. Fingers of ice splayed out from the river's edge, reaching into the center of the rapidly flowing, hundred-foot-wide stream. Now that the snow had stopped falling, the nighttime temperatures would plummet, and the river would freeze over completely.

Will looked north, studying the course of the winding river. A cold breeze caressed his nose and cheeks—not strong enough to sway the trees or dislodge their coatings of snow.

By traveling due east as he had, Will reckoned he'd reached the river ten or twelve miles north of where the Overland Trail crossed it at North Platte Crossing. Perhaps he should follow the river south, where he might hook up with a stagecoach. Maybe he could find his uncle and help him get food back to the camp. Bullfrog Charlie Munro's cabin would be someplace between here and the river crossing. That was another possibility.

A flicker of movement under the cottonwoods along the bank caught his eye. A hundred yards away, an antelope buck flicked his white tail. Was he signaling other members of his band? Were there females nearby? Will wanted that buck. That's why he'd come here in the first place.

"Quiet, Ruby," he whispered. He led the mule down the slope a few yards to a large tree and looped her halter rope around a branch. He slipped his hands out of his mittens and untied his carbine from the packsaddle. The buck stood unmoving, looking in the opposite direction. The north wind blew Will's and Ruby's scents away from the antelope.

The shot would be a long one from here, but the carbine's .52-caliber, metallic, rimfire cartridge provided an effective range of five-hundred yards, under ideal conditions. He must remember to aim low, since the Spencer had a tendency to fire high. But he didn't have a shell in the chamber. He'd packed the carbine unloaded for safety. If Ruby had fallen in the snow and the weapon had discharged accidentally, the shot might've killed the mule. He would have to lever a round into the chamber before he could shoot.

He took a deep breath and pointed the carbine toward the antelope. He tried to ease the trigger guard lever down and back up to chamber the round, but a deafening click filled the silence around him.

The buck had heard the sharp noise and bounded away.

"Dang it!" Will muttered. "Sorry, Mama." His mother, God rest her soul, had always chastised him for cussing. He tried to remember not to, but sometimes the curse slipped out.

"Ruby, you stay here. I'm going after that buck." Why he thought it did any good to tell the mule to stay where he'd tied her, he didn't know. Nobody else to talk to he supposed.

Will struggled down the slope on the snowshoes. Perhaps he should take them off. But the snow was deep and he'd probably bog down without them. He just needed to tread carefully.

He reached the spot where the buck had stood. Tracks led a few paces down to the river's edge and then turned south. Will trudged along the bank, easily following the trail the antelope left in the snow.

Hee-haw! Ruby brayed loudly.

Will looked back up the slope over his shoulder. The buck stood frozen not far from where he'd tied Ruby. The antelope had circled back and surprised itself by coming face to face with the mule.

Will swung around to get into position to fire, and in so doing stepped on the right snowshoe with the left one. He stumbled and slid backward down the sloping riverbank. He threw his arms up, in an attempt to regain his balance, and struck an overhanging branch with the barrel of the carbine. His finger jerked on the trigger. The weapon discharged with a loud bang.

The force of the recoil tumbled him farther down the slippery slope. The snowshoes tangled in the underbrush and ripped from his boots. He landed on his back on the ice along the river's edge.

A cracking sound exploded beneath him. His weight broke the fragile ice. He dropped the carbine and sank.

Wow! That was cold.

His back side bumped on the bottom of the stream, as his body submerged. He got his legs under him and stood up. Fortunately, the river was only waist deep near the bank. But he had to get out of the freezing water—fast!

He grabbed an overhanging cottonwood limb and pulled. The brittle branch broke off, and he fell back into the water.

Once more he stood and stepped toward the bank.

A dull snap from beneath the water's surface surprised him.

Oh no! An excruciating pain, far worse than the cold, engulfed his ankle.

He'd stepped into a beaver trap.

CHAPTER 4

Jenny McNabb entered the Wells Fargo station, closed the door behind her, and brushed a light dusting of snow from her shawl. She removed her old bonnet, shook off more snow, and hung it on a peg beside the entrance. "Papa, I think it's letting up. I can see patches of blue through breaks in the clouds."

"That'd be good. Maybe we can get a stage headed west before the day's over."

Alistair McNabb had been hired the preceding fall by Wells Fargo to manage their home station at Laramie. It'd been a godsend for what remained of the McNabb family. They'd buried Jenny's mother last summer at Virginia Dale, Colorado, and after they'd moved on in their covered wagon on the Overland Trail, they'd been attacked by Cheyenne Indians. Jenny had been kidnapped and spent several days in captivity before Will Braddock, with the help of Lone Eagle, rescued her. When she was reunited with her father and younger brother, Duncan, she'd learned her older sister, Elspeth, had gone to work for Mort Kavanagh as a dance hall girl in his Lucky Dollar Saloon in the Hell on Wheels town of Cheyenne.

Jenny worked as the station's cook, preparing meals she sold to the stagecoach passengers for a dollar and fifty cents. Meals were available only at what Wells Fargo designated as "home" stations, located about fifty miles apart. At intervals of ten to fifteen miles between the home stations, "change" stations provided a place where fresh horses were hitched to the coach after a six-horse team had run as far as they could go. Passenger amenities weren't provided at the change stations.

The fourteen-year-old girl had gained a reputation for serving the best meals between Julesburg, Colorado, and Salt Lake City. Drivers and shotgun messengers were replaced at each home station with a new crew. The incoming crew took a few hours' rest before their next run. When laying over at Big Laramie Station, the resting crew looked forward to one of Jenny's meals.

Jenny's father, a former Confederate cavalry officer, had lost his left arm at the Battle of Yellow Tavern. Even with one arm, he still did the work of two men. Her nine-year-old brother helped her father and the two stock tenders water, feed, and groom the two dozen horses they stabled. Duncan particularly liked assisting the drivers in changing the teams each time a stagecoach passed through. When he wasn't busy with the stock, he practiced Morse code. One of the stock tenders doubled as the home station's official telegrapher, but Duncan was determined to learn.

This latest snowstorm had brought all stage travel to a halt. Coaches heading west could get no farther than Big Laramie Station, and no stages had reached that point from the west for a week. Mail bags destined for Utah and California continued to accumulate. It was hard to walk through the place without stumbling over a mail bag—or a smelly passenger, for that matter. A dozen passengers had stayed, but many had given up and gone back east. Those who remained took turns sleeping in the few beds the station offered, often double bunking. A pungent odor permeated the small building.

The station's door flew open and Sean Corcoran stepped inside. "Well, Alistair," he said, "what do you think? This storm finally blowing itself out?"

"I hope so. We've got passengers and mail that have to move

west, and I know you're anxious to go."

"Are you feeling well enough to travel, Mr. Corcoran?" Jenny asked.

"Yes, thanks to you."

"I think Fort Sanders' doctor had more to do with your getting well than I did."

"Well, he helped, I'm sure . . . but it was your care that really did it." Corcoran had arrived a week ago on the last stage to make it through to Laramie from the home station at North Platte Crossing before the blizzard had shut down operations.

Jenny recalled that day, when driver Butch Cartwright had shouted for help before the coach rolled to a stop. "Hey, McNabb!" The driver had a peculiar, high-pitched, scratchy voice that carried a long distance.

Jenny's father had stepped outside at the call. "What is it, Butch?"

"Got a very sick man inside. Says his name's Corcoran, Sean Corcoran. Claims to be a railroad surveyor."

Jenny recognized the name immediately. She'd never met him, but she knew he was Will Braddock's uncle. She helped her father get the man out of the coach and into the station. He shivered uncontrollably, yet burned with fever.

"Mr. Corcoran?" Jenny had tried to get his attention. "Mr. Corcoran, what happened?"

He mumbled something, but he was incoherent, almost delirious.

They laid him on one of the beds and piled on blankets. She set to work making broth and tea while her brother rode for Fort Sanders' doctor, five miles away.

The Army doctor knew the sick man and confirmed he was indeed Sean Corcoran. He examined the patient and left medicine for Jenny to administer. Jenny insisted Corcoran be left at the station under her care, rather than be moved to the fort's infirmary.

Shortly after the doctor had returned to the fort, Lieutenant Luigi Moretti arrived. Moretti told Jenny he had served with Corcoran during the recent war and wanted to check on his friend. Jenny had met Luey, as most people called him, the preceding fall—the day Will had brought her to Fort Sanders after he'd rescued her from captivity by the Cheyenne.

"Luey, why do you suppose he turned up here?" Jenny asked.

"Don't know." The Italian-born officer pulled on the ends of his waxed mustache to straighten them. "Wonder where the other members of his team are."

Jenny stared at Moretti. Will was part of Corcoran's team. Where was he? What had happened? She placed her hand over the eagle talon she wore beneath her dress and felt its scratch against her skin. It'd taken Jenny three days to get Sean Corcoran back on his feet. During that time, she learned he'd left his team in Will's care when he'd gone to seek help. Corcoran thought he'd escaped the strange illness that'd felled his team members, but shortly after reaching Bridger's Pass on the Overland Trail he felt the symptoms.

Corcoran had told Jenny he'd been disappointed to learn neither food nor medicine were available at the Bridger's Pass change station. Even though he was feeling the onset of the illness, Corcoran made the decision to proceed east to North Platte Crossing in the hopes the larger home station would have provisions to spare. When he got there, he was too ill to stand. The station manager had decided to send him on to the closest doctor, who was at Fort Sanders.

That had been seven days ago.

"Listen up, folks." Jenny's father stood in the center of the room and addressed the passengers. "The storm's let up enough that we'll send a coach out this afternoon."

Applause and cheers greeted his announcement.

"Don't have enough room for all of you, so we'll board you in the order you arrived here. With the exception that I'm placing Mr. Corcoran on this coach. He's got a team of sick surveyors that have been snowbound out there for a week. They are in desperate need of food and medicine."

Jenny and Duncan helped Butch Cartwright harness the teams and pack the coach with mail bags. The passengers would have to sit atop them, but Jenny's father wanted to get as many people and as much mail as he could moving west.

Corcoran tied two horses to the rear of the coach—his saddle horse wore a McClellan saddle, the pack horse bore a load of provisions. He planned to take the stage as far as Bridger's Pass where he would leave the coach for the cross-country ride back to Rawlins Springs.

"Jenny," Corcoran said, "it was a pleasure to meet you. I know why Will was determined to rescue you last fall. You're a special young lady. Thank you for nursing me back to health."

"You're welcome. Please give my best to Will."

"I'll do that." He climbed into the coach.

Butch snapped the reins. "Giddup!" The coach lurched on its thoroughbraces and rumbled away.

Jenny caressed her eagle talon. Was Will still alive out there?

Chapter 5

Paddy O'Hannigan walked across the hard-packed dirt floor of the large circus-style tent that enclosed the main dance floor and gaming tables of the Lucky Dollar Saloon. At midday, the piano was silent and no dance hall girls circulated among the empty tables. Only Randy Tremble, the bartender, was at work wiping the top of the long wooden bar that extended the length of one side of the tent. Randy didn't look up. That was all right with Paddy. He didn't have anything to say to the heavyset, bearded, ruffian who doubled as a bouncer.

Paddy stepped up onto the narrow wooden floor of the false-fronted saloon and knocked on the door of Mortimer Kavanagh's corner office.

"What is it?" Kavanagh's gruff voice called from within.

"Paddy, Mort."

"Come in."

Paddy entered the small office and removed his bowler hat. "Well, and they're gone, Mort."

"What do you mean, they're gone?"

"Sure, and Chief Tall Bear's camp ain't there no more."

"Where did they go?"

"Now how would I be knowing that? They didn't leave no painted sign telling me where they'd gone."

"Don't get smart with me, Paddy O'Hannigan." Mort leaned back in his swivel chair and cradled the back of his head in his interlaced fingers. "You're lucky I still keep you around."

Outwardly Paddy remained calm—internally he seethed. When his temper rose, his scars itched. With his left hand he caressed the older scar that ran down his left cheek. With his right hand he rubbed his left chest muscle where his shirt concealed the newer scar, the one inflicted on him last year by Will Braddock's knife stab.

The sixteen-year-old wasn't sure how much more abuse he could take from his godfather. Kavanagh was his mother's cousin, and after Paddy's father had been killed by Major Sean Corcoran during the New York draft riots of 1863, Mort had agreed to take his godson under his wing. It was Corcoran's saber that'd sliced Paddy's cheek open when he'd stepped in to defend his father.

But Paddy hadn't found a way yet to break away from Kavanagh. He needed the money he earned at the Lucky Dollar Saloon to support his mother and younger sister in Brooklyn, where they struggled as laundresses.

"Sit down," Kavanagh said. "Tell me what you actually found out there."

"Well, d'ye see, there's nothing left of that Cheyenne camp, to be sure." Paddy dropped into a chair in front of Kavanagh's desk, pulled his Bowie knife from his boot top, and sliced a chaw off a twist of tobacco he pulled from his vest pocket. "Sure, and I didn't find any tracks leading away. Snow's too deep, don't ye know, to reveal much. Them Injuns must've skedaddled outta there before this storm struck. That's the best I make of it."

"The railroad's what caused it," Kavanagh said.

"Well, now, how d'ye figure the railroad done it?"

"Buffalo don't like crossing the iron rails. Those Cheyenne had to move to find buffalo, since the herd won't come to them now."

"Hmm." Paddy spat a stream of tobacco juice at a spittoon

sitting beside the corner of the desk. "And what will ye be doing now to slow construction?" Paddy knew that the longer it took the railroad to move the tracks west, the more opportunity the so-called mayor of Hell on Wheels had to sell whiskey to the workers.

"That band of Cheyenne did a good job scaring the pants off the railroad last year. The track layers had to keep one eye peeled all the time, never knowing when they'd be attacked."

Kavanagh bit the end off a cigar and spat it into a wastebasket, then lit the cigar with a lucifer match. "The Sioux are still attacking the line between here and the Platte River, but I've got to come up with another scheme once the railroad moves west of Laramie."

"Well now, what is it ye'll be wanting me to do?" Paddy asked.

Kavanagh blew a smoke ring across his desk. "Right now I've got to get ready to move out of Cheyenne. It's just a matter of days until the UP finishes laying track over Sherman Summit and heads down to Laramie. I want to be there ahead of them."

Paddy spat another stream at the spittoon, wiped a dangling string of tobacco from his lip, and waited for Kavanagh's instructions. When Hell on Wheels moved to Laramie he'd be closer to Sean Corcoran. He knew the surveyor and his team were working out ahead of the track layers. If there was one thing Paddy wanted to do even more than get away from Kavanagh, it was revenge on Corcoran—and Homer Garcon, the former nigger slave—not to mention Corcoran's nephew, Will Braddock. Yes, Corcoran, Garcon, and Braddock had been the cause of a lot of grief for Paddy, and he intended to even the score.

"Get out of here for now," Kavanagh said. "Don't go far. I'll let you know when I need you."

Paddy nodded. "Sure, and I'll be around."

When Paddy opened the office door he confronted Sally

Whitworth and Elspeth McNabb.

"Ah, now, darlin's, what a lovely sight ye be. 'Tis nice of ye to come to greet me."

"Get out of the way, you slimy Mick," Sally said. The pretty redhead had been Kavanagh's favorite for as long as Paddy had been working at the Lucky Dollar. He wondered if Sally was aware Mort might replace her in that spot with Elspeth. He'd seen the lovely blonde secretly caress Mort when she didn't think anyone was looking.

Chapter 6

Will's teeth chattered. He'd never known what cold was before. If goose bumps could have goose bumps, he was sure his had them. The flow of the North Platte bumped chunks of ice against him. His hat had stayed on because he'd tied the bandana around it to keep his ears warm, but he'd dropped his carbine into the river.

"Will. You hear me, Will?"

It took a moment for Will to realize that someone was standing on the bank looking down at him. "Y . . . yes," he stammered.

Bullfrog Charlie Munro, the old mountain man, extended a hand to him. "Come on. You gotta get out of the river."

Will shook his head. His lips trembled. "Can't . . . leg . . . trap."

"Leg? Trap?"

"Umm-hmm."

"Yer leg's caught in a trap?"

Will nodded.

"Hold on there." Bullfrog stepped into the river in front of Will. He slid down into the water, up to his neck. Will heard the old man's labored breathing as he struggled against the cold. He felt Bullfrog's hands search down his legs.

"Agh!" He winced when Bullfrog's hand hit the top of the trap that clamped his ankle. Then Bullfrog inserted his thumbs between Will's leg and the jaws and pried them apart. The pain eased.

"Put yer hands on my shoulders, Will. Lift yer leg outta there while I hold it open."

Will lifted his leg clear of the trap. He heard a muffled snap when Bullfrog let go of the jaws. The mountain man wrapped his arms around Will's waist and hauled him up onto the bank.

"Let's take a look at that leg."

Will lay on the bank shivering while Bullfrog examined him. The mountain man's slouch hat covered thick white hair that flowed over his shoulders. His full mustache obscured his mouth, making it impossible to see his lips move when he spoke. His beard reminded Will of a picture he'd seen once of the Prophet Moses.

"Yer boot took most of the blow. Can't tell if the jaws' teeth broke the skin, or not. But I don't wanna take yer boot off out here. Got to get you to the cabin."

"Ruby." Will pointed up the slope.

"Yer mule?"

Will nodded.

"Yeah, I see her. Heard her first. Right after I heard a shot, she started braying like she was trying to send a signal. I figured it weren't no Indian. So I come a looking."

Will could see Bullfrog shivering. "You're wet and cold, too," Will said.

"Yep. That's for sure. I'm gonna rig up a travois for Ruby to drag you upriver a piece to my cabin. I got an old raft I use to cross the river there. Cabin's on the other side."

Bullfrog drew a large knife from his belt and attacked a nearby sapling. "Ruby'll get wet though. She'll have to swim. But it ain't too wide there."

The sun had set by the time Bullfrog got Will to the cabin. The mountain man untied the travois and lowered the two poles that comprised the sled's sides onto the ground behind Ruby. From flat on his back, Will watched Bullfrog lead Ruby into a lean-to stable attached to the cabin, tie the mule alongside two horses, and kick some fodder in front of her.

Bullfrog helped Will rise from the travois and hop into the cabin, where he assisted Will out of his wet clothes and boots. Before changing into dry clothes himself, the old man cleaned Will's ankle, applied a poultice that smelled strongly of sage, and wrapped the wound with a bandage.

A fire blazing in a rock fireplace warmed the one-room home of the mountain man. Bullfrog draped their wet garments over three-legged stools in front of the hearth and upended their boots over stakes he drove into the dirt floor near the fire.

Will huddled under a buffalo robe on a cot. He'd almost stopped shivering. He watched Bullfrog hang a kettle on an iron hook suspended from a bar that spanned the fireplace opening.

"This here stew'll be hot right soon." The old man looked back at Will. "It'll get yer insides warmed up."

Will held up the eagle talon he wore suspended around his neck on a leather thong. "Bullfrog, I think Lone Eagle's talon brought you to my aid."

"Well, maybe . . . maybe not. But it didn't keep you from stepping in that old trap. Sorry 'bout that. I forgot where it was. I always marked 'em with a stake, so I could go back and find 'em . . . but that stake must've got knocked over somehow. With the beaver all gone from these parts, I don't keep traps set no more. I reckon that ole trap's been there for years."

Bullfrog spooned stew from the kettle into a wooden bowl and brought it and a carved bone spoon to Will. "Sit up there a spell so's you can eat this. Swing that leg out from under that robe, and let me have a look at it."

Bullfrog unwrapped the bandage and inspected the puncture wounds on either side of the ankle where the trap's teeth had penetrated the skin. "I'm gonna replace that poultice with a fresh one. Ground up sage works wonders getting the swelling down. Star Dancer, she was Long Eagle's mom, taught me that old Indian trick."

Bullfrog replaced the poultice and bandage while Will ate.

"How's that antelope stew?"

"Good." Will set the empty bowl on the cot beside him and wiped his mouth with the back of his hand.

Bullfrog handed Will a strip of bark. "Chew on this. Something about willow bark helps a body heal. Let's see if you can stand on that leg."

Will pushed himself up from the edge of the cot. "Ow!" He immediately took the weight off his left leg.

"I'll whittle you a crutch. Reckon it'll be a spell afore you'll be walking regular like. If yer boots hadn't been sturdy, that trap would've cut a lot deeper . . . maybe even broke the bone."

Bullfrog reached up to a peg on the wall behind him and retrieved a buckskin coat. He handed it to Will. "Here, put this on. Keep you warm while yer clothes is drying."

Will slipped into the knee-length jacket. He ran his hands over the leather and rippled the fringe that extended down the outside seams of each arm and encircled the bottom hem. "This is really soft," he said.

"Star Dancer made that for Lone Eagle. But the boy growed out of it so fast, it ain't hardly been worn. Been hanging on the wall there ever since he went away to that boarding school."

Will fingered the buttery leather and fastened the coat across his front with its four leather ties. There weren't any pockets in the coat, but he could remedy that problem by carrying a haversack to hold his knife, flint, and other odds and ends.

"Star Dancer chewed that antelope hide for days to make it real soft. Just like she did when she made this work shirt for me." He brushed his hands down his worn, buckskin shirt, then sighed. "She made the dress she's wearing on her burial scaffold out there behind the cabin, too. She was right handy at making clothes."

Will eased himself back down onto the edge of the cot.

"Why don't you keep that?" Bullfrog said. "Looks real nice on you."

"Maybe Lone Eagle will want it."

"Too small for him, now. I reckon, Star Dancer would be mighty proud to have you wear it, seeing as how you saved her son from the quicksand last year."

"Thank you, Bullfrog." The buckskin coat was certainly more impressive than the old wool jacket the railroad had given him. "I'll be honored."

"Now you jest lay down there and rest. Need to get your strength back. Don't you worry 'bout nothing."

Will had promised Homer he'd return not later than tomorrow night with food. He'd failed. What was he to do? But he was too tired to think about it now. He pulled the buffalo robe up beneath his chin and closed his eyes.

CHAPTER 7

Will hobbled out the door of the cabin on the crutch Bullfrog had fashioned for him the evening before. Snow covered the ground, but the early morning sun felt warm against his face. Fluffy clouds scudded across a brilliant, blue sky. The blizzard had finally blown itself out.

He wore a pair of Bullfrog's moccasins. His swollen ankle wouldn't fit into his boot. He leaned on the crutch and wiggled his left leg. It wasn't as painful as it'd been yesterday. Bullfrog had replaced the bandage and changed the sage poultice again this morning. The swelling was going down. If he could just put weight on the leg. He needed to get back to the surveyors' camp. He'd told Homer when he'd left camp yesterday morning he'd be back by tonight. What would his uncle think of his actions? He'd refused to take Homer's advice—now he was injured and unable to help his teammates.

His clumsiness had caused him to fail. If he hadn't been in such a hurry to get a shot at that antelope, he wouldn't have fallen into the river. If he'd just taken a little more time, been more deliberate, he could have bagged that buck and been on his way back with it. Instead, he had nothing to take to his sick companions at Rawlins Springs.

Bullfrog appeared from around the side of the cabin. "Just watered and fed the animals. A little crowded in the lean-to with two horses and the mule . . . but Ruby's getting along fine with Minnie and Ida." He set a bucket down by the cabin's door. "And how're you doing this morning?"

"Better. I can get around on the crutch. Thanks for making it."

Bullfrog waved a hand. "Yer welcome. Now, you just gotta rest so's you can get back to yer team in a couple of days."

"I've got to get back to the camp now. I promised Homer I'd be back there tonight . . . with food."

"Well, yer not fit to be going anyplace."

"I can't let them starve. The food was about gone when I left. I don't know when Uncle Sean will make it back and Homer will think I've been killed. I have to get food to them."

Bullfrog looked steadily at Will for a moment, then sighed. "I'll go. I've got a haunch of elk I can take."

"I can't ask you to do that, Bullfrog."

"You don't have no choice." Bullfrog surveyed the sky. "Weather's fine now. Sun's gonna start melting the snow. I can ride Minnie, and I reckon Ruby can lug the elk."

"I was hoping to take some feed for our horses, too."

"I'll pack some fodder along."

"And Homer wanted me to bring willow bark for Otto and Joe. He thought it'd help them get over the fever."

"He's right about that. I've got extra willow bark."

"Thanks, Bullfrog."

"I reckon I best get packed up, then. I can make it there by nightfall, for sure. Probably can't make it back tonight though. You be all right by yerself?"

"Yes."

"You said yer camp's just this side of the Divide, right on the line of them survey stakes. Rawlins Springs you called it?"

"Right. You'll see a white, Army wall tent and six horses, including Buck. His black coat will stand out against the snow more than the tent will."

"Oh, I don't reckon I'll have trouble finding the camp. That spring's been known to the Indians and trappers out here for years. Stopped by there many a time. It just never had no name afore."

Will dropped his eyes and felt himself flush. Why had he thought it necessary to tell the old mountain man how to find the camp? He looked back up. He couldn't see Bullfrog's lips, but he could tell he was smiling the way the bushy mustache curled up at the ends.

CHAPTER 8

Jenny rode astride her horse beside Lieutenant Luey Moretti. She'd given up riding sidesaddle, which she'd done in Virginia. Here on the frontier it was more practical to emulate the ways of men when it came to riding. Plus, riding like a man gave her more control over the animal in the rugged terrain. Her father had taught her before the war how to handle horses—grooming, saddling, and feeding them. At the Big Laramie home station, Jenny often lent a hand with the stock. She could harness the stagecoach teams as well as anybody.

"There it is." Moretti pointed to a sprawl of buildings and tents in the valley below them. "Cheyenne."

"Why it looks just like Julesburg," Jenny said.

"Hell on Wheels looks the same no matter where it is." Moretti turned in his saddle toward the column of troopers who rode behind him. "Sergeant Winter!"

From the rear of the column of a dozen cavalrymen a horseman galloped forward. He pulled up beside the lieutenant. "Sir?" Sergeant Winter saluted.

Moretti returned the salute. "Take the detachment on to the fort, Sergeant. I'll escort Miss McNabb into town."

"Yes, sir." The sergeant wheeled his horse about. "Detachment! Left turn. Ho!" The column of twos turned to the north and rode cross-country to where Fort D. A. Russell could be seen two miles northwest of Cheyenne.

Wells Fargo was transferring Jenny's father from Big Laramie to the home station at North Platte Crossing, eighty miles farther west. Jenny had convinced her father she should make an attempt to get Elspeth to return to the family before they increased the distance between themselves and the Lucky Dollar Saloon where Elspeth had worked since the preceding fall. With no stage traffic between Cheyenne and Laramie, Jenny hooked up with Moretti's cavalry detachment. Her father wouldn't let her make the two-day trip by herself.

Last night the detachment camped with Grady Shaughnessy's construction crew near Sherman Summit, the highest point the railroad must cross in the Laramie Range. The tracks now extended well beyond Cheyenne and would reach the summit in a matter of days. Shaughnessy had told them General Dodge planned a spike-driving ceremony to commemorate the momentous occasion and had even telegraphed a request for Sean Corcoran and his team to join him there.

Jenny had thought a lot about where Will might be ever since Corcoran had left Big Laramie three days ago. She prayed Corcoran had found Will and his team safe and well.

After descending the slope into the new town, Moretti and Jenny reigned in before the Lucky Dollar Saloon.

Moretti tugged on one side of his mustache to straighten it. "Jenny, you sure you'll be all right by yourself?"

"I'll be fine, Luey. Elspeth and I may have differing opinions about where our lives should go, but we're still sisters. She won't hurt me . . . and she won't let anybody else hurt me, either."

"Where will you stay tonight?"

"They have a hotel here. I'll get a room. I can take care of myself." She lifted back the skirt of her jacket to reveal a pocket revolver stuck in her waistband. She'd bought the Colt Model 1849, .31-caliber pistol, a favorite of women, from an itinerant peddler with some of her earnings from preparing meals for the

Wells Fargo passengers.

Moretti smiled. "Guess you're right. If you could withstand the rigors of captivity in a Cheyenne camp, you ought to be able to fend for yourself in a hotel."

"I can." She returned his smile. "But thanks for worrying."

"We'll head back to Laramie in the morning. I'll finish my business with Colonel Stevenson this afternoon while Sergeant Winter and the men gather up the resupply items. You'll ride back with us?"

"Yes. Papa and Duncan plan to go on to North Platte Crossing day after tomorrow. I told Papa I'd be back to travel with them. That's the only way he'd agree to let me come to talk to Elspeth."

Moretti waved her a smart salute and rode away. Jenny dismounted and tied her horse to a hitching rail in front of the Lucky Dollar Saloon. She crossed the board sidewalk, entered through the swinging bat-wing doors, and spotted her sister immediately.

Elspeth's blonde hair stood out in the drab confines of the tent-like structure that served as the saloon's dance hall. She was serving drinks to two scruffy men seated at a table near the back. When Elspeth turned away from the table, Jenny locked eyes with her sister and crossed the hard-packed dirt floor toward her.

"You look like a man, Jenny." Elspeth wrinkled her nose, shook her shoulder-length curls, and sniffed. "And smell like a horse."

"I just spent two days riding over the mountains to see you, Elspeth, and I certainly wasn't going to do it in a dress. Besides, I work at a stagecoach station and have to help shovel the manure."

Elspeth's bright red dress barely extended beneath her knees. Her calves were bare down to the tops of her high-button shoes.

"Don't you think that dress is a little revealing?" Jenny reached out and pulled up the neckline of Elspeth's low-cut dress.

"Stop it!" Elspeth yanked the neckline back down over her shoulders, revealing creamy skin. "This is the way all the girls have to dress if they want to work here."

"You don't have to work here. You should be with us. We're moving to North Platte Crossing. The family could use your help."

"You wasted your time coming if you thought you could talk me into leaving. I'm happy working for Mort Kavanagh, and I intend to continue."

A half-dozen early drinkers turned from the bar to watch the two sisters. Jenny felt self-conscious in her dirty trousers and ragged jacket.

Elspeth guided Jenny to the back wall of the tent, away from the bar. She took both of Jenny's hands and turned them over to study the palms. "Just look at your hands. They're callused and chapped. What would Mother think?"

"Mother's dead, Elspeth."

"You don't have to remind me of that. I meant, what would she think if she were still alive. You know how she wanted us girls to take care of our complexions."

Jenny sighed. "I don't have the luxury of that anymore. I have to work to help Papa."

"And how much do you make, cooking for stagecoach passengers?"

"After paying for the food, I get to keep about ten dollars a week."

"Humph! I make that much in a day. No, Jenny, I'm staying right here."

"How am I going to explain to Papa?"

"I don't care what you tell him, Jenny. But I'm not coming back with you."

Chapter 9

Paddy pushed through the canvas-flap door into the rear of the Lucky Dollar Saloon and stepped onto the hard-packed dirt floor. A half-dozen candelabra suspended from the rafters supporting the tented dance hall produced more smoke than light in the large enclosure. He nodded to Randy Tremble, who ignored him and continued polishing glasses behind the bar along the side wall.

Sliding his Bowie knife out of his boot top, Paddy sliced an end off a twist of tobacco. This twist was running low. He'd have to roll a drunk soon to get another. He surveyed the few card tables that were in use. No likely victims among the customers he saw. It was late afternoon, but *tools down* hadn't sounded yet for the railroad workers, and there weren't many customers. He stuck the chaw into his mouth with the point of the blade, then bent down to return the knife to his boot.

When he raised up, he recognized Elspeth McNabb and her sister, Jenny, against the opposite wall. He stepped into the shadows along the outer edge of the tent and sidled around the perimeter. He wanted to get close enough to hear what they were saying without being seen.

"I can imagine Papa's disappointed in me," Elspeth said. "But that's not enough to make me want to work in a stable. I didn't like the stable when we lived in Virginia. What makes you think I'd like it out here?"

"You don't have to work in the stable," Jenny said. "You can help serve meals in the station."

"Ha! And collect big tips for gouging the stagecoach passengers a dollar and a half per meal?" Elspeth shook her head. Her blonde hair brushed across her shoulders. "No thanks."

Paddy had slipped close enough that he'd heard the last exchange between the sisters. Jenny spoke with a mild, southern drawl. Elspeth laid hers on more thickly.

"If you're moving to North Platte Crossing," Elspeth said, "that'll put you right close to that young man you've got a hankering for. What was his name? Will Braddock?"

Paddy leaned closer. This bit about Will Braddock could be interesting.

"Yes," Jenny replied. "I haven't seen him since last fall, though."

"Maybe he's found somebody else." Elspeth laughed.

"That's possible. I just hope he's all right."

"What does that mean?" Elspeth asked.

Paddy listened to Jenny tell her sister about Corcoran's illness and how his team, including Will and Homer, had been snowbound near the Continental Divide. Ah, Paddy thought, how convenient. He'd have to keep an eye on North Platte Crossing and Jenny McNabb. All three of his enemies were quite close. Sooner or later they'd show up.

"I have to return to Big Laramie in the morning, Elspeth. I'm going to get a room at the hotel for the night. You can find me there."

"Don't hold your breath waiting for me, little sister."

"I'm worried about you, Elspeth. Who's going to take care of you?"

"I'll be fine. You don't need to worry about me."

Even though Jenny was dressed in trousers and an old coat, Paddy could tell she was as attractive as he'd remembered when he'd held his Bowie knife at her throat last summer atop the

Laramie Range. He was also reminded of his fight with Will Braddock that day. He reached up and rubbed his chest, next to his left shoulder, where Braddock had stabbed him.

"Sure, Jenny McNabb, and ye're going to be leading me to my enemies," he whispered to himself.

Jenny moved away from the wall of the tent, paused, and looked back at her sister. "Take care of yourself, Elspeth. Goodbye . . . for now."

Elspeth did not reply. Jenny walked out the front door of the saloon.

Paddy stepped out of the shadows. Elspeth's eyes narrowed when he confronted her.

"Ah, now, darlin'. Don't ye worry yer pretty little head. Paddy'll take care no harm comes to ye." He grinned when she frowned. "Sure, and that's the truth of it."

Chapter 10

Will stumbled down to the river using his crutch. He filled a leather bucket with water and struggled back up the slope to the rear of the cabin, entering the lean-to stable where Bullfrog Charlie's pack horse stood tied. "Morning, Ida. Bet you'd like a little water, and maybe some hay, wouldn't you?"

He set the bucket in front of the horse. Steadying himself against the stable's wall, he dragged some hay out of a corner with his crutch. Ida fidgeted and snorted. She didn't seem interested in Will's offerings. She kept her head turned back, looking toward the stable's open entrance. She whickered, her ears pricked forward, her eyes opened wide, her nostrils flared.

A rustling in the bushes beneath the cottonwood trees behind the cabin drew Will's attention, but when he stepped outside he saw nothing. Ida continued to snort and shuffle about in the stable. "Guess you'll eat when you get hungry."

He returned to the cabin and spent the morning cleaning his revolver. The soaking in the river wouldn't be good for it. He didn't want it to rust. The waterlogged paper cartridges resisted extraction—the black powder caked the back of each chamber. He dug out the bullets and wadding one at a time.

The extra cartridges he carried in his bullet pouch were useless from the time they'd been submerged in the river. Bullfrog didn't have a revolver, so he'd have to wait until he rejoined his uncle's team to be able to reload his pistol. He reached for his leather-flapped holster, which lay in front of the fire, and ran a hand over it. It wasn't quite dry enough to accept the freshly oiled revolver, so he laid the Colt on one of the stools near the hearth.

"Halloo the cabin!" Bullfrog's gravelly voice announced his return. Hopefully, Bullfrog had found Will's teammates in better health than Will had left them.

Will hopped on the crutch to the door. Just as his hand closed around the latch rope, a loud roar reverberated through the cabin walls.

"Wagh!" Bullfrog's cry pierced the air.

Will pushed the door open in time to see Minnie, Bullfrog's horse, rear and tumble the mountain man backward out of the saddle.

"Humph!" Bullfrog bellowed when his back thumped the ground.

A grizzly bear towered on its hind legs over Bullfrog. The bear's head surged forward, jaws opened wide—spittle glistened on long fangs.

Minnie whinnied a scream and raced away. Ida neighed and kicked the side of the lean-to stable. She wanted out. The presence of the bear must have been what had been troubling her earlier.

Another roar!

"Bullfrog!" Will stumbled out the door.

The bear swatted the mountain man in the face. Blood and strips of skin flew from deep gouges across his cheek. Bullfrog pulled his long-bladed Bowie knife from its sheath and stabbed upward into the bear's thick fur. The grizzly knocked the knife out of his hand with one giant paw and swiped the other against the side of the old man's head. Bullfrog's left ear ripped away.

"Will! The Hawken! Shoot!" The Hawken rifle lay on the ground near the old man.

The bear scraped a paw down Bullfrog's chest, ripping the

buckskin shirt, spraying more blood.

"Wagh!" Bullfrog rolled to his side.

Will hobbled over, dropped his crutch, and picked up the powerful, single-shot, big game rifle. A percussion cap perched on the nipple beneath the hammer. Was the gun loaded? He would only have one shot.

The bear roared and clamped his jaws over the top of Bullfrog's head. Shreds of scalp and white hair came away in the fangs when the bear pulled back. Blood stained Bullfrog's hair.

"Shoot, Will! Shoot!"

Will raised the heavy rifle and pulled the butt into his right shoulder. He leaned forward in a standard shooting stance, but his throbbing left foot wouldn't take the pressure. He let his weight shift backward into an awkward, unnatural position.

He'd never fired a Hawken with its set triggers. He pulled the rear cocking trigger—a click activating the hair trigger. He aimed at the bear's head. A body shot would be easier, but he didn't know if the Hawken's stopping power could fell such a big animal. He inhaled deeply, held his breath, and squeezed the front trigger. An explosion accompanied a flash of fire from the muzzle. The recoil of the heavy rifle slammed back against his shoulder, knocking him onto his butt.

The grizzly roared, reared upward, stepped toward Will—then collapsed. His shot had pierced the bear's left eye, penetrating the brain. The bear lay motionless before him.

Will dropped the rifle and turned to the bloodied man. "Bullfrog," he whispered. He sat down and cradled the old man's head in his lap.

"Good shootin', son." Bullfrog gasped.

"I never shot a Hawken before. Wasn't sure if I knew how."

"You done fine." Bullfrog wheezed. He coughed harshly. A trickle of blood oozed from his lips, the red stain spread down his long, white beard.

"I've got to get you inside." But how was he going to do that? His left leg barely supported himself.

He retrieved his crutch and hobbled back into the cabin. He dragged the buffalo robe off the cot and gathered up a length of rope. He returned and spread the robe on the ground above the injured man's head. He sat on the edge of the robe behind Bullfrog and grabbed the old man beneath the arms. He hauled Bullfrog toward him until he had the wounded man resting against his chest. He scooted himself backward a few inches, reached out, and pulled Bullfrog backward again on the robe, dragging him a short distance with each pull.

"Agh!" Bullfrog groaned each time Will tugged.

After a dozen pulls, Will had Bullfrog centered on the buffalo robe. He tied each end of the rope onto opposite corners of the robe at the mountain man's feet. Since he couldn't put pressure on his injured leg he positioned himself on all fours, looping the closed circle of rope over one shoulder, across his chest, and beneath the opposite arm. Then he heaved forward in a crawl, slowly dragging the robe and its burden toward the cabin. The rope cut deeply into his neck, and he understood more fully the benefit of a horse collar.

Will knew he couldn't lift Bullfrog onto the cot, so he pulled him to the hearth and settled him on the floor in front of the fire.

"That old griz hibernates in a cave on Elk Mountain." Bullfrog blew out his breath. "He came out early this year. He's snooped 'round afore . . . but he never bothered me."

Bullfrog was in bad shape. Will brushed a tear off his cheek with the back of his hand. Mustn't let the mountain man see him cry.

Chapter 11

Will managed to stop most of the bleeding from Bullfrog's chest and body wounds. The scalp still oozed, and the buffalo robe beneath the mountain man's head was sticky with blood. Bullfrog's skull showed through the row of deep gouges across the top of his head. Will fashioned a bandage to cover the grotesque hole left in the side of the old man's face. Surprisingly, there was little bleeding from where the ear had been ripped off. He tried to clean the long, white beard, but did a poor job—the hair remained matted and caked with dried blood.

Bullfrog moaned and murmured to himself throughout the night, drifting in and out of consciousness. Will didn't understand much of what the old timer said, but he did catch something about trapping with Jim Bridger—calling him Old Gabe. It reminded Will of the tall tales with which Bullfrog had regaled General Dodge's party the night Will had first met the mountain man a year ago. Will also heard him mumble about Star Dancer, telling her he was coming and to wait for him.

With sunrise, Will hobbled on his crutch down to the river and brought back a bucket of water. He stepped out of the early morning sunlight into the dim cabin.

"Will?" Bullfrog raised his head and looked around the cabin.

Will almost dropped the bucket. Bullfrog was awake.

"How long've I been here?" Bullfrog asked.

"Since yesterday."

"That when the bear attacked?"

"Yes."

Bullfrog moaned and laid his head back. "Ain't gonna make it this time, Will."

"What do you mean? Yes, you are."

"No. Reckon that ole bear got me good. Ain't got no strength left. Jest too old, I reckon."

"I heated up the antelope stew. Once you eat something, you'll start to feel better." Will stepped over Bullfrog and filled a wooden bowl from the kettle hanging over the fireplace. He leaned down and offered the food to the mountain man.

"No."

"You have to eat, Bullfrog."

Bullfrog shook his head. "Food won't fix what them bear claws done to me." Bullfrog closed his eyes and remained silent for a while.

Will thought he might have drifted off to sleep. But the old man sighed and opened his eyes again. "Almost forgot. I found your camp."

"Figured you had, since Ruby wasn't with you."

"Your uncle had returned with food and medicine for your friends."

"Good. I'm glad he's safe."

"Said he got sick . . . like the others. Said Jenny McNabb nursed him to health over to Big Laramie Station."

"Jenny?"

"Yep. Your uncle said Jenny's pa is transferring to North Platte Crossing. That's real close by. You're to meet your uncle there, soon's you're well enough to travel. I told him I'd see you got there." Bullfrog drew a deep breath and groaned. "Reckon I won't be doing that, now."

"Yes, you will."

"No, won't." Bullfrog shook his head slowly. "Promise me something, Will."

Will blinked away a tear. "What?"

"Keep an eye on Lone Eagle." The old man coughed and drew a deep breath. "Old Chief Tall Bear has kept them young bucks off Lone Eagle's back, but his grandpa ain't gonna live forever. When he's gone there won't be no Cheyenne what will want a half-breed hanging around. He'll have trouble adjusting to white man's ways when he has to leave the camp. Promise you'll help him."

Will nodded. "I'll try. I owe him for helping me rescue Jenny last year."

"One more thing. Bury me."

"Bury you?"

"I know it'll be hard, what with your leg."

"My leg's fine." Will stepped on his injured leg and immediately gritted his teeth. "But let's not talk about that. You're going to get better."

Bullfrog shook his head. "Not in the ground, mind you. Put me in the trees . . . with Star Dancer. Think you can get me up there?"

"I won't have to if you'll just eat and get well."

Bullfrog sighed. "After I'm gone take the Hawken to Lone Eagle. He liked that old rifle."

"At least try some of the broth." Will held the bowl out again.

Bullfrog raised a hand to push it away. "Take Ida. Minnie may come back . . . may not. Reckon some Injun'll get her."

Bullfrog drifted back into unconsciousness. Will sat on a stool and watched the old man. From time to time he wakened, called out something unintelligible, then fell quiet again. His breathing became more labored. Early in the afternoon, Bullfrog coughed harshly. His chest heaved. A trickle of blood flowed out of his nose. His chest sank back and did not rise again.

★ ★ ★ ★ ★

Will cut his crutch into two pieces and bound them on either side of his leg with leather thongs. The makeshift splint allowed him to put some pressure on the injured ankle. The ankle would probably swell again, but it couldn't be helped. He needed to be able to use both hands, and that wasn't possible holding onto a crutch.

He saddled Ida and rigged her with the travois Bullfrog had fashioned for him after his fall into the river. He dragged Bullfrog's body out of the cabin wrapped in the buffalo robe and rolled him onto the travois. He took the hand axe from beside the fireplace and a coil of hemp rope that hung on the wall.

He led Ida, using her to drag the travois into the cottonwood trees behind the cabin. Star Dancer's body, covered with a buffalo robe, lay lashed to a scaffold high above ground—out of the reach of any man. Will would do the same for Bullfrog.

He selected four sturdy cottonwoods standing close together to serve as the corner posts for his platform. He cut and trimmed a dozen saplings with the axe. He fashioned the two thickest saplings into long poles and chopped the smaller ones into shorter pieces to serve as cross braces. He cut several short lengths off the coil of rope and stuffed them into his waistband.

He rolled Bullfrog's body off the travois. Then he mounted and guided the horse to the first tree, dragging one of the long poles with him.

"Steady, now, Ida." The mare whinnied and shook her mane. "Easy!"

Ida calmed and stood still beside the tree. Will reached as high as he could and lashed the end of the pole to the trunk. He repeated the process three times until he had both long poles lashed parallel to one another ten feet above the ground. Then he tied a dozen cross braces between the two long poles to complete the platform.

He dismounted, wincing when his foot hit the ground. While mounted, the pressure was off the leg and he worked comfortably. Now came the hard part. He had to get Bullfrog's body onto the scaffold.

He wrapped several turns of rope around the body and knotted it. He threw the loose end over a limb that extended out over the scaffold, tied it to Ida's saddle, and led her slowly away. Bullfrog's body inched upward. When he had the mountain man positioned even with the level of the scaffold, he used a trimmed sapling to push the body over onto the platform.

He remounted and eased the horse up next to the scaffold. "Now stand easy, Ida."

Grasping the side pole of the platform he stood up on the horse's back. Ida whickered and shifted under the unusual act. "Steady, Ida. Steady."

From his standing position he straightened Bullfrog's body and lashed it to the platform. He'd wrapped the buffalo robe completely around the body, covering the face in order to protect it from scavengers and hiding the old man's features.

Will placed a hand on Bullfrog's chest. Perhaps some words were in order. It was a funeral—of sorts. But he didn't know what to say. He didn't know whether Bullfrog had been religious or not.

"Goodbye, old friend. I wish you a speedy journey on your way to join Star Dancer."

He tapped his own heart with a hand and felt the eagle talon beneath his shirt. He lifted the thong from around his neck and looped it around one of the scaffold poles next to Bullfrog's body. The eagle talon swayed gently in the breeze beneath the platform. "May this talon bring you good luck in your after life—just as it did for me in this one."

Thirty minutes later, Will took a last look around the cabin.

He wore Lone Eagle's buckskin jacket and held Bullfrog's Hawken rifle. He stepped outside and pulled the door closed behind him, ensuring the latch engaged, and paused to glance at the two scaffolds in the cottonwood stand.

He gathered up Ida's reins and placed a foot into the stirrup, then paused. The carcass of the grizzly lay twenty yards away. He went back into the cabin and returned with the hand axe, hobbled across to the bear, and chopped the claws off each paw.

Chapter 12

"Jenny, you tried," her father said. "Now you'll just have to forget it."

"Papa, I can't forget her. She's my sister."

"I didn't mean forget *her.* I meant forget about trying to influence what she's going to do with her life."

Jenny sighed. She took her bonnet from the peg beside the station door and turned to survey the interior of the Big Laramie home station. The two little, sod-roofed, cedar-log buildings, connected by a breezeway, had been their home for the past six months. Now they were moving farther west where her father would take up the same duties managing the home station at North Platte Crossing. There they would be eighty-five miles closer to the McNabb family's original destination. They should have reached California, or perhaps Oregon, late last year. But the fates were against them it seemed and they'd just have to make their way west at a slower pace. Jenny tapped the eagle talon that hung beneath the neckline of her dress. Maybe it would bring her some good luck.

"Ready?" Her father held the door open.

She nodded and stepped outside. Her brother, Duncan, sat perched on top of the coach in the midst of the passengers' baggage. This was one of the new Concord coaches. Its pomegranate red body, set off with black, metal trim, sparkled in the bright sunlight. *Wells, Fargo & Company,* painted in large, gilt letters, ran along the headboard above the door and windows. Matching letters on the door read *U.S. Mail.*

"Come on, Jenny," Duncan called. "Butch's ready to go."

"I'm coming." She looked up at the driver and smiled. Jenny knew Butch Cartwright's real name. She was probably the only one here who did, but she kept that to herself.

Butch returned Jenny's smile and adjusted the ribbons, as the reins were called in the stagecoach trade, between the fingers of thin, silk-lined, buckskin gloves that enabled precise control of the six-horse hitch. The driver held a whip in the right hand, with a booted right foot propped against the wooden brake lever that was affixed to that side of the coach.

This hitch of horses would pull the coach to the next swing station, fourteen miles distant, where they'd be exchanged for six fresh ones. Before reaching their destination at North Platte Crossing, the teams would be changed five times. The horses never walked except on extremely steep hills. The driver kept them at a brisk pace, averaging nine miles per hour, cracking a whip over the horses' heads when they needed encouragement. Time was money and Wells Fargo did not intend to lose either.

Slim Dempsey sat on the seat beside Butch. As the shotgun messenger, his job was to defend the coach's passengers against attack and to safeguard the valuable contents of the strongbox. A sawed-off, double-barreled, shotgun lay across his lap. A lever-action, Henry repeating rifle sat propped against the seat beside him. At his waist he wore a Colt revolver. His feet were planted firmly atop the green, iron-bound, Wells Fargo strongbox.

The shotgun messenger seemed to thoroughly enjoy Jenny's cooking. Where Slim put all the food he consumed, she had no idea. He truly resembled his name. During his layovers at the station, Jenny liked to sit and chat with him after he'd eaten, while he cleaned his collection of firearms. He was particularly proud of the shotgun, which he'd used during the war while a member of the North Carolina cavalry. He'd sawed the barrel off his father's favorite British-made, 12-guage, Perkins shotgun when the war started. He'd said his father had threatened to whip him for it, but since he was going off to fight for the South, he'd been forgiven. Slim enjoyed telling the passengers stories about the battles he'd fought in. But he'd never been able to get Jenny's father to engage in any conversation about the war. It was a topic Alistair McNabb avoided.

"Come along, Jenny." Her father handed her up and she took a seat with her back to the front of the coach beneath the driver's box.

Even though Jenny had been inside a coach when it was parked at the station, she had yet to ride in one. This standard nine-passenger model had three seats. The middle seat was the least desirable, because the only back support was a net of leather straps.

Mail bags jammed the floor space between the seats, forcing the passengers to place their feet in an uncomfortable manner on top of them. "Sorry about the mail bags, folks," her father said. "Still trying to get caught up after that blizzard. Wells Fargo's government contract specifies mail takes precedence over passengers."

Alistair bumped Jenny as he slipped into the window seat next to her. "Sorry," he said. "It's going to be a bit crowded."

"It's all right, Papa." Jenny sat in the center of the seat with her back to the front of the coach. A male passenger occupied the other window seat beside her. Seated between the two men, she would be shielded somewhat from the constant dust that blew through the uncovered windows.

Nine passengers had squeezed into the coach. By having Duncan ride topside, Jenny's father had managed to maximize the paying customers on this trip.

"Giddup!" Butch called to the team and snapped the ribbons. The coach lurched and rolled into motion.

"Mmm," Jenny moaned. Was this what sea-sickness felt like? Her father had warned her to be prepared to feel woozy in the beginning. The egg-shaped, coach body, suspended between the wheels on two oxhide thoroughbraces, caused the coach to sway like a hammock. How could a passenger tolerate this rocking back and forth and pitching side to side for a thousand miles to reach the west coast? She was glad she only had to ride the eighty-five miles to North Platte Crossing.

CHAPTER 13

Will leaned on a crutch he'd fashioned after reaching North Platte Crossing. His ankle didn't hurt much, but he thought it best to keep the weight off it a little longer. He watched the Wells Fargo stage approach the home station. A cloud of dust floated around the churning wheels.

The driver hauled back on the ribbons and stepped hard on the brake lever. "Whoa!" The harness jingled as the teams halted beside the corral, adjacent to the station. The coach swayed slightly, then settled onto its thoroughbraces. Before the driver and the shotgun messenger even dismounted, two stock tenders were busy changing the tired teams for fresh ones. The coach would be on its way west in less than an hour—just enough time for the passengers to eat their meal.

"Hey, Jenny!" Duncan yelled from atop the coach. "Look who's here."

Jenny's head appeared in the window and Will smiled when he saw the broad grin appear on her face.

"William Braddock." Jenny's initial grin was replaced with an open-mouthed expression of shock. "What happened to you?"

Will shrugged and hopped toward the coach on his crutch. "Nothing much."

"And where'd you get those fancy buckskins?"

"I'll tell you all about it when we're alone." He nodded at the other passengers who were crowding into the station to get a seat at the meal table.

Thirty minutes later, Jenny laid her fork beside her plate and leaned back on the bench. "That's the first meal I've eaten in a stagecoach station in six months that I haven't prepared myself. Guess I'll be fixing the next meal for the passengers. Have to start eating my own cooking again."

"And good cooking it is, too." Will's uncle had stepped into the station. "I can assure you of that. I enjoyed several of your meals at Big Laramie Station. It's nice to see you again, Jenny."

"Hello, Mr. Corcoran. You seem to be doing well."

"I'm fine now. Thanks once more for nursing me back to health. Maybe you can put your healing touch to work on my nephew." He pointed a piece of paper he held at Will, who sat opposite Jenny at the table. His uncle shook the paper back and forth. "This telegram from General Dodge directs us to meet him at Sherman Summit right away."

"Sherman Summit?" Will asked.

"Doc Durant and a host of dignitaries are coming from New York to drive a commemorative spike where the Union Pacific's tracks cross the highest point on the line. The bridge over Dale Canyon is almost complete, and the tracks will soon reach Laramie. General Dodge has invited the survey inspection team to attend the ceremony."

"Can I come, too?" Will asked.

"He said bring the whole team. You're part of the team, aren't you? Unless that leg injury of yours has you immobilized."

"I don't need the crutch anymore," Will said.

"Good. I'll leave you two to get reacquainted while I get Homer and the boys started with the packing." His uncle stepped out through the door.

The other passengers had finished their meal and had stepped outside to smoke and chat before re-boarding the coach.

"We're alone now, Will," Jenny said. "Are you going to tell me what happened?"

Will explained about stepping into the beaver trap and being rescued by Bullfrog Charlie. A tear trickled down her cheek when he described the bear attacking the old mountain man.

"I left my eagle talon on his burial scaffold. Maybe it will bring him luck in his journey to rejoin Star Dancer."

"I hope so," she said.

He watched Jenny rub her fingers across the front of her dress. He knew she was feeling her eagle talon beneath the neckline.

"What is that you're wearing around your neck now?" she asked.

Will lifted the leather thong over his head and dropped the necklace on the table with a clatter. "Claws from the bear that killed Bullfrog."

Jenny looked at Will, then back at the necklace. She gathered it into her hands and rubbed each of the claws. "They're huge. They're as long as my fingers."

"I made the necklace to remind me of Bullfrog. I won't wear it much . . . probably look ridiculous. I just finished making it this morning."

Jenny reached across the table and hung the necklace around his neck. "It's a nice keepsake, whether you wear it or not."

"You remember Ida, Bullfrog's pack horse?" Will asked. "You and I rode her down from the Laramie Range to Fort Sanders last year."

"Yes, I remember Ida."

"She's here in the corral. I've got Buck, so I don't need Ida. She's gentle riding. She can be your saddle horse. Bullfrog would be happy to know you have her."

"Oh, thank you, Will. That's very thoughtful. You can be sure I'll take good care of her."

"I guess I'd better go help Uncle Sean."

While she'd been eating, Jenny had told him about riding to

Cheyenne to try to talk her sister into returning to the family. She reached across the table and placed a hand over one of his hands. "You be careful, Will. Hell on Wheels will soon be in Laramie and I know Paddy O'Hannigan will be looking for you."

"Paddy?"

"Yes. You didn't kill him last year . . . like we thought. He was in the Lucky Dollar Saloon in Cheyenne. I don't think he realized that I saw him, but I did. He's not to be trusted, Will."

Chapter 14

Will and his uncle stood alongside the tracks at Sherman Summit, awaiting the arrival of the special train from Cheyenne. The wind blew strongly from out of the west across the flat, barren summit. Will's buckskin coat defended him well against the cold blasts. An occasional fierce gust forced him to clamp his hand over his old slouch hat to keep it from blowing away.

Jack Casement stepped across the tracks to join them. Will liked the diminutive former Army general who held the contract with the Union Pacific for the construction of the railroad.

"Good morning, Corcoran," Casement said. "Morning, Will. Glad you could join us." Casement slapped the riding crop he always carried against his leather boot.

"Does the wind ever stop blowing up here, General Jack?" Will's uncle asked.

"Seldom. Nothing much will grow up here . . . except that limber pine over there." Casement pointed to a gnarled, twisted tree growing out of the center of a jumble of boulders not far from where they stood. The tracks curved widely around the site.

"We didn't have the heart to cut down the only tree on the summit," Casement said, "so we bent the tracks around it."

"Looks old," Will said.

"One of the track layers is an amateur botanist," Casement said, "and claims limber pines can live a couple thousand years."

A train whistle diverted Will's attention from the tree. A laboring engine belched a black cloud from its diamond-shaped smokestack as it struggled up the long slope. Will had ridden by horseback over these mountains west of Cheyenne the previous summer with his uncle's team when they confirmed this was the best route. Still, the grade had been pushed to the maximum of two percent in order to cross the Laramie Range. Any steeper and the 4-4-0 locomotive wouldn't be able to pull a load.

Even with the west wind blowing, Will heard the chuffing of the steam engine as it drew nearer. A huge elk antler rack adorned the massive headlight on the front of the boiler. The train slowed to a crawl. The engineer blew a long blast on the whistle and clanged the bell repeatedly. Steam hissed from the cylinders in front of the driving wheels and the big locomotive ground to a stop right beside him.

Will waved to the engineer and the fireman as he fell into step behind his uncle and General Jack. They moved toward the single passenger car attached at the end of a string of eight freight cars.

Conductor Hobart Johnson alighted from the coach and placed a stool below the short steps that descended from the rear platform. A tall, lanky, slightly stooped gentleman stepped off the train behind Johnson.

"There's Doc Durant," Will's uncle said. "He arrived in style . . . in the Lincoln car."

"Hard to believe he actually refurbished Lincoln's funeral car to use it as his personal rolling palace." General Jack shook his head. "The arrogance of the man."

Will had never seen the vice president and general manager of the Union Pacific. A drooping mustache concealed the man's mouth above an unkempt goatee. He lifted a narrow-brimmed, straw hat and brushed his slicked-down hair back with a slender hand. He looked at Will and his companions. He didn't say anything, although Will was certain he had to know General

Jack, and probably even his uncle.

"And Silas Seymour, the *Insulting Engineer,*" General Jack said.

Conductor Johnson held the hand of a heavyset man who struggled to step from the train. Once on the ground, Seymour popped open his ever-present umbrella.

The surveyors and tracklayers had bestowed the rude title upon Seymour last year because of his meddling in the route General Dodge had selected for crossing the Laramie Range. Will remembered Seymour always insisting on being addressed as "Colonel," even though he'd never been in the Army. He worked under Durant's instructions to make sure the route was not necessarily the shortest or straightest, since the government paid the company for the miles of track laid. It didn't matter to Durant whether or not a route was the best, if he could finagle a way to get more money.

Will held up a hand in greeting to General Grenville Dodge when he stepped from the coach. Dodge grinned and nodded at Will's gesture. The Union Pacific's chief engineer was the real brains behind the construction of the eastern portion of the transcontinental railroad. A surveyor in his own right, Dodge knew almost instinctively which route was best. Being an engineer, he knew how to grade the route, how to lay the tracks, and how to construct the bridges. His mustache and beard appeared more gray than when Will had seen him last fall, but he was still a handsome man who stood ramrod straight.

A half-dozen other civilians and an equal number of military officers alighted from the passenger coach and followed Dodge and Durant to the front of the train. Dodge stepped up onto the locomotive's cowcatcher and raised a hand to silence the conversations of the gathering.

"Thank you all for coming to Sherman Summit for this special occasion," he said. "Today, the sixteenth of April, 1868, the Union Pacific Railroad crosses the Rocky Mountains at eight-thousand, two-hundred, forty-two feet . . . the highest elevation yet reached by *any* railroad in the world."

Dodge raised his hand again to silence a sprinkling of applause.

"Some of you may not know Samuel Reed, but I want to recognize him today." Dodge gestured to a man who stood quietly at the outer edge of the assemblage. His wavy hair, full beard, and mustache were speckled with gray. He nodded his head toward Dodge.

"Sam's primary job is to keep the UP's supplies moving forward from Omaha to wherever end of track happens to be. Without his efficient effort the whole construction process would grind to a halt. But over the past several weeks he's also been supervising the erection of a seven-hundred, thirteen-foot-long trestle over Dale Creek. It's the largest bridge the UP will have to build anyplace along our right-of-way. It's a mighty big bridge to cross a small brook that one could easily step over . . . but without it, we'd be stuck here at the summit."

The dignitaries turned toward Reed and clapped.

"So, gentlemen." Dodge stepped down from the cowcatcher. "Today we celebrate two major achievements in the construction of the Union Pacific. Thomas Durant . . . Doc Durant . . . the vice president and general manager of our railroad, will now drive a spike to make these accomplishments official."

Durant raised a sledgehammer and struck the ceremonial spike a blow. While the crowd applauded and shook Durant's hand in congratulations, Dodge walked over to Will and his uncle.

"Corcoran." Dodge shook hands with Will's uncle. "Rough winter I understand."

"Yes, sir. We all got sick, but we're fine now."

Dodge looked Will up and down. "Where'd you get that fancy

buckskin coat?"

"Bullfrog Charlie gave it to me."

"And you're limping," Dodge said. "I was looking out the window when you walked toward the rear of the train earlier."

"A little. Caught my foot in a beaver trap, but it's almost healed now."

"You always seem to be getting into some kind of trouble." Dodge laughed. "How's the arm wound?"

Will slapped his bicep. "Good as new, General."

Dodge turned to Will's uncle. "I have an assignment for you, Corcoran. I want you to go to California and check on the progress of the Central Pacific. I want to know what problems they face and how fast they'll be able to proceed across Nevada once they're clear of the Sierra Nevada. See if you can start negotiations with one of their officials about establishing a suitable place for the two railroads to join."

Dodge motioned for Sam Reed to join them.

"Sam will accompany you as far as Salt Lake City. He's going to try to negotiate a contract with Brigham Young for the Mormons to grade for us when we get into Utah. I talked with Young last fall and he promised to consider it. When you press on to California, leave the rest of your team with Sam so he can start surveying north of the Salt Lake. I want the UP to get at least that far, and hopefully well into Nevada, before we join up with the CP. Any questions?"

"Well, sir. Will's not officially part of the team."

Dodge glanced at Will, then back at Will's uncle. "Take him to California, if you like."

"You know, Grenville," Reed said, "Doc Durant has directed Seymour to accompany me."

"Yes, can't be helped. Maybe between you and Corcoran you can keep him from messing up things too much."

Dodge placed a hand on Will's shoulder. "What's this I hear

about Bullfrog Charlie Munro dying?"

Will told Dodge what had happened.

Dodge shook his head. "Sorry to hear that. Guess there won't be any antelope steaks for a while. Sure would've tasted good."

"I'll get one for you, General," Will said. "After all, I've been the team's hunter for several months."

Dodge grinned. "Fine. But be careful out there. A band of Cheyenne attacked the Dale Creek bridging crew last week and we lost some men."

Chapter 15

Will rode Buck, and led a pack horse, north from Sherman Summit, heading in the direction of Cheyenne Pass. He stayed just below the ridgeline on the eastern side of the Laramie Range so that his silhouette would be obscured. Hopefully, the Indians who'd attacked the tracklayers earlier weren't still around. But he didn't want to make it easy for them to spot him—or for an antelope to see him approach.

He'd ridden a couple of miles before he spotted his prey. He eased back on the Morgan's reins. "Whoa."

Two hundred yards ahead, four pronghorns ranged along a small stream. Three small ones, females, grazed in a loose cluster. Standing guard nearby, a larger antelope appeared to be frozen in place. The male protector held his head high, bigger horns evident against the skyline, the only movement the occasional flicker of his white tail.

Will stepped out of the saddle and dropped Buck's reins to the ground. The Morgan was trained to stand in place when the reins trailed downward. Will looped the pack horse's lead rope over Buck's saddle horn. "You two stay here," he whispered, "and be quiet."

He'd loaded Bullfrog's old Hawken rifle before leaving the railroad tracks. He was far enough away from the antelopes that he could cock the weapon without the clicking noise alerting them. He checked to be sure the percussion cap sat securely in place on the nipple beneath the hammer.

The morning breeze caressed the left side of his face, blowing from the west, over the crest of the ridge, and down the slope. He slipped downhill a ways before turning to approach the stream, trying to keep the slight wind from blowing his scent toward the antelopes. He crouched and moved slowly through knee-high grass.

From time to time he stopped to ensure the pronghorns hadn't moved. He looked back up the slope to where he'd left the horses, hoping they'd continue to remain quiet. Satisfied he was below the point where the wind could give his presence away, he crept a little closer.

He'd practiced enough with the Hawken to become comfortable with his ability to hit his target. The effective range of the old muzzle loader was less than the Spencer carbine firing its conical bullet, but the Hawken's .50-caliber ball packed more wallop. He needed to get close enough to the antelope to ensure a clean kill.

When he was less than a hundred yards away, he knelt behind a large bush. Maybe he could get the buck to come to him by using an old Indian trick. An inquisitive animal by nature, the antelope was known to check out curious objects. Will lifted his slouch hat above his head on a twig and waved it slowly back and forth.

The buck's head swung in his direction.

Will gently moved the twig. The hat swayed above it. The antelope took a dozen steps toward him, then stopped.

He wedged his decoy into a bush in front of him. The limbs supported the twig, allowing the hat to sway slightly in the breeze. The antelope took two more steps his way.

Will eased the Hawken's stock up to his cheek. The pronghorn stood eighty yards away. A good range. He cocked the rear-set trigger, turning the front one into the hair trigger. He sighted down the barrel, compensated for the crosswind, took a shallow breath, and held it. He squeezed the trigger. The blast drove the rifle back against his shoulder. White smoke at the muzzle momentarily clouded his vision, but the breeze quickly cleared the air.

He rose and walked toward the stream. The three smaller antelopes gazed at him for a moment, then bounded away. In front of him lay the buck—dead in the grass.

Looking up the slope to where he'd left the horses, he puckered his lips and whistled Morse code for the letter B. *"Tseeeee, Tse, Tse, Tse."* One long and three short notes. Buck knew the call and trotted to him, bringing the pack horse along.

"That's my antelope you shot."

Will jerked around at the sound of the unexpected voice.

An Indian rode toward him on a spotted pony, a broad grin creasing the young warrior's face. He wore a buckskin shirt and trousers and clutched a bow in one hand. A single eagle feather hung downward from a red, trade-cloth band tied around his head. Vermillion and yellow paint stripes accented his pronounced cheekbones.

"Lone Eagle." Will hadn't seen the mixed-blood Cheyenne since the previous fall. "It's good to see you. Sorry I beat you to the antelope."

"That buckskin coat looks familiar. And the rifle, too." Lone Eagle slid off his pony from the right side, the way an Indian dismounted.

"Your father gave me the coat. He asked me to give you the Hawken."

"My father?"

Will told Lone Eagle about his father's death. He showed him the bear claw necklace he'd made from the grizzly that'd killed Bullfrog.

Lone Eagle caressed one of the claws. Will noticed a glistening of tears in the young man's eyes.

"And the talon I gave you?" Lone Eagle asked.

"I hung the talon on his burial scaffold. I thought it might bring him luck in finding your mother in the great beyond."

"Thank you. I will go there now."

"To Bullfrog's cabin?"

"Yes. I am no longer with the tribe. Grandfather Tall Bear is dead. This winter was hard on our band. Buffalo hunting was not good and we did not have enough food. Grandfather was too old to survive on starvation rations."

"I'm sorry to hear that. I liked your grandfather. But why do you leave the tribe?"

"Black Wolf is the new chief. My grandfather protected me, but Black Wolf says a half-breed is not a real Cheyenne. He does not want me there."

"What will you do?"

Lone Eagle shrugged. "Maybe I will stay in the old cabin. I was born there. I can become true to my name . . . a lone eagle . . . a lone man."

Will held out the Hawken. "Take it, please. It belongs to you. Your father wanted you to have it." He lifted the flap on his haversack and retrieved a leather pouch containing the spare ammunition for the rifle, handing it to the Indian, too.

Lone Eagle took the rifle and ammunition, then swung onto his pony. "Thank you for helping my father with his journey to his final hunting ground. I owe you another favor."

"You can return the favor for me now."

"How?"

"See that Jenny McNabb stays safe."

Will told his friend about Jenny's family taking up residence at North Platte Crossing, not far from Bullfrog's cabin. "I'm going to California with my uncle and won't be back for some time. You can protect her. Particularly from Paddy O'Hannigan."

Lone Eagle nodded sharply, kicked his pony's flanks, and rode up the slope.

CHAPTER 16

Mort Kavanagh swung his chair around from the window where he'd been watching the traffic pass down the dusty street of the newest Hell on Wheels in Laramie. The motley conglomeration of tents and shacks had recently been relocated from Cheyenne. Mort leaned back and blew a smoke ring at the ceiling. He tapped the ash off his cigar and stuck it back into the corner of his mouth. "Paddy, I've got a surefire plan for slowing down the railroad."

Paddy sat across the desk from his boss, carving a plug off a twist of tobacco with his Bowie knife. "Sure, and what'll that be now, Mort?" He returned the knife to his boot top.

"Blow up a railroad tunnel."

"And just who will ye be getting to do that, now?"

"You."

"Me?"

Kavanagh nodded.

"By myself?" Paddy jammed the tobacco plug into his cheek.

"By yourself."

"Ah, now, I can't lift no keg of black powder alone."

"You won't use black powder."

"Sure, and I won't? And just how am I gonna pull off this explosion?"

"Nitroglycerin."

"Nitroglycerin!" Paddy almost choked on his chaw.

"That's right."

"Well, and I don't know a thing about using nitro, don't ye see."

"You'll learn."

"Sure, and that stuff's mighty dangerous, Mort."

"And mighty powerful." Kavanagh tapped a copy of the *Sacramento Union* that lay on his desk. "According to an article in this paper, nitro's eight times more powerful than black powder."

"Sure, and the UP didn't use nitro to blast their new tunnel through Rattlesnake Hills. Even they think the stuff's too dangerous to keep around."

"We're not going to get the nitro from the UP."

Paddy cocked his head to the side and stared across the desk at Kavanagh. What was going on here?

"We'll get it from the CP."

"The Central Pacific?"

"That's right." Mort shook the paper open and scanned the article. "Says here the CP's blasting long tunnels in the Sierra Nevada with nitro. They brought in a Scottish chemist, name of James Howden, to mix the stuff on the spot for them."

"So, ye're gonna hire this chemist Howden away from the CP?"

"Nope. You're going to convince him to teach you how to mix the stuff."

"Ah, now, Mort. I don't know about that."

Mort glared at Paddy across the top of the newspaper. "Who's paying your salary, Paddy O'Hannigan? When Casement fired you for stealing from the railroad, I had to start paying you myself. Or have you forgotten? Sometimes it's sorry I am that as your godfather I made that foolish promise to your ma to look after you."

Paddy's left eye twitched. He ran his hand down the scar on his cheek. It throbbed when his temper rose. He bit down on the plug of tobacco and forced himself to remain silent. Someday—he promised himself for the thousandth time—someday, he was going to get out from under Mort Kavanagh's thumb. But Paddy still needed money to send to his mother and sister in Brooklyn. And working for his godfather was the only thing he had going for him right now.

"Go to California and find this chemist. Get the ingredients from him. There are only three . . . glycerin, nitric acid, and sulfuric acid. According to this article, they're safe until they're mixed. You get him to teach you how to make nitroglycerin. Find out how much it'll take to blow up a tunnel, and get a little extra."

"You have a tunnel in mind?"

"Yeah, Rattlesnake Tunnel."

"Rattlesnake Tunnel!" Paddy narrowed his eyes and stared at Kavanagh. "The Army's building that new Fort Fred Steele right near that tunnel, Mort. Sure, and there are too many soldiers too close to that tunnel to blow it up."

"We'll see. You just get the nitroglycerin and let me worry about the target."

Paddy spat a stream of tobacco juice at a spittoon. "When is it ye'd be wanting me to go find this CP chemist?"

"Leave tomorrow. I'll give you money to bribe James Howden. If he won't part with the stuff for cash, you know how to convince him."

Paddy felt the smirk crease his lips. Now we're talking. Sure, and he wouldn't be wasting money on a chemist when a Bowie knife can do the job quicker. He could almost count the bonanza he was going to be able to send to his mother. There'd be enough for him to pocket a little extra spending money, too.

"Here's the cash." Mort tossed a fat envelope onto the desk. "Get moving."

Paddy rose, stuffed the envelope inside his vest, squared his bowler hat on his head, and walked out of Kavanagh's office.

He stepped down onto the dirt floor of the dance hall. Elspeth McNabb stood at the bar. She kept her back turned to him when he stepped up behind her.

"Well, d'ye see, darlin', ye need to be remembering who it was that was responsible for getting ye this job." He would like to run his fingers through those long blonde ringlets that brushed the tops of her bare shoulders.

Elspeth snorted, but did not turn around.

"Ye'll be mine someday, darlin'," he whispered. He ran a finger across the soft skin of her back that was revealed above the neckline of her low-cut dress.

He laughed when she shuddered.

Paddy didn't like the look the stage driver gave him when he tossed his valise up to have it placed on top of the coach. Was it a look of recognition? There hadn't been regular stagecoach service in Cheyenne, so the last place Paddy had seen any Wells Fargo employees was in Julesburg. He didn't remember seeing this driver, and Paddy prided himself on having a good memory for faces. He made it a point to keep mental track of any potential enemy.

"Hurry along, folks. It's a nice morning to start a long ride." The station manager herded the half-dozen passengers out from the station building. "Everybody on board, please."

The driver had no trouble wedging Paddy's small bag in among the piles of luggage strapped between the low railings that encircled the roof of the coach. Maybe the driver was just fascinated with the scar on his cheek. But the look wasn't one of revulsion, like he got from other folks. The driver got busy adjusting the luggage tie-downs and didn't look at him again.

Paddy shoved his way to the front of the line and took the far window seat with his back to the coach's front. He wasn't about to be stuck in the uncomfortable center seat.

The station manager glared at him as he handed up the final passenger, a young lady. Paddy watched the manager's eyes drop to the Bowie knife protruding from his boot top. He looked back at Paddy, then closed the door. "They're all aboard, Butch," the manager said. "On your way."

"Giddup." The driver snapped the ribbons and the coach rolled away from the Big Laramie Station.

This wasn't going to be such a bad ride. That final passenger was a real looker, and she was sitting in the center seat directly opposite him.

Paddy didn't plan to ride the coach the eighty-five miles from Laramie to North Platte Crossing, where Jenny McNabb might see him. Toward the end of the day, after passing through narrow Rattlesnake Canyon, a notorious place for Indian ambushes, the coach reached the Pass Creek swing station. Here, sixteen miles east of the North Platte River, was the last opportunity to leave the stagecoach at a point of some civilization. He would spend the night at Pass Creek, arise early in the morning, steal one of the station's horses, and ride around North Platte Crossing before rejoining the stage on the other side of the river.

"I'm getting off," Paddy said. He leaned forward, bringing his face close to the young lady as he rose, and breathed in her perfume. "Ma'am, ye'll be excusing me if I disturb ye."

The woman had looked at him briefly when she'd first taken her seat. After that, she'd avoided eye contact, keeping her head bowed. She raised her head now and grimaced. Paddy grinned his widest gap-tooth smile. He didn't care that his foul breath probably offended her.

Two stock men hurriedly changed the six-horse team. The stop would only be for a few minutes. Passengers were not permitted to dismount during the changeover at a swing station. It interfered with keeping to a schedule.

"Where do you think you're going, mister?" The driver looked down at him from the seat high on the front of the coach. "We're not to the end of the run."

"Sure, and I got business to attend to hereabouts. I'll catch up further along, don't ye know. Toss me down that carpetbag."

The driver wrapped the reins around the brake lever and climbed back into the pile of luggage. Paddy's bag had been one of the last loaded, so it was easy to retrieve. The driver dropped the bag into his waiting arms and stared at him with a fixed expression.

Paddy didn't know what was troubling that driver, but he didn't care for the look he was getting.

CHAPTER 17

"Hello, the cabin!" Paddy cupped his hands around his mouth to amplify his challenge. He sat the stolen horse on a high bank that rose steeply above a thicket of cottonwoods spread out below him. Through the branches he could see a small log cabin in a clearing that extended to the North Platte's edge.

"Hello, down there!" he called again. It wouldn't be wise to ride into that clearing without ensuring someone wouldn't greet him with gunfire. He leaned forward in the saddle and held his hand to the brim of his bowler hat to shield his eyes from the bright sun, and waited.

A few minutes later, a figure stepped out of the trees and looked up at him.

Paddy's mouth fell open. He hadn't expected this. He'd heard Bullfrog Charlie Munro had a cabin along the river. He'd somehow stumbled across it.

Lone Eagle, dressed in a buckskin, looked up the slope. He said nothing, he didn't motion, he just stared back at Paddy.

Paddy kicked the mare and headed down the steep cliff toward the clearing. As he descended, he studied the young man who awaited him below. The mixed-blood Cheyenne's black hair, tied back into a ponytail with a red cord, glistened in the noonday's sunlight. Paddy chuckled to himself. Lone Eagle probably slicked it down with bear grease, like Paddy had heard all savages did. But Lone Eagle looked more like a mountain man now, than a warrior.

"Well, sure, and if it's not the half-breed." Paddy reined the horse to a stop in front of the cabin.

Lone Eagle cradled in his arms a large bundle wrapped in a red trade blanket, which was decorated with bead and quill work.

"Scrawny Irishman," Lone Eagle said. "I told you before, I will cut your throat if you continue to insult me."

"Aw now, that ain't no insult. Sure, and it's just the truth." Paddy laughed.

Paddy's horse shuffled and snorted. A pungent odor assailed Paddy's nostrils. The stench coming from the cottonwood grove must be what was unsettling his mount. He spotted the scaffolds mounted between tree trunks.

"Them yer folks buried in the trees?" Paddy asked.

"My father is."

"Sure, and I heard tell the old man fought a grizzly and lost." He cackled. "Bet that was some sight to see, don't ye know."

Lone Eagle did not respond.

"What's that ye're holding in the blanket?" Paddy asked.

"These are the bones of my mother, Star Dancer."

"I see two scaffolds yonder. Why ain't her bones up there?"

"My mother lay there for many years." Lone Eagle shook the blanket roll. The contents rattled. "Now she is here."

Paddy cocked his head to the side and furrowed his brow in an unspoken question.

"Only her bones are left. I will take them to Elk Mountain and bury them in a cave with our ancestors."

Paddy's eyes widened and he reared his head back. He hadn't heard of this custom.

"It is a Cheyenne tradition." Lone Eagle continued. "Many tribes do it. After only the bones are left, the family places them in a sacred place. Someday my father's bones will join my mother's."

"Sure, and ye savages should be burying yer kin in the ground, like god-fearing white folks do."

"We are not savages," Lone Eagle said. "We honor our dead after they depart this life. We do not dump dirt on their faces and abandon them to the dark."

"Well, suit yerself."

"What are you doing here, O'Hannigan? What do you want?"

Paddy sensed the anger in Lone Eagle's terse questions.

"Sure, and I'm searching for a place to ford this cussed river, don't ye know. I'm on my way to California. Secret kinda mission, ye might say."

"There is no ford here."

"Well, and just how do travelers get across?"

"They use the ferry at North Platte Crossing . . . or swim."

"Well, d'ye see, I ain't going to be using Wells Fargo's ferry and if ye remember, I don't swim. And what be that I see tied up yonder? Sure, and it looks to me like it's rigged to be a ferry."

Paddy motioned to a log raft resting on the near bank. A series of ropes stretched from it to trees on opposite banks of the river.

"My father's old raft. He used it to take himself across the river. Not big enough for animals. They have to swim."

"I'll pay ye to take me across."

"I don't want your money, Irishman. I will take you over just to be rid of you."

Paddy drew his Navy Colt from its holster and cocked the hammer.

"Don't get no ideas about dumping me overboard . . . or I'll blow yer brains out."

Paddy watched Lone Eagle gently place the blanket bundle on a log bench beside a travois that leaned against the front wall of the cabin. He glared back at Paddy, then strode toward the riverbank. "Come, Irishman."

Paddy took a deep breath and wished he hadn't. He choked back a gag. He couldn't wait to get away from here. The smell of Bullfrog's decaying body was more than he could stomach.

Chapter 18

Jenny laid the buckskin dress on her cot and brushed it flat with her hand. She'd folded it last autumn and placed it in a small trunk her father had given her for storing the few belongings she owned. Everything she'd brought with her from Virginia had been burned in the covered wagon that night last year when the Cheyenne had abducted her. This was the first time she'd taken the dress out since the McNabbs had arrived at North Platte Crossing.

She removed her tattered, woolen shirt and pulled the dress over her head, smoothing it down over her trousers. She fingered the blue and yellow bead work that decorated the bodice of the soft leather. She shuddered when she thought about the time she'd been forced to wear the dress. She placed her palm against the side of her neck. She could almost feel the rawhide thong Chief Tall Bear's wife, Small Duck, had kept tied around her throat to lead her around the Cheyenne village like a horse while she did the old woman's chores. The only decent thing Small Duck had ever done for her was give her this beautiful buckskin dress. But Small Duck hadn't done that out of love or respect. The chief didn't want Jenny wearing a white woman's clothing in the camp.

Jenny sat on her cot and replaced her work boots with the moccasins she'd worn during the weeks she'd been a slave in the Indian village.

The door to the back room where the three McNabbs slept

swung open. Her father stood in the doorway.

"My goodness, what's the occasion?" he asked.

"No occasion. I was moving the trunk so I could sweep beneath it and decided to take a look. I hadn't opened the trunk since we moved here." She grinned at her father.

"It is a nice dress, Jenny, but not suitable for wearing around our passengers. There'll be a stage coming in within the hour. We wouldn't want to frighten the folks, would we?"

The front door to the station banged open.

"Pa! Come quick!" Jenny's brother shouted. "There's an Indian out by the corral."

"What?" Her father headed for the front door, reaching with his right arm to pick up his carbine from where it leaned in a corner.

"Franz has his rifle on him, Pa. But the fellow won't quit petting Buck. Maybe he plans to steal Will's horse."

Duncan stepped aside to let his father pass.

Jenny hurried out behind her father and brother.

"Step away from that horse!" Jenny's father cocked the hammer of the carbine. Because he only had one hand, he held the weapon low beside his waist, keeping the stock pressed against his side with his elbow.

The buckskin clad man turned slowly to face Jenny's father, but kept his hand pressed against Buck's forehead.

"No, Papa," Jenny said. "Wait. It's Lone Eagle."

Her father paused and looked at her. "The half-breed that captured you?"

"The Cheyenne warrior who spared my life . . . and helped me escape."

Lone Eagle stood before her in buckskin shirt and trousers. The last time she'd seen him, he'd been bare-chested and clad in a breechcloth. He still wore his black hair tied back with a red cord—but there was no beaded band, nor any feather, adorning his head. Hanging around his neck she saw his eagle talon amulet.

Jenny brushed her fingers along the talon she wore around her own neck, concealed beneath her clothes.

Her father eased the hammer down on his carbine. "It's all right, Franz. You can lower your rifle."

Franz Iversen pointed his rifle down, but left it cocked. "You sure, Mr. McNabb?"

Franz served as the stockman for the station, caring for the horses and changing the teams when a stagecoach arrived. Jenny and her brother helped him when they didn't have other chores.

"Yes," her father said. "Jenny knows him."

"What brings you here, Lone Eagle?" Jenny asked.

"I promised Will Braddock I would keep an eye on you while he is gone to California. I need to talk with you."

Jenny turned to her father. "It will be fine, Papa. He's not going to hurt me. Let me talk with him alone, please?"

Her father looked from Jenny back to Lone Eagle. "Franz, move back into the stable, but keep your rifle handy. I'll step back into the station. Only a few minutes, Jenny. We have to prepare for the incoming stage."

"Yes, Papa."

Her father motioned for Duncan to join him, and they entered the station.

Her father did not close the door. Jenny could see him standing back in the shadows of the station's interior. He continued to hold his carbine.

Jenny walked over to Lone Eagle. "Will told me what happened to Bullfrog," she said. "I'm sorry about your father's death."

"Thank you, Jenny." Lone Eagle's eyes scanned her up and down. "You are wearing the buckskin dress you wore in our camp. Why?"

Jenny chuckled. "You sound like my father."

"What?"

"Never mind. I haven't worn this dress since I returned to Fort Sanders last year. I came across it in my trunk and decided to put it on. No reason. Simply coincidence that it happened when you arrived."

"You look nice in it."

She pulled up the hem of the buckskin dress, revealing the old blue pants she wore. "Yes, I'm sure I do."

She dropped the hem and grinned at Lone Eagle. "What is it you want to tell me?"

"Paddy O'Hannigan came by my cabin yesterday. Will asked me to protect you from him. I wanted to be sure you were safe."

After the stage had arrived from Big Laramie last evening, Butch Cartwright told Jenny something she hadn't told her father. Butch told her about the scrawny, scar-faced fellow who'd left the stage at Pass Creek with a flimsy excuse about having local business to conduct. From the description, she knew it was Paddy O'Hannigan. But what business could that ruffian have with the stock handlers who looked after Well Fargo's stage horses at that tiny swing station? There wasn't anything else at Pass Creek. And why had he felt it necessary to leave the stage and avoid coming to North Platte Crossing?

"What did Paddy want?" she asked.

"He wanted to get across the river, but he didn't want to come here to do it. I ferried him over. He said something about going to California on a secret assignment. I do not know more than that."

Jenny sighed. "Thank you, Lone Eagle. I'll send a telegram to Will. He needs to know Paddy is on his way to California."

She wished Paddy had told Lone Eagle more about why he was making the trip. All she could do was warn Will to be on the lookout for the nasty Irishman.

CHAPTER 19

Will, his uncle Sean, and Jacob Blickensderfer walked toward the Continental Hotel in Salt Lake City, a half-dozen steps behind "Colonel" Silas Seymour and Sam Reed. Reed's request for a meeting with Brigham Young had been postponed numerous times, but now they were to have an audience. Seymour kept wagging his finger at Reed, lecturing him on what Doc Durant would expect Reed to say to the great Mormon leader.

Blickensderfer had been waiting for them when they arrived in Salt Lake City three days ago. Will had met the brilliant engineer last year, when he served as the government's inspector charged with determining where the Rocky Mountains started, that magical point at which the railroad had the right to draw on bonds at $48,000 per mile for construction costs. That was three times what the government paid for work on level ground and twice that for effort in the foothills. General Dodge had hired Blickensderfer away from the Department of the Interior to work for the Union Pacific and had assigned him the task of planning the construction across Utah.

Blickensderfer spoke in a low voice to Will's uncle. "I don't know who's worse, Seymour or Reed. That trumped-up, self-titled colonel creates consternation wherever he goes. And Reed used to have a stronger backbone than I've seen him exhibit lately."

"Reed can't seem to decide who he works for," Will's uncle said. "He's having a tough time walking the tight-rope between

General Dodge and Doc Durant. Dodge and Durant are at each other's throats all the time lately. Sometimes it's hard to believe they both work for the same company."

Since their arrival at the foot of the snow-capped Wasatch Mountains, Will had struggled to understand the way of life of the people who inhabited this lovely valley. Polygamy was officially illegal in the United States—but then Utah wasn't yet a state. Traditional religious thinking didn't accept the idea of multiple marriages. Will remembered Reverend Kincaid railing against the Latter-day Saints' practice on numerous occasions from his pulpit in Burlington, Iowa. Until the Mormons abolished polygamy, Utah would probably continue to be denied statehood.

While they'd waited for the meeting to take place with Brigham Young, Will had found plenty of time to walk around this largest city between the Mississippi River and California. His inspections confirmed that the Mormons were indeed industrious and prosperous. The clean streets were wide, with man-made streams of clear, mountain water running down each side.

The houses, surrounded by trees and flowers, were mostly constructed of adobe and logs. The two houses the men walked past now stood out as exceptions. These two-story edifices were built of adobe and sandstone. The Beehive House was larger than the Lion House, but it had been pointed out to Will on one of his earlier walks that they were both the homes of the Mormon leader.

"Uncle Sean," Will asked, "why does Brigham Young need two houses?"

His uncle laughed. "It's rumored he needs the room to house his multiple wives and numerous children."

Will looked ahead to where Seymour continued to shake his finger at Reed. "Remember, Samuel," Seymour said, "be noncommittal about our route through Utah. Even though

Young's a stockholder in the UP, Durant doesn't want him to know we don't plan to run the railroad through Salt Lake City. Young doesn't have to know yet that we're staking out a route around the northern end of the lake."

An hour later, as their meeting drew to a close, Brigham Young leaned back in his swivel chair and folded his hands over his ample stomach. He stared across his desk at Reed and Seymour. Above his close-trimmed beard, he clamped his clean-shaven upper lip down firmly onto the lower one. "Gentlemen, I think we can reach an accommodation. However, I'd feel more comfortable if you could assure me the railroad intends to come into our capital city."

"Well." Reed shifted in his chair. "That's a question you'll have to pose directly to the vice president and general manager . . . when he comes here next."

"I intend to do that."

"This contract will be for grading, tunneling, and bridge building from the head of Echo Canyon into Ogden, only," Reed said. "The Irish tracklayers will follow. We'll do our best to keep the Irish separated from your workers."

"I appreciate that. Most of our fellows have the fortitude to avoid strong drink, which is a good thing, since our beliefs forbid it. But avoiding the temptation in the first place is part of the battle."

Reed stood and extended his hand across the desk. "So, we're agreed?"

"Agreed." Young stood and grasped Reed's hand. "Our men need the work. The locusts have destroyed our crops the last three years running. We still have to feed our families."

Will was glad he didn't have to exert the effort necessary to feed such a large family. He remembered how hard he and his mother had struggled just to take care of the two of them.

★ ★ ★ ★ ★

The next day, Will and his uncle said goodbye to Reed and Blickensderfer outside the Wells Fargo stage station. Since Seymour wasn't an early riser, they'd managed to avoid him.

"Homer," Will's uncle said, "stay with Otto and Joe until we return. The three of you can help Sam with his survey work north of the lake. I'll send a telegram to Sam when we're on our way back, and you can come back in to Salt Lake City and rejoin us here."

"Yes, sir," Homer said. "What 'bout Otto and Joe?"

"I'll leave them with Sam until I learn what General Dodge has in mind for the team."

"All aboard, folks." The Wells Fargo agent announcement came from the boardwalk that ran in front of the station.

Half-a-dozen passengers crowded aboard the coach, jockeying for the best seats for the six-hundred-mile journey to Carson City, Nevada. Will and his uncle didn't manage to get the seat under the driver, but they did avoid the center one. The rear seat would force them to eat more dust, but at least they'd have a solid backrest for the fifteen-day trip.

The driver snapped the ribbons, cracked the whip, and the coach rolled away from Salt Lake City's home station. Will leaned out the window for a final look at the pleasant community. He did an immediate double-take. That looked like Paddy O'Hannigan walking into the Wells Fargo office.

Chapter 20

"Call me Stro, Mr. Corcoran. My friends call me Stro." James Strobridge's voice boomed like a field boss trying to get the attention of some faraway worker. He winked at Will and his uncle with his one good eye. He wore a black patch over his right eye, which he'd lost to a delayed blast of powder when the Central Pacific constructed the Bloomer Cut, four years ago.

Will thought the six-foot-two Strobridge would make a great pirate.

"All right, Stro. Then you'll have to call me Sean."

Strobridge guffawed. "Right, Sean! We Irish have to stick together, don't we?"

"That we do," Will's uncle said.

"Let's sit a spell and let that supper digest." Strobridge motioned to two rocking chairs on the converted boxcar's recessed verandah. "It's a cool evening, but at least it isn't snowing. We've been shoveling snow for three months to clear the grade for laying the connecting tracks between Summit Tunnel up above and Truckee down here. Just finished that job last night."

"If the tracks weren't laid all the way through, how'd you get the rolling stock and the rails here?" Will's uncle asked.

"Dragged everything down the wagon road on ox-drawn sleds—hundreds of trips. Had to break the locomotives into manageable pieces, then reassemble them here."

Will sat on the floor of the narrow porch, between the two

men in their rocking chairs, and dangled his feet off the edge. It reminded him of last year, when he'd ridden across Nebraska in General Dodge's boxcar stable with the door open. Except then, it'd been warm. Mr. Strobridge was right—this evening was cool. Will pulled his buckskin jacket closer around him.

"Tell me, Sean, are you a drinking Irishman?" Strobridge asked.

"I enjoy a good Irish whiskey from time to time."

"Not me. Teetotaler. Don't touch the evil stuff."

Will's uncle didn't have to make a response because Hanna Strobridge stepped out onto the verandah with a steaming pot she held with a towel. "More coffee, gents?"

"Yes, please," his uncle said.

She filled his cup and then her husband's. "Would you like some, Will?"

"No thanks, ma'am. I had enough with supper. And thank you again, ma'am, for that good meal."

"You're most welcome." Mrs. Strobridge stepped back into the portable home she shared with her husband and two children. She'd converted the railcar into comfortable family accommodations, even hanging curtains over windows cut into the boxcar's walls. A canary chirped away in a cage hung at one corner of the verandah.

Strobridge's combination work-home train sat in Truckee Canyon, far below the Summit Tunnel, the highest and longest of the twelve tunnels the Central Pacific had dug through the Sierra Nevada. To keep from falling behind in their race with the UP, the CP had worked on both sides of the mountain range the previous year. Now that the rails were joined, CP trains could roll straight through from Sacramento, California, to Reno, Nevada.

Will watched the shadows creep across Donner Lake as the sun descended behind the mountain peaks. Here, at the eastern end of the beautiful lake, the ill-fated Donner Party had been forced to spend the winter twenty-one years ago. It was rumored they'd committed cannibalism to stay alive. Will had heard that story told many times.

Crowded around the lake's shore and flowing up the slopes on both sides of the broad valley, tall fir trees stretched their needle points upward. Will thought the Union Pacific would love to have access to such wonderful stands of timber.

With the loss of sunlight, the blue of the lake water turned to deepening shades of gray, as did the green boughs of the trees. Gradually, they all blended into black on the valley floor.

"So, Sean," Strobridge said. "Dodge sent you to start negotiations for a meeting point."

"Right. And since you're the CP's construction superintendent, I thought you'd be the man to talk to."

Strobridge's laugh boomed again. "Well, that's not my decision to make. I'm more like your Jack Casement in the chain of command. I just build what they tell me. I suggest you talk to Monty."

"Monty?"

"Samuel Montague. He's our chief engineer . . . like your General Dodge. He, and to be fair about it, Louis Clement, his assistant, engineered the Summit Tunnel and designed the snow sheds you see all along the cliffs up there." He pointed with his coffee cup to where the final rays of the sun still illuminated the heavy-timbered structures that hugged the side of the mountain where the CP had blasted out the path for their tracks. The shed's roofs were buried in snow, but that kept the tracks within them clear. "We'll be building more snow sheds. Expensive . . . but cheaper than shoveling that bloody stuff all the time."

"Where'll I find Montague?" Will's uncle asked.

"I'll take you to him tomorrow. If Monty ain't got the authority to agree to a meeting place, you'll have to talk to Cholly Clocka."

"Cholly Clocka?"

The "pirate" threw his head back and bellowed a harsh laugh. "Yeah. That's what the Celestials call him. Charley Crocker. He's the one of the 'Big Four' that calls the shots for the CP."

The Central Pacific's "Big Four." Will had read their names in the newspapers and heard General Dodge talk about them. They were the force behind building the western half of the transcontinental railroad. Leland Stanford, a former governor of California, served as president of the CP. Mark Hopkins oversaw the company's finances in Sacramento, while Collis Huntington guided their political maneuvering in the nation's capital. Charles Crocker stayed out on the line making sure work progressed as fast as possible. All four were Sacramento merchants who'd made their fortunes selling supplies to the forty-niners during the gold rush.

"Who're the Celestials?" Will looked up at Strobridge.

"That's what we call the Chinese. I didn't want 'em in the first place. Thought they weren't big enough to do the work. But the bloody Irish kept getting drunk all the time, and threatening to strike, so I finally let Crocker talk me into trying a few of them. Best dang workers we've ever had. Almost all our crews are Celestials now. Still use Irish for supervisors. But the Chinese don't drink, don't fight, don't strike, and have clean habits . . . generally speaking. Sunday's a down day for us and that's when the little runts relax, do their gambling, and smoke their opium. Filthy habit, but they don't overdo it. They're never too hung over to come to work."

Strobridge rocked back and forth sipping his coffee. "The Chinese are real powder monkeys too. They seem to have a natural love for fireworks. When we made the cut high up on Cape Horn we didn't have any room to work . . . it being so narrow. The Celestials came up with the scheme to get the job done. They lowered each other down the cliff face in wicker baskets. Hanging in those baskets they pounded holes in the cliff with hand drills and packed the holes with powder. They cut the fuses to varying lengths so an entire round of charges would go off at the same time. The louder the blast, the more they thought it scared off the evil spirits."

He laughed, then paused. "We didn't lose a single one of them on that job. That's what really convinced me they knew how to work."

Strobridge leaned forward and set his cup on the railing. "Only real problem we had with them weren't their fault. Bunches of 'em started heading back to San Francisco a few weeks back. Refused to work in the Nevada desert. I tracked the source down to some rascals who were telling them there were giant snakes out there that'd swallow a man whole. Once we got that rumor squashed, they came back."

Will grinned at the story. Rattlesnakes were bad enough—they didn't have to be giant to scare him.

"Getting a little chilly out here now the sun's gone." Strobridge stood and lifted the bird cage from its hook. "If you'll excuse me, I'll call it a day. Got to get this canary back inside. Hanna will have my hide if it freezes to death. You fellows can bunk down in my office car if you like. You'll have to spread your blankets on the floor, but at least it's warm. It's the next car up."

Chapter 21

Early the next morning, Strobridge took Will and his uncle from Truckee Junction, at the foot of Donner Lake, up the eastern slope of the Sierra Nevada toward Donner Pass and the Summit Tunnel. They rode an empty construction train headed back for a load of rails.

The three of them stood in the open doorway of an empty boxcar as it climbed the steep, twisting route, higher and higher away from the lake. At Horseshoe Bend, three miles up a narrow defile created by Clear Creek, the train doubled back on itself crossing the tumbling waters on a rickety bridge to get to the other side of the canyon. On the sharper curves, Will could see the 4-4-0 locomotive pulling their train belch large balls of black smoke from its diamond smokestack with each stroke of its driving pistons.

Shortly after crossing the creek, the train dove into Tunnel Thirteen, the first of many before they would reach the summit. Inside the narrow confines of the tunnel the engine's smoke engulfed them. Will covered his nose, but couldn't suppress a cough.

"You'll look like a coal miner by the time we get there." Strobridge laughed.

They emerged from the tunnel and the train clattered around a sweeping curve on the outer edge of a sheer cliff. Far below, the crystal, blue waters of Donner Lake came into view.

"Wow!" Will exclaimed. "Spectacular!"

Strobridge laughed again. "We're better than halfway to our destination at this point. We've gained eight hundred feet since we left Truckee Junction, eight miles back. We'll gain another five hundred before we get to Summit Tunnel . . . six miles ahead. We'll be over seven thousand feet at Donner Pass."

Snow covered the steep slope all the way down to the lake, five-hundred feet below the tracks. White sprinkles clung to the branches of the fir trees. The beautiful view ended abruptly when the train ducked into a snow shed. It wasn't as dark as a tunnel, but the smoke concentrated almost as thickly.

"Much fire danger?" Will's uncle pointed to sparks emitted from the smokestack that clung to the heavy rafters overhead.

"It's a problem," Strobridge answered. "We spray the timbers with water to keep them damp. But sometimes a fire gets started that we can't put out. We've had to rebuild some of the sheds."

They chugged out of the snow shed and immediately plunged into a tunnel.

Will counted seven tunnels and twice that many snow sheds, strung tightly together, until they finally emerged onto an open stretch of track not covered with a shed. Far below Donner Lake looked no bigger than a pond.

"Tunnel Six is just ahead," Strobridge said. "We call it Summit Tunnel. It's twice as long as any other. Almost seventeen-hundred feet. Completing this tunnel is what held up connecting the rails for so long."

The smoke wasn't so thick in this tunnel, which Will thought strange since it was the longest. Partway through the tunnel the train passed beneath a shaft of sunlight.

"We dug this tunnel from both ends and the middle at the same time," Strobridge said. "We dropped this central shaft down from the top of the mountain and had teams work in both directions outward until they met up with the teams coming in from each end. The shaft provides ventilation and helps keep the smoke level down."

Since they'd departed Truckee, the slight grade of the tracks caused Will to lean toward the front of the train, now his balance suddenly shifted rearward. They'd passed the highest point of the Sierras. The train headed downward toward an expanding point of light approaching from ahead. They steamed through the western portal of the tunnel, straight into another snow shed, then slowed to a halt.

"We're here." Strobridge jumped down from the open boxcar door. Will and his uncle followed. Strobridge led them, still inside the snow shed, to an opening in the heavy timbered walls.

Will stepped out of the shed's dimness into brilliant sunlight. He threw his hand up to shield his eyes from the glistening snow. The area adjacent to the shed and several nearby buildings had been cleared of snow, but several yards away the drifts towered over the heads of workmen who scurried about the site.

"Snow's eighteen feet deep on the level here," Strobridge said. "We keep half the workforce busy just shoveling the stuff." He waved a hand toward the distant snowbank where dozens of men filled hand carts with snow.

Stumps covered the ground between Will and the shovelers. The Central Pacific had denuded the forest for a hundred yards away from the tracks for the timbers they needed for the massive snow sheds.

"Let's go see if we can find Monty." Strobridge led them toward a large wooden structure attached to the snow shed. "He's probably over here in the maintenance facility."

"Uncle Sean," Will said. "If you don't mind, I'll just look around out here for a while."

"Sure thing." His uncle stepped in behind Strobridge, following him along a depressed pathway that had been worn in the snow.

The shovelers wore neat blue coats and trousers. Umbrella-shaped, woven straw hats, covered their heads. Pigtails extended down their backs. Sunglasses shielded their eyes—a good precaution against the snow blindness that would render them ineffective, otherwise. Will wished he had a pair. The glare was overpowering.

Scattered among the shovelers, a few taller individuals wore the ragtag remnants of Army uniforms, both Union and Confederate. Will was used to seeing the same thing on the Union Pacific's workforce. It didn't take long to determine they were the Irish supervisors. They slapped whips against a boot or tapped clubs into the palm of a hand.

"Hurry up with that tea!" one of the supervisors shouted. "It's break time."

" 'Scuse prease." Will looked over his shoulder to see where that strangely accented comment had come from. A shorter figure, dressed in blue, shuffled up behind him, balancing a long pole across his shoulders, on each end of which hung wooden barrels. Will recognized them as the standard, black powder, storage kegs.

"I said hurry up with that tea!" The supervisor snapped his bullwhip and nipped the young man in the side.

"Ow!" The slender youth jumped sideways and dropped the pole. Brown tea flooded from the barrels, sinking into the snow.

"You good for nothing, yellow-bellied Celestial!" The Irishman stepped toward the Chinese boy and raised his whip. The shovelers stopped all along the snowbank and looked.

Will stepped between them. "It was my fault, sir. I was blocking his way."

The Irishman towered over Will. "And just who are you?"

Chapter 22

Before Will could give the supervisor his name, a hand clasped his shoulder from behind. "He's with me," Strobridge said. "Get on about your business, MacNamara."

"Yes, sir." The Irishman slapped the whip against his boot and turned toward the snowbank. "Back to work! All you bloody Celestials, get back to work! No tea break."

"Sorry, Mr. Strobridge, I didn't mean to cause them to lose their tea break."

"It's all right, Will." Strobridge looked unsmilingly at him, then winked with his one good eye. "They'll get plenty of tea."

Will's uncle stood behind Strobridge. He shook his head, but said nothing.

"Come on, Sean," Strobridge said. "Monty's down along the tracks inspecting a collapse in the shed's roof. The snow gets too heavy sometimes. We'll find him down there a ways."

"You coming, Will?" his uncle asked.

"No, sir. I'll see if I can help remedy my mistake here."

"Be careful." His uncle stepped in behind Strobridge who strode off down the outside of the snow shed.

The tea boy regained his feet. He lifted his pole and buckets back onto his shoulders.

"I'm sorry," Will said.

"You friend of One-eye Bossy Man?"

"One-eye Bossy Man?"

The Chinese youth nodded in the direction of Strobridge.

Of course, Strobridge only had one good eye. "Mr. Strobridge . . . yes," Will said.

The youth bowed slightly. " 'Scuse prease." He turned and walked up the snow path.

"Wait." Will followed him. "I'll help."

"How?" The Chinese youth kept walking.

"I can carry tea. The men will be extra thirsty when they finally get their break. I was in your way. I caused the problem."

"Problem caused by big Mac, not you."

"But I want to help."

The Chinese youth stopped and turned abruptly. Will had to duck to keep from being leveled by the swinging pole and the bucket.

Will threw up his hands. "Whoa. You don't have to knock me down just because I caused you to fall."

A grin creased the Chinese youth's lips. He bowed again. "Apologies."

"Apology accepted. Now can I help? My name's Will Braddock, by the way."

"Chung Huang." The youth bowed slightly. "Come." He turned and led Will up the narrow path through the snow.

They circled the large wooden maintenance facility and disappeared into a snow tunnel. Chung Huang didn't say anything as he led Will deeper into a maze hollowed out beneath the drifts. Small shacks lined each side of a wide pathway carved through the packed snow. Each shack was set back into the snowbank. Dim light filtered through a roof of snow that overarched the pathway from bank to bank.

Chung Huang opened a door into one of the shacks and stepped inside. He laid his pole and buckets on the wooden floor beside a potbellied stove standing in the center of the room. A metal stovepipe passed upward through the roof of the structure. Will surmised it penetrated on through the snow above. Along the walls Will counted eight sets of double bunks. Even though water dripped from the wooden ceiling, the hut was warm.

An elderly man, the only other occupant, stirred a pot on the stove.

Chung Huang bowed to the older man. "Prease to present, Will Braddock."

The old man nodded to Will.

"Hsi Wang is cook for our gang," Chung Huang said.

"How do you do," Will said. He didn't know whether or not to shake hands.

Hsi Wang nodded again and continued stirring the pot.

"Each gang has its own hut?" Will ask.

"Yes. Cholly Clocka pays head man wages for gang each week. Head man gives money to cook for food, then pays gang members from what is left."

On the stove next to the pot containing the food, a pot of tea boiled. Chung Huang scooped the tea into his barrels with a ladle.

"This is a very confining, gloomy place to live," Will said. The only light in the hut came from candles and the glow from the stove.

Chung Huang shrugged. "Snow gone soon. Then nice."

"Do you get any time off?"

"Sunday."

"And what do you do on Sunday?"

"Read books."

"Read books?"

"Yes, read on Sunday. Old men smoke opium. Me . . . no. Don't like it."

"How long have you been here?"

Chung Huang filled one bucket with steaming tea and started on the second. "Me . . . long time. I join gang last summer."

"Did you come from China?"

"No. San Francisco. I send money to my auntie."

"That's nice."

Chung Huang completed filling the second bucket and stooped to lift the pole. Will bent to help.

"No, my job," the Chinese youth said. "You bring cup."

Will took the tin cup Chung Huang lifted from his belt and handed it to him.

They returned to the snowbank where Chung Huang served tea to the shovelers. Will couldn't imagine the tea being hot by the time they'd walked back through the cold weather with it, but the workers smacked their lips with pleasure as they sipped the lukewarm beverage. The Irish supervisor MacNamara stood to one side, slapping his whip against his boot and sipping from a pocket flask. Whiskey no doubt. He glared at Will and Chung Huang. Will stared back.

Strobridge had commented on the train ride this morning about another benefit of using Chinese workers. They stayed healthier by drinking tea instead of the creek water that the Irish consumed. Boiling the tea water killed the germs that plagued those who consumed untreated water.

"Break's over!" MacNamara shouted. "Back to work!"

Chung Huang picked up his pole and empty buckets and headed back toward the snow tunnel. Will followed.

Whoom!

An explosion shook the ground beneath Will's feet. Looking up, he watched a cloud of snow erupt skyward, then float back down, above the location of Summit Tunnel.

Chung Huang pointed up the slope, beyond the maintenance facility. A thin column of black smoke hung in the air, beside a small shack nestled amidst a rocky formation. "Nitroglycerin," he said.

"Nitroglycerin?" Will looked at his companion.

Chung Huang nodded. "Shack belongs to chemist, James Howden. My cousin works there as his assistant making nitroglycerin."

A muffled pistol shot caused Will to look back toward the shack.

"May be problem there," Chung Huang said. "Shot came from inside shack."

"Let's go see," Will said.

Chung Huang dropped his pole and raced past the maintenance building.

Will chased after him. Behind the building a winding path climbed toward the shack. Will, the faster climber, reached the plateau ahead of Chung Huang, just as the door of the shack flew open. A short man stepped through the doorway, saddlebags in one hand and a pistol in the other. He looked directly at Will with eyes partially concealed beneath the brim of a bowler hat. A scar ran down his left cheek. Paddy O'Hannigan!

Chapter 23

Paddy had arrived in Truckee the day before. He'd avoided the railroad yards in the bustling new town. He had business with the Central Pacific, but nothing he intended to pay for, and not in Truckee. It made sense not to let anyone connected with the railroad get a good look at him.

He hitched a ride with an old Irish teamster heading back up the wagon road to Donner Summit. Even though the railroad tracks were now connected through to Truckee, the CP was not yet offering regular service. Most freight still moved across the Sierras by wagon, just as the teamsters had done it for twenty years hauling supplies to the silver mines in Nevada, and more recently construction materials for the railroad.

The teamster had been glad for the company and hadn't charged Paddy anything. He'd told Paddy it was a pleasure to talk with someone on the slow, steep climb—someone who understood the tribulations of a fellow immigrant from the Emerald Isle.

The climb from Donner Lake to Donner Pass took the better part of the day. The road snaked back and forth through one hairpin curve after another. Snowdrifts lined the road in those places except where the shear drop precluded the snow's accumulation.

The teamster told Paddy he'd hauled supplies for the CP from the very beginning. He claimed his team of mules knew the road so well they didn't need a skinner. But he fussed at them all the way anyway. "Up Charlie! Up Elmer! Git a move on thar! Not too close that cliff's edge, mind you. Up, I say! Pull!"

Paddy sliced an end off his tobacco plug with his Bowie knife. He grinned when he saw the driver examining the knife out of the corner of his eye. He chewed his tobacco wad, spitting off to the side of the wagon from time to time, and let the old man do most of the talking. Paddy extracted the information he needed about his destination by pretending to be fascinated with the experiences the old man related about the construction work on the railroad while he'd driven his rig alongside the route of the tracks over the years.

"Well now, you say they used nitroglycerin to blast them tunnels up yonder," Paddy said. He pointed across the steep slope that rose above the wagon road to where the tracks wound around the mountainside.

"Yep. They stopped me up here at the summit more than once. Held me there, they did, until they finished their blasting and all the rubble rolled down the mountainside. Good thing, too. Ever once in a while them rocks landed on the wagon road. Been kilt for sure."

"That nitro's dangerous, I understand."

"Well, I aim to tell ya it is. They keep it stashed away from the tracks in a separate shack. Thataway I 'spose if it blows up, wouldn't be too many folks hurt."

"But that shack couldn't be too far away, or they couldn't get to it without a lot of bother."

"Oh, the shack where they mix the stuff sits on a rocky outcrop right above the Summit Pass tunnel."

Paddy parted ways with the teamster at the top of the pass. He waved goodbye to the talkative old driver and watched the wagon roll away down the road. "Sure, and I thank ye, old timer," he muttered. "Ye made my job a lot easier, and that's for certain."

Paddy traveled light. He only carried a pair of saddlebags. What few personal belongings he owned were stashed in the bottom of one pocket. The other pocket was empty.

He stepped off the road and found concealment in a thick stand of fir trees. He shivered in the cold air of Donner Pass, even though morning sunlight bounced off the snowbanks. Only a light breeze blew across the summit. He wouldn't want to be up here in bad weather. Wagons and groups of riders on horseback passed along the road at irregular intervals. Finally, he saw what he needed. A solitary rider approached.

Paddy spit out his tobacco chaw, making a dirty brown scar in the snow. He drew his revolver, stepped out of the trees in front of the rider, and pointed the pistol at the man's chest. "Hold it," he said. "Get down. Slow and easy like, don't ye know. And keep yer hands up."

The rider stepped from the saddle and raised his hands. He wore a heavy wool coat. If he were armed, the weapon would be beneath the coat's long tail. It wouldn't be easy for him to reach it.

"Lead that horse over into them trees," Paddy said. He followed the rider. "Sure, and that's far enough. Don't turn around."

"You can have the horse," the man said. "Just don't shoot me."

"Sure, and I'll have the horse." Paddy hit the man hard over the head with his pistol butt. "And I'll have whatever money ye've got on ye, and that nice warm coat, too."

After leaving the knocked-out rider concealed in the trees, it took Paddy only a few minutes to find the explosives shed exactly where the teamster told him it would be. The stiff winds that regularly blew across the summit scoured most of the snow away, providing a decent path for riding. Paddy guided the stolen horse up to the side of the shack and dismounted. He lifted the saddlebags off the horse's rump and stepped around to the front of the building. He drew his revolver and opened the single door.

A diminutive Chinaman, dressed in a blue jacket and trousers, looked up when Paddy stepped inside. Paddy motioned with the pistol for the man to raise his hands. The Chinaman was alone in the tiny structure. A workbench extended the length of one wall. Glass bottles of various sizes lined shelves above the workbench. Three large barrels stood along the opposite wall.

"Speak English?" Paddy asked.

The Chinaman nodded. "Yes."

"James Howden . . . the chemist. He here?"

The Chinaman shook his head. "Gone to Sacramento."

"This the nitroglycerin shack?"

The Chinaman's pigtail bobbed when he nodded again.

"Sure, and yer gonna show me how to mix the chemicals to make nitroglycerin. Understand?"

Another nod.

"Well get to it! Mix a sample in that little bottle there so's I can see if it works." Paddy pointed his revolver at the smallest bottle on the shelf.

The Chinaman took a glass beaker to the barrel labeled nitric acid and measured liquid from it. He returned to the workbench and poured the acid into the small bottle. It smelled and looked like strong horse urine.

The Chinaman brought a beaker of sulfuric acid from the second barrel and added an equal amount of it to the bottle. Paddy snorted. This stuff stunk of rotten eggs.

From the third barrel the man brought back glycerin. He poured the thick glycerin slowly into the bottle. Paddy hoped the Chinaman knew what he was doing.

The Chinaman sealed the bottle with a cork, rocked it back and forth gently, and set it on the workbench. The three chemicals combined, coating the interior of the glass with an oily, yellow film.

Paddy noted the quantities of each chemical the Chinaman had measured. Now he knew how to mix nitroglycerin. At least, he thought he did.

"Test it," Paddy said. He waved to the open door with his pistol.

"What?"

"Throw it out there. Let's see if it explodes."

The Chinaman carried the bottle to the open door and threw it far down the slope.

Whoom!

The explosion shook the tiny shack. The snow pack where the bottle landed erupted in a powdery cloud. A thin column of black smoke rose from the site.

"Sure, and that's the stuff all right." Paddy smiled. "Now put some of each chemical in separate bottles and seal them." He pointed to larger bottles.

The Chinaman filled the three large bottles, pushed a cork into each, and sealed them with paraffin wax. Paddy wrapped the bottles with his spare clothes and placed them in the saddlebags.

The explosion would have alerted the workers in and around the maintenance facility. Maybe they would think it was just an accident, or a test. But, no use taking a chance on the Chinaman sounding an alarm. Paddy shot him in the thigh.

"Agh!" The man doubled over and grasped his wound. Paddy whacked him over the skull with the pistol barrel. The Chinaman crumpled.

Paddy stepped outside and froze. A man ran up the slope toward him.

Will Braddock!

CHAPTER 24

When Will saw Paddy raise the pistol and cock the hammer, he dove behind a large rock outcropping. Paddy fired. The bullet ricocheted off a boulder, showering Will with slivers of granite. Will scooted farther down the slope, deeper into the jumble of rocks. A second bullet zinged past his head and buried itself into a snowbank, with a swish.

Chung Huang reached the plateau and dove into the rocks alongside Will. When he landed, his broad-brimmed straw hat fell down his back. The chin strap kept him from losing it.

"Giddup!"

Will heard Paddy's shout and eased his head above the rocks in time to see the Irishman slap his horse's flanks with the reins and disappear around the back of the shack. Paddy came back into view above the shack, riding up the slope toward the trees. The snowdrifts were less deep on the windswept summit, which would give Paddy a good start, but when he reached the deeper drifts at the tree line, he would have to slow down.

"Come on," Will said. He raced toward the shack. Chung Huang pulled his hat up and followed.

They stepped into the small explosives building. The chemist's assistant lay on the floor. Blood soaked the man's trouser leg. His eyes were closed, his breathing shallow.

"No!" Chung Huang dropped to the floor. "Cousin Ming, speak to me."

Will grabbed a rag from the counter and handed it to Chung.

"Press this onto the wound to stop the bleeding. I'm going after Paddy."

"You know him?"

"Yes, I know him."

Will drew his pistol from its flapped holster. He quickly checked the loading in each cylinder and the seating of each percussion cap. "You stay with your cousin. Help will be here soon."

As Will stepped through the open door, he saw groups of workers struggling up the slope through the snow. He slipped along the side of the shack and peered behind it. Paddy, approaching the tree line, paused before riding beneath the cedar trees, raised his pistol, and fired at Will. The bullet flew high, thumping into the wooden-walled shack above Will's head.

"Humph." Will snorted. Paddy can't shoot. That's good.

Will raised his revolver, braced his forearm against the edge of the shack with his free hand, took aim, and fired at Paddy.

Paddy's bowler hat flew off his head. He turned back and fired another shot at Will. This shot flew wide of the shack. Paddy kicked the horse in the flank and disappeared into the trees. Will raced across the rocky summit past an air vent that he suspected was the one connected to the central opening that extended down through the solid granite into Summit Tunnel, a hundred feet beneath him.

Will stopped at the tree line. Paddy's path led farther up the mountain through the deep snow. Will would have the big trees to hide behind if Paddy should fire at him again. But could Will catch the Irishman on foot? He might, if he had Otto's snowshoes. But he didn't.

Ahead of him, Will heard Paddy urge his horse forward. Why was Paddy struggling through the snow in the forest? Riding down the wagon road would have been easier.

Then it dawned on Will. It would be a simple matter for the

CP officials to telegraph down to Truckee and set a posse out to catch Paddy when he got down to Donner Lake. Paddy was up to no good and knew he'd have to evade capture. But what was he doing here in the first place? And what might it mean for the Union Pacific?

The deep snow soon soaked Will's trousers and filtered into his boots. His feet grew colder. On foot he wasn't going to catch Paddy.

"Whew." Will blew out his breath. A cloud of steam hung in the frigid air in front of his face. He jammed his revolver into his holster and turned back.

Will reached the explosives shack just as two Chinese workers carried Chung Huang's cousin out of it on a stretcher. They crossed the snow field and headed down the slope toward the tracks.

Chung Huang stepped out of the shed and raised his eyebrows at Will.

Will shook his head. "Snow's too deep. I couldn't keep up with the horse."

Chung Huang nodded.

"How's your cousin?"

"Flesh wound."

"Passed clean through?"

"Yes," Chung Huang said.

"He'll be fine then. I know." Will unconsciously rubbed his left bicep where the wound from the arrow still throbbed when he thought about it.

"Also, has bad lump on head," Chung Huang said. "Ming say man hit him with gun after shooting him."

Will shook his head. He knew how much a whack on the skull hurt, too. "Your cousin say what Paddy wanted here?"

"Chemicals to make nitroglycerin."

"Nitroglycerin?" What did Paddy O'Hannigan plan to do

with nitroglycerin?

A few minutes later Will rejoined his uncle and Mr. Strobridge at the CP's maintenance building. He told them about Paddy O'Hannigan taking the ingredients for making the explosive.

Strobridge reached into a coat pocket and handed Will a telegram. "This might have helped . . . had it arrived earlier."

Will unfolded the single sheet, glanced at it, then read it aloud.

PADDY COMING CALIFORNIA STOP SLIPPED SECRETLY ACROSS NORTH PLATTE ON MAY 9 STOP BE CAREFUL STOP JENNY

"May 9," Will said, "that was over a month ago."

"That telegram's been sitting in our Sacramento headquarters since it was sent," Strobridge said. "It was addressed to William Braddock in care of Central Pacific. The telegraphers didn't know what to do with it. There's no William Braddock on the CP's payroll. I had sent a report to headquarters about you and your uncle's visit yesterday. When they received it, they evidently made the connection and re-routed the telegram back here."

"Jenny knew I was coming to California," Will said, "but I didn't tell her where. I didn't know where myself."

"But how did Jenny know Paddy was coming to California?" his uncle asked.

Will shook his head. "That's a good question, Uncle Sean."

CHAPTER 25

Will waited on the platform at the Summit Station alongside James Strobridge while his uncle talked with Charles Crocker and Samuel Montague. His uncle had briefly introduced him to the Central Pacific's construction manager and chief engineer when they'd stepped down from the train now stopped on the track beside the station. Montague stood a head taller than his uncle and Crocker a head shorter.

Crocker defended his ground like a bulldog—short, thick, pugnacious. He couldn't seem to speak in a normal voice, and his only facial hair, a sharply pointed goatee, bounced beneath his chin when he bellowed. "No, Corcoran. You go back and tell your General Dodge and Doc Durant that the CP has no intention of agreeing to a meeting point this early. Collis Huntington is prowling the halls of Congress daily drumming up support from every senator and representative who'll listen that we have the right to press across Nevada and as deep into Utah as we can. We'll make it to Ogden before the Union Pacific, and you can bet on that."

"I'll tell them, Mr. Crocker. But it seems a waste of money and effort."

"Ha!" Crocker roared. "We'll see about that. The UP will have more miles of road than the CP, and collect more acres of free government land along your right-of-way, no matter what. And you were building most of your track over level prairie, until you reached the Rockies."

Montague stood silently, rubbing his thumb and forefinger over his mustache and down through his closely trimmed beard. The evening Will and his uncle had sat with Strobridge on the porch of his railcar home outside Truckee, Strobridge had described Montague as one of the smartest men working for the CP. He'd been the one who had solved the engineering problems that many said precluded the construction of a railroad across the Sierra Nevada Mountains. But Strobridge had also said Montague wasn't comfortable with the politics that were the purview of the "Big Four," of which Crocker was perhaps the most outspoken.

A conductor leaned from the steps of the leading passenger car. "Mr. Montague," he said, "we're ready."

"Time to board, Corcoran," Montague said. "This is a red-letter day for the CP. First passenger train to run from Sacramento, across the mountains, and into Nevada. Even though you're the competition, we've arranged for seats for you and your nephew to Reno." A broad grin creased his face. "Our compliments."

"Thank you, Monty," his uncle said. He turned to Will. "Ready?"

"Yes, sir."

"And thank you, Stro." His uncle shook hands with Strobridge, then Montague.

"Sure thing, Sean. Always glad to help a fellow Irishman." His laugh boomed over the hissing steam escaping from the engine's driving cylinders.

"Mr. Crocker, I'll convey your message to my superiors. Thank you for meeting with me." His uncle extended his hand to the corpulent man.

Crocker shook the offered hand. "Good luck, Corcoran. And may the best company win." His laugh shook his heavy waistline.

Will's uncle boarded and Will stepped onto the car's steps

right behind him. He paused and looked up the slope to the explosives shack, then down to the snowy path beside the maintenance facility. Chung Huang trudged along carrying his buckets of tea.

Will jumped off the step and raced across the platform. He cupped his hands around his mouth and shouted. "Chung Huang!"

The Chinese youth looked up and grinned. He walked toward Will, raising a hand in greeting.

"Your cousin all right?"

Chung Huang nodded, his big straw hat bobbing. "He will be fine, thank you."

"Maybe we'll meet again when the rails join."

"Maybe. I hope by then to be a tracklayer, not just a tea boy."

"I'll look for you next year. Someplace in Utah, maybe."

The train's whistle sounded two short blasts. Steam hissed from the cylinders as the engineer released the brakes. The locomotive chuffed and lurched forward. The couplers on the string of passenger cars banged one after another as the slack between them was taken up.

Will dashed back to the train, leaped onto the step, turned, and waved goodbye to Chung Huang.

The first through passenger train from Sacramento arrived in Reno shortly after eight on the evening of June 18, 1868. Shouting crowds, an occasional gunshot, and clanging bells from the local churches and the fire station greeted the debarking passengers. Will felt like a celebrity when he stepped off the car. Nevada's newest town occupied a prominent place along the route of the transcontinental railroad. Carson City, the state's largest town, was too far off the direct route to entice the railroad to make the detour necessary to reach it. Just as the

Union Pacific would bypass the capital of Utah, so would the Central Pacific bypass the capital of Nevada.

After spending the night in a Reno hotel, Will and his uncle boarded a mud wagon for the thirty-five mile, six-hour trip over rugged terrain to reach Carson City. Wells Fargo still used the capital city as its principal stagecoach station in western Nevada. During the ride, Will's uncle remained silent. Will knew he was brooding about not being successful in his mission to get the Central Pacific to agree to a meeting place. His uncle would be concerned about the reaction of General Dodge when he had to pass along the bad news. And Will was worried about the future of the survey inspection team and his own job.

The Wells Fargo Concord coach for their journey back to Salt Lake City wouldn't depart until the following morning, so Will and his uncle spent the afternoon strolling the streets of Carson City. Will paused in front of a stationer's window to study a display of books.

"You suddenly develop an interest in reading?" Will's uncle asked. "Plan to buy one?"

"Not for me."

"Wouldn't be for some black-haired young lady I know, would it?"

Will felt his face flush. He looked sideways to see his uncle's broad grin.

"Jenny's family lost their library last year in the wagon fire." Will looked through the window and pointed to a volume. "I think she might enjoy that one by Charles Dickens."

"*A Christmas Carol*? Yes, she probably would."

"Only one problem," Will said.

"What's that?"

"I don't have enough money. Could you advance me a little on my salary?"

His uncle threw his head back and roared with laughter.

"Well, if it were for anybody else, I'd say no. But since it's for Jenny McNabb, I'll agree."

CHAPTER 26

Will, his uncle, and Homer Garcon waited to board the stagecoach at Bridger's Pass Station for the final thirty miles of their journey. Will looked forward to the end of the three-and-a-half weeks of riding over the dusty, bumpy roads. They'd spent fourteen days traversing from Carson City to Salt Lake City, and another ten days to get to Bridger's Pass. The Union Pacific's rails had been extended across the North Platte River to the new Hell on Wheels town of Benton, a few miles east of Rawlins Springs. North Platte Crossing, the coach's final destination, now served as Wells Fargo's connecting point with the railroad. No stagecoaches ran farther east.

"Well, if it isn't Butch Cartwright." Will's uncle tipped his hat to the diminutive driver perched on the seat atop the Wells Fargo coach that pulled up in front of the station.

"How'd do, Mr. Corcoran." Butch spoke with a scratchy, high-pitched voice. "You look much fitter this time than when I last seen you."

"Will," his uncle said, "this is the driver that took me to Big Laramie Station when I came down with the sickness."

"Hello, Mr. Cartwright." Will held his hand above the brim of his slouch hat to shade his eyes from the morning sun, when he looked up at the driver.

"Just Butch. Don't cotton to the mister part."

"All right . . . Butch." Will couldn't remember any other stagecoach drivers they'd encountered on their trip to and from

California who didn't hide behind a scruffy beard. Few men in the West went clean-shaven. His uncle being one—and himself. He ran his fingers across his chin feeling for the elusive whiskers. No need to shave regularly, yet.

"This ugly mug beside me is Slim Dempsey," Butch said. "He's my shotgun messenger."

Will and his uncle both acknowledged the introduction with a wave. Slim touched the brim of his hat with his shotgun.

"Time to board, folks," Butch said.

The driver heaved their luggage onto the roof of the coach while Will, his uncle, and Homer took their seats.

"Giddup!" Butch called. The whip snapped and the six-horse rig lurched forward.

Less than two hours later, the coach stopped briefly at Pine Grove swing station. Scanty evergreen and aspen trees, the only vegetation other than scrub brush along the nine-mile run from Bridger's Pass, lined the creek bed beside the one-room log building and gave the station its name. Snow melt coursing down from the Continental Divide nourished the trees during the spring, but now in mid-July the creek bed was dry. The passengers didn't disembark during the five minutes it took the station's stock tenders to change the teams.

Butch drove the six horses at a trot on eastward toward Sage Creek Station, ten miles distant. The pungent odor of sage wafted into the open windows. Will wrinkled his nose. A little sage goes a long way, and there was more than a little out there. The gray-green bush dotted the landscape on both sides of the Overland Trail, as far as he could see. He was reminded of the sage poultice Bullfrog Charlie had applied to his leg earlier in the year.

Will sat by the window on the rear seat. Most travelers chose the comfort of the front seat, but Will preferred the view forward. He liked to see where he was going. When he wasn't admiring the scenery, he read a few pages in the Dickens' novel he'd purchased for Jenny.

The coach topped a ridge and headed down a gentle slope. The solitary bulk of Elk Mountain came into view on the horizon. Will knew the North Platte River flowed just this side of that prominent peak. They were close to their destination.

"Everybody look alive!" Butch screamed down to the passengers from the driver's box. "Indians attacking Sage Creek Station!"

Will stuffed the book into the haversack he wore over his shoulder, drew his Colt from its holster, checked the seating of the percussion caps, and brought it to half-cock. Other passengers pulled revolvers from carpetbags or holsters. A middle-aged woman in the middle of the front seat grabbed the arm of the man beside her. "Oh, Elmer, we're going to die."

"Hush, Agnes," her companion said. "No, we're not. There are too many of us here with guns." The woman leaned against him, whimpering.

Will stuck his head out the window. A column of smoke spiraled upward from the shake roof of the log station. Riders on ponies circled the burning building. The station's two stock tenders lay dead in front of it. Gunfire punctuated the war cries. *"Aiyee, aiyee, aiyee!"*

"We're gonna run straight through, folks," Butch yelled. The whip cracked. "Hie! Hie! Giddup." The whip cracked again and again. "Hie! Hie!"

The Indians broke away from the station and swung in along both sides of the stagecoach. Bullets smacked into the wooden sides, spattering wood chips and dust into the coach. From the driver's box, the sharp crack of Slim's carbine returned the fire of the attackers. Will fired his pistol at an Indian, but missed. The bouncing coach made accurate shooting difficult.

"Let's concentrate our fire on that lead pony!" Will shouted to the two men who leaned out the center and front windows next to him. "The pony's a bigger target."

"Right," the man beside him said.

Three revolvers roared together. The pony stumbled and the brave flew over its neck.

"Yeah!" The other man shouted from the front window.

But they'd only stopped one of a dozen pursuers. A shot zipped through the window and plowed into the wood above the middle-aged woman's head. She screamed.

"Hush, Agnes! Your screaming won't help!"

Gunfire reverberated inside the coach. The acrid black powder smoke hung in the confined space. Will's lungs burned—his eyes watered. Bullets and arrows kept slamming into the rocking, bouncing stage.

"Aiyee, aiyee, aiyee!" The attackers didn't back off.

"Slim!" Butch cried from above. "No, Slim!"

The body of the shotgun messenger tumbled from the top of the coach, past the window where Will sat, and thudded onto the trail. Now the driver was unprotected. If Butch were shot, who'd drive?

Will jammed his revolver into its holster. He squeezed through the window and reached up to grab the luggage railing along the top of the coach.

"What are you doing?" Will's uncle yelled.

"I've got to help Butch!" A bullet splintered the wood in the window edge next to him. He felt a sharp blow against his side from what had to be another bullet, but since he was still alive he pulled himself up onto the roof and crawled forward.

"Humph." Butch slumped just as Will took the shotgun messenger's seat.

"You hit?" Will asked.

"Yeah." Butch sat up and took a deep breath. "In the arm. Stings like the devil."

The shotgun messenger's Spencer carbine lay in the footwell of the driver's box. Will picked it up and levered a shell into the chamber. He turned and fired. He levered the trigger guard again. No shell came up into the breech.

"Behind the seat." Butch gasped. "Extra tubes."

Will pushed a pair of saddlebags aside. Beneath them lay half-a-dozen loaded ammunition tubes. He extracted the butt cover from the carbine, tipped a tube against the opening in the butt, and slid the replacement rounds into place. He crawled over the seat back, eased along the top of the coach, and lay prone, facing the rear.

The lead Indian rider looked up. Black paint obscured his face from his eyes down. Black Wolf's Cheyenne band! Will steadied the carbine across a valise. He sighted at Black Wolf's pony. He waited for the coach to bounce into the air, and when it dropped back hard, bottoming onto its thoroughbraces, he pulled the trigger. The pony dropped. Black Wolf pitched off.

Will levered another shell into the chamber and took aim at the next rider. Again he waited for the coach to bottom. The carbine roared and that pony fell.

The Indians gave up their pursuit.

Will climbed back into the driver's box. Butch breathed hard. "That was some shooting," the driver said. "Didn't think we were gonna make it."

Will studied the grimace on Butch's face. "You're hurt pretty bad."

"Agh!" Butch slumped against him.

Will grabbed the bundle of reins that slipped through the driver's gloved hands. Now what? He'd only driven a two-horse team. What did he do with all these reins?

Butch stirred beside him. "Can you drive it?"

"Don't know."

"You have to try." Butch blew out a sharp breath. "Change

seats. Brake's on this side."

Will stepped up behind Butch and lifted the bundle of reins while the driver slid beneath them to the left. Will settled into the driver's right-hand seat and braced his foot against the brake handle.

"Now," Butch said. "Ribbons for the near horses in your left hand."

"Ribbons?"

"Reins. Off horses in the right hand. Lace the ribbons for the lead team between the fore and middle fingers."

Will adjusted the reins.

"Good. Swing team between middle and ring fingers." Butch paused to suck in a breath through clenched teeth. "Wheel team between the ring and little fingers."

Will struggled to get the bundle of reins into place in his bare hands.

"Your hands are too big for my gloves," Butch said. "Sorry."

"I'll manage."

"Slow 'em down, Will." Butch looked back. "The savages aren't chasing us anymore."

Will slowed the teams to a trot and drove the rest of the fourteen miles from Sage Creek Station to the North Platte River in under two hours. The horses kept up a steady pace without much urging—still his hands were bloody and raw from the biting ribbons. At the river's edge, he guided the stage onto the ferry and once across, he drove it up the opposite bank.

"Whoa!" Will hauled back on the reins and pushed his foot down on the brake lever. The coach rocked to a stop in front of North Platte Crossing Station. The teams blew hard—white, foamy sweat covered their coats. Butch lay passed out on the seat.

"Uncle Sean! Homer! Help me get Butch down."

"Will?" Jenny McNabb stepped out of the station's door.

"What're you doing?"

"Trying to drive this thing. Butch's been shot."

"Where's Slim?"

"Dead."

The passengers tumbled out of the coach, all telling their own version of the hair-raising experience to Alistair McNabb and the driver waiting to take the stagecoach on the next leg of their journey.

Will handed the semi-conscious Butch down into the up-stretched arms of his uncle and Homer, then jumped down from the driver's box.

"In here," Jenny said.

Will's uncle and Homer passed sideways with their burden through the narrow door Jenny held open, and eased the wounded driver down onto a bench in the station's main room. Will and some other passengers entered behind them.

"Hold Butch steady, Will, while I examine the wound," Jenny said.

Will held the driver upright on the bench while Jenny checked the injured arm.

"Bullet went completely through the fleshy part of the upper arm," Jenny said. "Lots of blood, but no broken bones. I can take care of Butch."

"Butch is in capable hands with Jenny," Will's uncle said. "I know from personal experience. Let's get our gear off the coach, Homer. Will, you can stay and help Jenny."

The two men exited the station, leaving Will behind.

Blood soaked Will's hand where he'd supported Butch. "We have to get this shirt off and stop the bleeding," he said.

"Not here," Jenny whispered.

Will furrowed his brows. "Not here?"

"In the back room." Jenny nodded to a doorway at the rear.

"What's wrong with here? These folks have seen men without

their shirts on before." He swept a hand around the room indicating the passengers.

Jenny's blue eyes flashed gray at Will. "Butch is a girl!"

CHAPTER 27

Paddy rode into Benton, the latest version of Hell on Wheels, and dismounted behind the Lucky Dollar Saloon. If the countryside around the single dusty street weren't higher and dryer than along the Laramie River, he wouldn't have known the ramshackle town had moved. The shacks and tents occupied the same positions they did everyplace. Mayor Mortimer Kavanagh, though no election had earned him that title, controlled everything and everybody in this den of thieves. They were all bent on taking every last dollar off the railroad workers.

Paddy looped the reins around one of the ropes securing the rear of the big tent that enclosed the bar and dance hall of the Lucky Dollar. He slipped his Bowie knife from his boot, sliced the end off his plug of tobacco, then used his rotten, broken teeth to slide the chaw off the blade. He pushed through the canvas flap that served as a back door and stepped inside.

A good crowd occupied the candelabra-lit expanse for the noon hour. The patrons who bellied up to the bar wore blue uniforms, instead of coveralls—soldiers rather than gandy dancers. Benton was just a short ride from the Army's new Fort Fred Steele, which had been built on the west bank of the North Platte River. Paddy knew his godfather would be pleased. Until Hell on Wheels picked up and moved west to keep up with the railroad, Kavanagh would have the military to thank for providing him extra customers. Paddy noticed these customers' uniforms were piped in the light blue of infantry instead of the bright yellow of cavalry.

A group of laughing soldiers parted and Elspeth McNabb stepped out from their midst. She shook her long blonde hair and waved a pale hand at the admiring men. "Stay right here, boys. I'll be gone just a moment."

She swatted a hand away that attempted to pinch her and wagged a finger at the guilty party. "Now, now. None of that."

The soldiers guffawed and turned back to the bar.

Elspeth whirled away from the soldiers and froze. Her smile dissolved into a sneer.

"Ah, me darlin'." Paddy touched the tip of his Bowie knife to the brim of the new bowler hat he'd bought in Carson City to replace the one Will Braddock had shot off his head in California. "What a lovely sight ye be."

"Out of my way." She snarled and stepped sideways.

Paddy moved to block her way. He glanced over her shoulder to assure himself none of the soldiers were looking. He touched the point of the knife to Elspeth's cheek, causing her eyes to widen. He had her attention now. He reached out with his other hand and stroked her hair.

"Get your hands off me. Mort will have your neck if he catches you touching me."

"Ah, now, me darlin'. Mort don't scare me none."

"That's not what I've seen." She snorted.

He was tempted to push the point into that soft skin—just enough to draw a drop of blood. But he pulled the knife back and bowed his head to her. "Someday, my pretty. Someday, ye'll be all mine."

Paddy turned away from her and crossed the packed dirt floor to reach Kavanagh's office, tucked in the corner of the wooden false-front of the building. He rapped sharply on the door.

"Come in."

Kavanagh looked up from his desk when Paddy entered. "So, did you get it?"

"Sure, and I did."

"Where is it?"

"I hid it in a cave up on Elk Mountain. Not far from here."

"Good." Kavanagh leaned forward and scratched a lucifer match across the desktop. He held the flame to the tip of his cigar and sucked in his breath.

"But we may have a bit of a problem, don't ye know."

"How's that?"

"Well now, Will Braddock saw me stealing them chemicals. It's pretty sure I am that he can identify me. And maybe . . . just maybe I'm saying . . . he can associate me with you, Mort."

Kavanagh stared at Paddy, rolling his cigar around in his mouth. "And?"

"I came across Black Wolf's band of Cheyenne over near Elk Mountain, so I did. I engaged him, ye might say, to get rid of Braddock. And in the process he'd be doing me a favor by getting rid of Sean Corcoran and that nigger at the same time. All three of them are heading back this way on the stage. I told Black Wolf ye'd be giving him ammunition, if he was to get the job done proper like."

"You did?"

"Sure, and I did."

"Well, I hate to admit it," Kavanagh said, "but you used your head this time. I can arrange some ammunition for those Cheyenne . . . if they can shift the blame away from me."

Paddy sat up straighter. He hadn't been sure his boss would like him promising ammunition. He breathed a sigh of relief. And the beauty of this plan was his vendetta could be accomplished without putting himself at risk.

"I rode past Rattlesnake Tunnel on my way here," Paddy said. "Sure, and it's mighty close to that new Army fort."

"Yeah, maybe so, but you'll be away from there when the explosion takes place. And this is going to be even bigger than I thought. I've got a plan."

A soft knock on the door caused Kavanagh to look beyond Paddy. "Come in, sweetheart."

Sally Whitworth stepped in with a bottle and two glasses on a tray. "Here's the whiskey you asked for, Mort."

"Thanks, my dear. Just put it here on the desk."

Sally's red curls swished across her shoulders when she leaned forward to place the tray on the edge of the desk. She stood back and wrinkled her nose. "When's the last time you bathed, O'Hannigan?"

"Ah, now, darlin'. I just returned from a long, hard journey. Had I only known I'd be seeing yer beautiful face so soon, I'd of jumped in the horse trough before I came in." He blew her a kiss.

"Humph. Don't blow that foul breath in my direction." She spun away and left the room.

Kavanagh laughed. "She likes you as much as she always has." He drew deeply on his cigar and blew a smoke ring.

Paddy spat a string of tobacco juice into the spittoon beside Kavanagh's desk. "Well now, Mort, just what's yer plan?"

"I have it on the best authority that Ulysses S. Grant will visit end of track in a day or two. He's out west campaigning for the presidency. Now's my chance to really get his attention so that he'll order a slowdown in construction."

Paddy eyed the unopened whiskey bottle and the two tumblers beside it. "So, and what does General Grant's visit have to do with blowing up the tunnel?"

Kavanagh popped the cork from the bottle and splashed the golden liquid into the tumblers. He pushed one across the desk to Paddy and picked up the other. "You're going to blow up the tunnel with General Grant inside it."

CHAPTER 28

Jenny stepped out of the small back room and eased the door closed. Will sat at the central table cleaning his revolver. Travelers took their meals in this larger of the two rooms that comprised the North Platte Crossing Station while waiting for the next stagecoach to depart, but now it was empty except for Will.

He looked up and laid his pistol on the table. Cleaning rags, a small can of oil, and a brush lay in front of him. The Colt glistened with a fresh coat of oil. "How's Butch?"

"Sleeping," Jenny replied.

"And the wound?"

"It stopped bleeding."

He picked up his revolver again and wiped excess oil off the barrel.

"Will, are you going to keep this a secret?" she asked.

He shrugged in response.

"If Papa, or anybody else in Wells Fargo's management, finds out, it will cost Butch her job. She's the best driver the company has, even though they don't know who she is. Please do this for me . . . if not for her."

The door into the station opened and Jenny's father, Will's uncle, and Homer filed in. Jenny stared at Will, cocked her head slightly, and raised an eyebrow.

Will returned her stare for a moment, then nodded.

"Thank you." She mouthed the words silently.

The telegraph key, on a table beneath one of the two small windows, clattered to life.

"Where's Duncan?" Jenny's father asked. "Someone wants to send us a message."

"He's in the corral, Papa. I'll fetch him." She hurried outside, closing the door behind her.

Duncan wasn't in the corral. She walked around behind the station and found him lugging two buckets of water up from the river. One of his jobs was helping with the stock tending, the other was operating the telegraph.

"Duncan!" she shouted. "Somebody wants to send us a message!"

"Coming." He hurried into the corral and dumped the water into the trough. He joined Jenny and they entered the station.

Duncan sat at the table and tapped out his call sign. A moment later the telegraph key jumped up and down, emitting a string of dots and dashes. Duncan copied the message directly onto a pad in block capital letters. Jenny was proud of her brother. He no longer needed to write down the code first. She leaned over Duncan's shoulder and read the message as he transcribed the letters.

FROM GRENVILLE DODGE TO SEAN CORCORAN STOP MEET ME IN BENTON JULY 25 STOP GRANT TO INSPECT END OF TRACK BEFORE MEETING WITH DURANT AT FORT SANDERS STOP IMPORTANT

"The telegram is for you, Mr. Corcoran." Duncan handed the pad to Will's uncle, who read the message, then handed the pad back to Duncan. "Can you send a reply?"

"Yes, sir." Her brother poised a pencil over his pad.

"Corcoran to Grenville Dodge Stop Message received Stop Taking next stage to Benton."

When he'd finished copying the message onto his pad, she watched Duncan grasp the telegraph key between the thumb and first two fingers of his left hand and rapidly click out the message. "Done, Mr. Corcoran," he said.

"How much?"

"Twenty-five cents each word," Duncan said. He counted the words he'd written on the pad with a forefinger. "Thirteen words comes to three dollars and twenty-five cents, sir."

Will's uncle handed Duncan three silver dollars and a quarter, then folded Dodge's telegram and placed it in his pocket. "Will," he said, "I'm going on ahead on the stage. You and Homer come along with the horses and gear. Try to get to Benton by tomorrow. I'd like you to meet General Grant. He's probably going to be the next President of the United States."

Will nodded.

Will's uncle looked at Homer. "Can you do it?"

"I 'spects we can. We just gotta get the gear rounded up and ride to Benton."

"Good." Will's uncle turned to Jenny's father. "When's the next coach depart, Alistair?"

"It's a mud wagon. Leaves in less than an hour."

"I'll be ready." He left the station building.

"Papa," Jenny said, "since we're moving to the Green River home station next week, I'd like to go to Benton to see Elspeth before we go."

"The mud wagon's full, Jenny. Mr. Corcoran just took the last seat."

"Will and Homer are riding to Benton, Papa. I can ride Mr. Corcoran's horse along with them, then ride the wagon back."

"She's welcome to come with us," Homer said. "We's leaving in a couple of hours."

"All right," her father said. "Come on, Duncan, it's time to harness the teams."

Jenny's father and her brother left the station.

"I'se going to get started with the packing, Will."

"I'll put this revolver back together and be right there."

Homer nodded and stepped outside.

Jenny looked at Will, but said nothing.

"You didn't tell me you were moving," he said. "Didn't you think I'd be interested?"

"I didn't have a chance to tell you. I've been busy tending to Butch."

Will returned the pistol to its holster and lifted his haversack off the back of a chair. "Oh," he said. "I almost forgot."

Jenny watched as he took a book out of the haversack, and saw his mouth fall open.

"What's wrong, Will?"

She followed his stare as it concentrated on a large hole penetrating the center of the front cover. He opened the book and a musket ball clattered to the top of the table. "I bought this for you," he said. "But now it's ruined. I felt a thump against my side during the Indian attack, but didn't realize it was because a bullet had hit the haversack."

Jenny took the book out of his hands. "Charles Dickens' *A Christmas Carol.* How did you know it was one of my favorites? Papa used to read it to us children each Christmas."

"Well, it's ruined now. Sorry."

"No, it's not. I know the story so well I can easily fill in the missing words. Besides, each time I read it, I'll know that it probably saved your life."

She stood on tiptoe and planted a kiss on Will's cheek. She saw him turn several shades of red and his eyes opened wide. Yes, she thought. I like doing that to him.

CHAPTER 29

"Hyah!" Paddy slapped the reins against the neck of the horse, urging it up the steep slope of Elk Mountain. "Giddup, ye mangy old nag. Sure, and that cave's not far now."

Mort Kavanagh was determined to slow the pace of construction on the railroad even if it meant killing Ulysses S. Grant in the process. If Paddy didn't need the money, he'd tell his godfather to go to the devil. What would happen to him if he got caught tangled up in this plot? But he'd just received another letter from his sister informing him that their mother was ill and they couldn't afford to buy the medicine her doctor prescribed. Paddy shook his head and exhaled. He didn't know what else to do but go through with this harebrained scheme.

He'd have to be careful, that's for certain. Nitroglycerin was nasty stuff. He needed to remember what that Chinaman had said about mixing the chemicals, or he'd blow himself to kingdom come.

There's the cave up ahead. "Hyah!" He kicked his mount hard in the ribs. The horse snorted its objection to the abuse. At the base of a rocky outcropping he reined in and dismounted. He flipped the reins over a bush at the mouth of the cave and lifted the saddlebags off the horse's rump.

The early afternoon sunlight, unobstructed by clouds, streamed directly into the entrance. He wouldn't need a torch to find the chemicals he'd stashed here several days ago.

A half-dozen paces into the cave he located the niche in the rock wall where he'd hidden the three large bottles. "Ah, now, wouldn't ye know it." Paddy set the saddlebags on the floor of the cave. He hadn't planned this well enough. He'd only brought one pair of saddlebags, and their pockets were full of the vials he intended to fill with the nitroglycerin. He couldn't mix the chemicals until he got down to the railroad. The stuff was too volatile to transport already mixed. But how was he going to get the three, large chemical bottles down the mountain?

Just inside the cave's entrance, the charred remains of a fire indicated humans had occupied the cave recently. Perhaps something useful had been left deeper inside the cave.

He stepped back outside and selected a dead branch from beneath a Ponderosa pine. The dry needles would burn rapidly, but he could fashion a torch from it that would satisfy his needs. He reentered the cave, took a lucifer match from his vest pocket, and struck it against the rock wall. He held the match to the branch. The needles burst into flame.

He held the makeshift torch in front of him and moved deeper into the cave. He slowly swung the burning limb back and forth in an arc as he walked.

What was that? He stopped, holding the torch farther in front of him to get a closer look. A streak of red stretched across an opening in the side wall of the cave. The color was too consistent to be rock. He reached out and brushed his hand along the object. "A blanket," he said. "Sure, and what's a blanket doing here?"

That would do the trick though. He could wrap the vials in the blanket and sling it from his saddle horn. Then he could pack the chemicals in the saddlebags. What a bit of luck. He jammed the torch into a crevice in the wall to free his hands. The light from the cave's entrance would guide him back out. He wouldn't need the torch anymore. It'd burn out in a minute or two, anyway.

He pulled the blanket out of the niche and cradled it in his arms. Embroidery in trade beads and porcupine quills decorated the length of the red cloth. The bundle contained something that rattled. He shook the blanket and it unrolled. The contents clattered to the floor.

"Bones!" Leg bones, arm bones, and ribs littered the cave's floor at his feet.

"Agh!" The eye sockets of a skull stared up at him from the midst of the jumble.

"Ho, sure, and I'm getting out of here!" He scurried back to the sunlight with the blanket.

An hour later, Paddy approached a small, wooden railroad trestle spanning one of the many dry gulches. He dismounted and removed his bomb-making tools from the horse. He'd decided he'd better conduct a test to be sure he got the nitroglycerin mixture correct.

He smoothed out a spot in the sandy bed of the intermittent stream and lined up the three bottles of chemicals, side by side. He opened one of the small vials and nestled it firmly in the sand, piling grains halfway up its sides to stabilize it.

He blew out his breath, then took another one—a deeper one. "Sure, and I hope to get this right. By all the saints, don't let me make a mistake."

He must mix the chemicals in the proper order. He knew the two acids came first. His bottles weren't labeled, so he'd go on smell. He remembered the first one he wanted to pour into the vial, the nitric acid, smelled like horse pee. He peeled off the paraffin sealing wax and eased the cork out of one of the bottles.

The rotten egg smell assaulted his nostrils. "Whew!" Sulfuric acid. He slipped the cork back into the neck of the bottle.

He worked carefully. It took five minutes before all three ingredients were poured into the small container. He corked the vial, eased it out of its nest of sand, and gently rocked it back and forth. An oily, yellow film coated the inside of the glass container.

"Ah! Got it."

He walked the dozen steps to get beneath the bridge, holding the tiny bottle in front of him with both hands. The bottom timbers of the trestle spanned the dry creek bed five feet above his head. He inched up the sloping bank until he reached the place where the timbers were anchored into the ground. He set the vial on the top edge of the lowest beam and slid back down the slope. He breathed a sigh of relief. That should do it.

He repacked the chemicals into his saddlebags and led his horse farther away from the bridge. He needed to find a safe place to wait for the next passing train's vibrations to dislodge the vial and set off his test explosion.

Chapter 30

"Lone Eagle's cabin's just ahead," Will said, "in that stand of cottonwoods."

Will, astride Buck, rode on one side of Jenny, who was mounted on his uncle's horse. Homer rode on her other side, leading Ruby.

The cabin nestled in a thick grove of trees that extended away from the water's edge, along the east bank of the North Platte, and butted up against a steep embankment rising above the narrow plain a hundred yards from the river.

"Bullfrog certainly selected a beautiful stretch of the river to build his cabin," Jenny said.

Will recalled what he'd done the last time he'd been here. "And to serve as a burial place." He couldn't yet see the scaffold he'd built in the cottonwoods, but he knew it was there.

Lone Eagle stepped from behind a tree, blocking the path of the three riders. "It's a good thing you weren't trying to sneak up on me. I heard you ten minutes ago." He laughed.

"Guess we were a little careless," Will said.

"More than a little, Will. Hello, Jenny. And this must be Homer."

"Homer Garcon," Will said, "meet Lone Eagle Munro."

"How do, Mr. Munro." Homer touched the brim of his hat. "Heard lots about you."

"Lone Eagle will do." He motioned toward his cabin. "Don't have much, but you're welcome to share what there is. Come in. Have a cup of coffee, at least."

The riders nudged their horses forward and followed Lone Eagle, who walked ahead of them.

"What have you been doing since I last saw you, Lone Eagle?" Will asked.

"A little hunting . . . some fishing. Mainly staying away from the railroad. It's getting so crowded around here all the game's been scared away. Too many men up there." He nodded up the river to the north. "They erected a big bridge over the river for the tracks. And blasted a tunnel through the Rattlesnake Hills. The Army's built a new fort beside the bridge, too. It is not the same here, now. Not like when I was a boy."

As the riders dismounted in front of the cabin, Lone Eagle pointed to the skin of a grizzly bear pegged to the wall next to the door. "That is the one Will shot—the one that killed my father."

Lone Eagle glanced into the woods behind the cabin. Will followed his gaze and spotted the scaffold where he'd buried the old mountain man.

"I see you're wearing the claws," Lone Eagle said.

"In memory of Bullfrog." Will tapped the necklace with his fingers. "I don't wear them often, but since we were coming here today, I decided to show them."

"Come in." Lone Eagle held the door open.

After they'd settled themselves on the single cot and the two three-legged stools that comprised the cabin's furniture, Lone Eagle poked the fire to life. He soon had coffee boiling in an old iron pot. He passed around an assortment of mugs and poured the thick liquid into each. He scooped a handful of sugar from a sack, dumping it into his mug, then passed the sack to the others.

While Lone Eagle served the coffee, Will told him about his

run-in with Black Wolf on the stagecoach run from Sage Creek Station.

Lone Eagle shook his head. "I don't know why he would lead his warriors this far west. Black Wolf must have been paid a good price to do so. Might be that Irish thug, Paddy O'Hannigan. He passed through here a few weeks ago headed west. He's always up to no good. And he has a bone to pick with you, Will."

"I have the same thought," Jenny said.

Will nodded and stretched his feet out in front of him. He hadn't told Jenny about the nitroglycerin incident at Summit Tunnel.

"*Whoom!*" An explosion rocked the cabin.

A piercing whistle screeched.

"That's a locomotive whistle," Will said. "That's up where the tracks run."

"They were setting off those explosions when they built the tunnel," Lone Eagle said, "but they finished that work long ago. And those explosions weren't that loud."

The whistling continued unabated.

"That's not an engineer sounding a normal whistle. Something's wrong up there," Will said. "I'm going to take a look."

Jenny and Homer followed Will out to their horses and mounted. Lone Eagle ran down the slope and jumped onto his pony. The four riders urged their mounts into a gallop.

Chapter 31

Fifteen minutes later, the four riders approached the bridge across the North Platte. Beyond the bridge, to the north of the tracks and west of the river, Will could see the sprawl of Fort Fred Steele's complex. The dozens of new buildings were not surrounded by a protective stockade. Like the fort outside Cheyenne, the size of the garrison would ensure that Indians thought twice about an attack.

A handful of soldiers on a ferry pulled the craft toward the east bank of the river, their horses swimming in the water alongside. They too must be on their way to investigate the explosion and constant whistling. For a moment, Will wondered why they didn't just ride over the bridge.

A closer inspection provided the answer—the tracks crossed the span on open girders. A man could walk across, stepping from one railroad tie to another, but not a horse.

A quarter mile to the east of the bridge, Will saw the freight train stopped on the tracks. He wheeled Buck toward the train and raced parallel to the rails. The others followed.

Clouds of steam spiraled skyward from the locomotive, whose boiler tilted downward at a steep angle. Three men stood beside the cab of the engine. Will recognized one of them—Hobart Johnson, the conductor.

Will and his companions drew up even with the locomotive and reined in. Will stepped down from his saddle. "Mr. Johnson, what happened?"

"Hello, Will." Johnson pointed to the front of the locomotive. The leading wheels, beneath the cowcatcher, hung suspended in midair. The frame supporting the boiler rested on the trestle's abutment. "Bridge blew up. Whatever the explosive was, the vibrations transmitted from the train through the rails evidently set it off before we reached the bridge. Engineer Patton slammed on the brakes and kept us from plunging into the gulch. Boiler's cracked, though. Can't stop the steam escaping through the whistle."

"Vlademar, climb up there and knock that whistle off." Engineer Patton motioned for his fireman to step forward. "Careful. That steam will roast your hide."

The engineer handed the fireman a wrench and helped him clamber up the side of the locomotive.

The soldiers had gotten across the river and rode up to the engine. "What's going on here?" a sergeant shouted over the whistle's scream.

"Trestle blew up, Sergeant," Johnson said. "Damaged an engine, as you can see, and the telegraph line is down, too. The poles were mounted on the side of the bridge. They're gone now."

The sergeant turned back to the half-dozen men who sat behind him. "Arrest that Indian, Corporal." He pointed to Lone Eagle, who had ridden his pony down into the gully crossed by the bridge and was busy poking among the debris of timbers with his bow.

"Why?" Will asked.

"He's an Indian, isn't he? He must have had something to do with this."

"No, he didn't. He's with me."

"That's right, Sergeant," Johnson said, "he didn't have anything to do with it."

"Then who did?"

Conductor Johnson shrugged. "Don't know, but I did see a white man, wearing a bowler hat, riding away right after the explosion. What I do know is we've got to get this locomotive off the tracks, and more importantly, we have to get a crew out here to rebuild this bridge . . . fast. General Grant will be coming through here later today and there's no way to notify his train to stop until we reconnect the telegraph. We don't have much time."

The steady hiss of steam suddenly replaced the screeching. The fireman had succeeded in smashing the offending whistle off the boiler.

"Well, nothing we can do to help here," the sergeant said. "I'm taking my detachment back to the fort." He swung his horse around and motioned the column of soldiers to follow him.

"Will," Lone Eagle called from the gully. "Come see this."

Will eased Buck down the slope and joined Lone Eagle, who pointed with his bow to the ground several yards from the wreckage of the bridge. "One man's tracks only. Little mound of sand surrounded something there. And there are larger marks on the ground next to it."

Will dismounted and studied the mound. In the bottom of the fine sand he could make out the impression left by the bottom of a small jar. He ran his fingers over the marks remaining from three larger containers. "He mixed nitroglycerin here."

"That's an explosive, isn't it?"

"A very powerful, and dangerous one. I'm pretty sure I know who did this. Let's see if we can find any signs."

"*We?*" Lone Eagle grinned at him.

Will returned the grin. "You, then."

Lone Eagle slid off his pony and followed boot marks and hoof prints back into the brush, farther from the bridge. He waved for Will to accompany him.

"He waited here. Horse pranced around a long time before leaving." Lone Eagle followed some hoof prints across the dry creek bed and fingered several freshly broken branches where the horse had crashed through. "Guilty party rode east from here, along the railroad tracks."

"Strange. I would have thought he would ride back to the west. Return to Benton . . . where I'm sure he works."

"Who?"

"Paddy O'Hannigan."

Chapter 32

"What's east of here, Lone Eagle?" Will asked. "Why would O'Hannigan ride that way?"

"Rattlesnake Hills Tunnel. In those hills on the horizon there." He pointed to a low ridge that ran north and south across the tracks a couple of miles away.

"The tunnel . . . of course. That's his real target. This little trestle was just a test of the nitro."

Will mounted and tapped Buck's flanks, riding up the bank on the east side of the gully. Lone Eagle followed. Will reined in when he reached the tracks and called back across the narrow expanse where the trestle had fallen. "Mr. Johnson!"

"Yes?" The conductor raised his hand to signal Will had his attention.

"I think I know who blew up the trestle and what his next target is."

"You do? What is it?"

"Rattlesnake Hills Tunnel."

"I'll get that Army detachment back here to give pursuit."

"There's not time. Lone Eagle and I will go after him." Will glanced at his friend to see if he might refuse—he didn't.

"If you hurry, Mr. Johnson," Will said, "you can catch up to that sergeant and ride across the river on the Army's ferry. Take Jenny and Homer with you."

"I'se coming with you," Homer said.

"No. You get Jenny safely to Benton. Find Uncle Sean and

General Dodge and tell them what's happening."

"All right. Mr. Johnson, you can ride my mule, Ruby. It'll be faster than walking."

"Will," Jenny said, "you and Lone Eagle be careful. I know who you're going after and he's dangerous. He won't hesitate to kill you."

"I know." Will turned Buck back to the east and kicked his flanks. "Come on, let's ride."

By keeping their mounts in the cleared ditch that paralleled the railroad, Will and Lone Eagle had an unobstructed route and reached the Rattlesnake Hills in less than half an hour.

Will pulled up at the base of the hills where the tunnel cut through them. Heavy timbering reinforced the tunnel's opening and extended ten feet from the face to form a shed that would keep falling rock from tumbling down onto the tracks.

Lone Eagle slid from his pony and pointed to the ground with his bow. "Same horse prints here as in the gully. The horse pranced around here for a while . . . but then the tracks lead off to the south."

"He's gone already, then." Will dismounted and dropped Buck's reins, allowing them to trail on the ground. Buck knew he was to stay in place.

Lone Eagle stepped toward the entrance to the tunnel and stopped. "No!" He stooped and touched a red blanket rolled up beside the tracks. He looked off to the south, where Elk Mountain dominated the horizon.

"What?" Will asked.

Lone Eagle stood and shook out the blanket. He caressed the trade beads and porcupine quills decorating the length of red cloth. "This is my mother's shroud."

"How did Paddy get it?"

"He's been in the cave on Elk Mountain." Lone Eagle lifted the blanket to his nose. "Smells like rotten eggs."

"He used it to carry the chemicals for making the nitroglycerin. We have to be careful. Don't kick over any bottles we find."

Lone Eagle rolled the blanket and mounted his pony.

"Where are you going?" Will asked.

"I must return the blanket to my mother's bones." He pointed with his bow to Elk Mountain.

"Can you wait?" Will stepped to the pony and grasped its bridle. "I may need your help."

Lone Eagle looked at Will for a moment, then nodded. He dismounted and tied the rolled blanket to the rear of his Indian saddle.

"What we're looking for are small bottles. They'd be the same diameter as the indentation in that mound of sand you discovered in the gully. Doesn't take much nitro to blow something sky-high."

"That's not the only thing we have to look out for," Lone Eagle said.

"What else?"

"They don't call these the Rattlesnake Hills for nothing. This dark tunnel is a likely hiding place."

Will stepped into the tunnel's entrance. "Check the cross timbers. Paddy's probably placed the bottles on them, expecting the vibrations from the train to shake them off."

"Is that one?" Lone Eagle pointed above his head.

"Yes. I'll climb up and get it and hand it to you. Take it outside someplace away from the horses. Do not drop it, whatever you do."

Lone Eagle leaned his bow against the side of the tunnel shed.

Will stepped up on a crossbeam, holding on to a girder with one hand, while he reached up to grasp the glass bottle with the other. It fit easily into his palm. He tightened his grip on the girder and eased the small bomb off the timber.

Will slowly handed the bottle down to Lone Eagle, who cradled it between both hands. The Indian carried the bottle gingerly outside. Will eased himself down from the crossbeam and watched his friend head down the embankment from the tracks into the ditch. Lone Eagle walked fifty paces away and placed the bottle on a boulder, then returned.

"I don't see any more on this side of the tunnel, do you?" Will asked.

Lone Eagle shook his head.

They both crossed the tracks and scanned the opposite wall of wood.

"There." Lone Eagle pointed. A second bottle sat on a shelf at the same height as the first one.

Will once again stepped up onto a crossbeam and reached up to find a handhold.

Zzzzz.

A rattlesnake lay coiled on the timber where he'd placed his hand. The snake's diamond-shaped head hung poised right in front of his face.

"Hold still," Lone Eagle said. "I need my bow. I left it on the other side of the tracks."

Will held his breath. He didn't blink. He didn't move. He stared into the eyes of the big rattler. Its tongue flicked out and back.

Zzzzz.

The rattlesnake's head rose higher.

Zing!

Whap!

An arrow zipped past Will's ear and pierced the snake's head, pinning it back against the timbered wall.

The snake's body jerked and flopped. Its tail flipped around and knocked the bottle of nitroglycerin off the shelf.

"Grab it!" Will shouted.

He squeezed his eyes shut, expecting a loud explosion.

He heard a loud sigh instead.

Will looked down and let out his own breath.

Lone Eagle cradled the bottle in his hands. His bow lay at his feet.

Hanging beside Will was the largest rattlesnake he'd ever seen. With the head firmly affixed to the wall by the arrow directly opposite Will's nose, the body continued to twitch its full length. The rattles still sizzled down by his feet.

Will dropped to the floor of the tunnel. A final look around the entrance convinced him there were no more bottles. The two they had recovered rested on the large boulder outside.

"Let's bring the horses inside the tunnel and I'll shoot the bottles. We can't leave that explosive undetonated."

While Lone Eagle held the animals' heads, Will peered around the edge of the tunnel entrance and fired a carbine shot at the bottles. The ear-splitting explosion threw chunks of rock clear across the tracks in front of the tunnel. The horses whinnied and reared, but Lone Eagle held on to them.

Will stepped outside the entrance. Where the boulder once stood gaped a hole large enough to swallow both of their horses—and riders.

Chapter 33

Jenny, Homer, and Hobart Johnson raced into Benton on lathered horses. The conductor had borrowed a horse from the cavalry at Fort Steele after they'd crossed the river, allowing him more riding comfort than Ruby's packsaddle. Homer's mule trailed behind him on a lead rope.

"Where d'ya 'spose I'll find Mr. Corcoran and General Dodge?" Homer spoke to Conductor Johnson.

"Probably over to the Casement warehouse. Come on, I need to go there anyway to tell General Jack to assemble a bridge repair team. And I need to talk to General Dodge because he's the only one who has the authority to send a locomotive out to push the busted one into the ditch and clear the tracks."

"I have to find my sister," Jenny said. "I'll find you later to return Mr. Corcoran's horse."

"Sure enough, Jenny," Homer said.

The three riders parted at the center of the one-lane, dusty road that served as Hell on Wheels' only thoroughfare.

Jenny didn't have any trouble locating the Lucky Dollar Saloon. The tall, false-fronted structure occupied the center of the long row of shacks and tents making up the portable town, like it had in Julesburg, Cheyenne, and Laramie. Benton was just the latest iteration of ramshackle buildings the merchants and gamblers dragged along following the railroad west.

Jenny guided the horse up to the hitching rail that stretched along the boardwalk in front of the saloon. She dismounted, looped the reins over the rail, and brushed the dust off her clothes. She'd put on a new pair of work pants and a clean wool shirt when she'd left North Platte Crossing this morning, thinking the ride would be a leisurely one and she'd be presentable when she met her sister. But the race to the site of the explosion, and then the fast-paced ride on to Benton, had played havoc with her appearance.

She lifted her slouch hat and ran a hand through her hair, trying to gather the stray black tendrils back into place beneath her hat. She didn't need a mirror to tell her trail grime besmirched her face. She could feel the grit on her cheeks with her fingertips. Unless a passerby noticed how her curves filled out the shirt she wore, she might be mistaken for a man—a boy, at least.

She walked across the boardwalk and pushed through the bat-wing doors of the Lucky Dollar. She spotted Elspeth right away. Her older sister swayed from side to side on the end of a bench beside a piano player who banged away on the keys of the out-of-tune instrument. Elspeth's blonde curls, shining in the light cast from the dozens of candles crowding the big tent's chandeliers, brushed the tops of her bare shoulders. The half-dozen patrons in the dance hall at this midday hour clapped in unison, while Elspeth's clear voice sang the familiar Stephen Foster tune.

Oh! Susanna, don't you cry for me;

I come from Alabama,

With my banjo on my knee.

Jenny stepped down from the wooden floor of the narrow false-front onto the hardpacked dirt that extended from one side of the circus-style tent to the other. The music drowned out any noise her boots made as she walked to the piano, which sat against the back wall of the dance hall. She wished her sister would wear something that covered her shoulders—and bosom.

From where she stood at the end of the bench, she had a more revealing view down the front of Elspeth's dress than she deemed appropriate.

It took a moment for Elspeth to realize someone stood beside her, she was so wrapped up in singing. She turned sideways on the bench. "Well, look who the cat dragged in."

"Hello, Elspeth."

"Jennifer, you look worse than the last time I saw you." She wrinkled her nose. "And don't you ever take a bath? Whew! You smell like a horse."

"I just rode in on one. Of course, I smell like a horse."

"What are you doing here? It's a long ways from North Platte Crossing."

"I came to talk to you. Can we find a private corner?"

"Sorry, Michael, you'll have to carry on without me." She touched the piano player's arm, who nodded and kept playing.

Elspeth led Jenny to one end of the long, wooden bar that stretched the length of the tent. "This is as private as it gets in here." She leaned back against the bar and hooked the heel of a high-button shoe over the footrail.

Jenny stood opposite her sister, her back against the wall of the tent, giving her a view down the length of the empty bar. What customers there were occupied tables, while the bartender stayed busy polishing glasses at the far end of the bar.

"Well," Elspeth said. "Are you going to tell me why you're here?"

"We're moving again. Pa's being transferred to the Green River home station. We want you to come with us."

"Humph! I'll bet Pa never even mentioned my name. This is all your idea."

Jenny didn't want to tell her sister that she was right about their father never mentioning her. He'd given up on persuading her to rejoin the family. "He misses you, Elspeth."

"Why didn't he come? Did he send you?"

"No, he didn't send me. But he knows I'm here. The family should be together. We're working our way west slowly with Wells Fargo, and when the railroad is completed we'll go on to California, where we were headed in the first place."

"You forget, little sister, that I never wanted to leave Virginia." Elspeth's southern drawl caressed the name of their old home state. "California wasn't my choice. But as it turns out, I'm heading that way anyway. All I have to do is stay with Hell on Wheels and follow the railroad all the way to the *promised* land."

"What can I do to convince you to come home?"

"Home? Pooh. This is my home . . . for now." She swept an arm back, indicating the dance hall. "I'm socking away a nest egg that will let me eventually get away from that lecherous Mort Kavanagh. Once I do that, I'll be able to live in style. And what will you have, *dear* sister? You still making a dollar-fifty per meal?"

After buying the food, it was less than a dollar-fifty Jenny made selling meals to the stagecoach passengers. And she hadn't saved much of that, either. She used her meager profits to buy essentials for the family, and an occasional treat for herself. She didn't have a good response to Elspeth's snide comment.

"I've got to get back to work," Elspeth said.

Jenny suddenly ducked down and grabbed her sister's waist.

"What are you doing, Jenny? Begging won't make me change my mind. And get your dirty hands off my dress!"

Jenny peered around Elspeth's side and nodded toward the wooden front of the Lucky Dollar. "Is that Paddy O'Hannigan?"

Elspeth looked over her shoulder, following Jenny's gaze. "Yes. He's going into Mort Kavanagh's office in the corner there. He works for Mort."

"I don't want Paddy to see me. He tried to kill me last year."

Chapter 34

Will rode down the single street of Benton, Buck kicking up brownish yellow dirt with each step. Jenny stood on the boardwalk in front of Abrams General Store, next to the Wells Fargo station. She held a small parcel, probably containing something she'd bought in Benjamin Abrams' store.

Will reined in and stepped down from the saddle. "Been shopping?"

Jenny held up her package. "Just some salt and pepper. Don't want to have to haul a lot of supplies to Green River when we go."

"Did you see Elspeth?"

"I saw her. She won't come with me, though. Guess I didn't really expect her to."

Will took off his slouch hat and slapped it against his leg. A fine reddish spray flew from his trousers. "This alkali dust gets into everything."

"It surely does." She ran a hand down her cheek and held it out for him to see the deep ocher color staining the tips of her fingers.

"You didn't catch up with Paddy," she said.

"No. How'd you know?"

"He came into the Lucky Dollar Saloon while I was talking with Elspeth. You need to be careful, Will. Paddy won't hesitate to attack you . . . or me for that matter."

"You're right. Lone Eagle and I did manage to dismantle the

nitro bombs he'd left in the tunnel."

"Where's Lone Eagle now?"

"Headed back to his cabin . . . by way of a cave on Elk Mountain." He told her about Star Dancer's blanket shroud, and how upset Lone Eagle had been when he found out Paddy had desecrated it by using it to carry his chemicals.

"Oh, that is sad. I can imagine how he must feel."

The Wells Fargo mud wagon rolled down the street and stopped in front of the station. "Whoa!" Butch Cartwright called down from the driver's seat in her scratchy voice. "You going with us back to North Platte Crossing, Will?"

"No." He stuck his hat back on his head and smiled up at the driver. Now, of course, he could see she was female—but she'd fooled him for a long time—and she was still fooling everybody except Jenny and him apparently. He wondered how hard she had to concentrate on keeping the scratchy tone in her voice. Maybe she'd been masquerading so long it was second nature now.

Butch held a hand beside her mouth and shouted into the station building. "Time to go, folks, if we want to get to North Platte Crossing before dark!"

A half-dozen passengers came out of the building and tossed their luggage up to Butch, who stowed the pieces on the top of the wagon.

"Jenny," Butch said, "ride up here with me. I don't have a shotgun messenger this run. Can you fill in?"

"Sure." Jenny laid a hand on Will's forearm. "How long until I see you again?"

He shook his head. "Probably not until the railroad gets to Green River."

She stood on tiptoes and kissed him on the cheek. He felt his face flush under the soft touch of her lips.

"I see you blushing, Will Braddock." She laughed. "Until

Green River, then."

Jenny climbed up the side of the mud wagon and settled on the seat beside Butch. Butch took her foot off the brake, snapped the ribbons, and the six-horse team rolled away from the station.

Will waved once. Jenny raised the shotgun in a return salute. He watched until the coach disappeared from view where the narrow road turned south and dropped down a slope.

Benjamin Abrams stuck his head out of the entrance to his store. "How do, Will. Haven't seen you for a while."

"Hello, Mr. Abrams."

"Your uncle came into the store a little bit ago and bought some cigars. You want some candy today?"

"No, thank you. I have to find my uncle right now. Maybe later."

"Hey, Will!" Homer hurried down the street toward him.

"Hey, Homer. Where can I find Uncle Sean?"

"He's over to the Casement warehouse."

Will handed Buck's reins to Homer. "How about taking care of Buck for me while I go report to Uncle Sean? Buck needs rubbing down, fed and watered."

"Sure thing. All the other animals are over to the livery stable. I'll take him over there."

"See you later, Mr. Abrams." Will and the storekeeper exchanged waves.

Will headed down the street to where he could see the knockdown warehouse at the end of track, just beyond the western edge of Benton. He spotted his uncle standing with General Dodge, General Jack Casement, and Conductor Johnson alongside a work train. Grady Shaughnessy stood nearby directing workers in stacking timbers and other construction materials onto a string of flatcars.

Will greeted the four men as he approached. The last time

he'd seen the generals and Grady had been at the dedication ceremony at Sherman Summit.

"Will." All four men greeted him simultaneously and faced him with quizzical looks.

"What'd you find beyond the bridge?" Johnson asked. "We heard an explosion."

Will told them about the nitroglycerin planted in the tunnel and how he and Lone Eagle had disposed of it. He informed them he believed it was the work of Paddy O'Hannigan. He didn't mention the rattlesnake.

"Good work," General Jack said. "I'll keep an eye out for O'Hannigan. Had to fire that rascal once. Guess it's going to take more than that to put a stop to his conniving."

"I suspect there's someone putting him up to these tricks," Dodge said, "but proving it may be difficult."

General Jack turned to Shaughnessy. "You're going to have to rebuild that trestle in record time, Grady. Can you do it?"

"Shouldn't be a problem. These timbers were already cut for the next trestle. We'll just use them to rebuild the damaged one. The only thing that'll slow us down is waiting to clear that locomotive off the track."

"Conductor Johnson has the authority to direct the engineer on this locomotive to push the other one into the ditch," General Dodge said. He stepped back a pace and looked down the street. "Where's that telegrapher? He's got to go with you and hook up a wire so he can notify General Grant's train to stop."

"Here he comes," General Jack said.

A short, balding man, carrying a carpetbag, limped up the dusty street and stopped in front of the assembled railroad men.

"What's this, Elmo?" Dodge pointed to Elmo Nicoletti's leg.

"Fell off a ladder trying to hook up the line to the new station building yesterday."

"How're you going to climb a pole to make your connection?" Dodge asked.

"I'm not. Somebody else has to. I can tap out the message, but I can't climb the pole."

"I can do it," Will said.

General Dodge looked at Will, then at Will's uncle, who nodded his approval.

"All right, then. We have to act quickly. Better get started, Mr. Johnson."

"Yes, sir. Boooard!"

Will and two dozen workers clambered onto the flatcars.

A half-hour later Will stood on the west bank of the shallow ravine alongside Shaughnessy, Nicoletti, and Johnson, watching the damaged locomotive being shoved aside.

"All right," Johnson said. "Let's get the telegraph working."

Nicoletti pulled a spool of wire and a telegrapher's key from his carpetbag. "Will, take one end of this wire across that gully while I hook the spool up to the key on this side. Climb up that pole over yonder and twist your end onto that wire you see hanging up there."

Will grasped the end of the wire, scrambling down the embankment and up the other side. He looped the wire twice around his wrist and shinnied up the pole. When he had the wire connected, he waved to Nicoletti, who rapidly tapped out a message on his key.

After a pause, the key clattered a response.

"Too late, Mr. Johnson," Nicoletti said. "General Grant's train has already departed Medicine Bow with enough fuel and water to make it nonstop to Benton. They're highballing it . . . there's no way Medicine Bow can notify them this bridge is out."

Chapter 35

Even from where he clung to the telegraph pole, Will could see the disappointment on Conductor Johnson's face. He shinnied back down the pole and crossed the gully to rejoin the conductor and the telegrapher.

"The only way to stop that train now is to flag it down. Will, you're younger than me . . . and a whole lot faster at running, I'd allow. Can you run down the track as far as you can and flag the engineer?"

"Yes, sir."

Johnson gave Will a red flag and instructions on what to do. "On your way, then," he said. "Tell General Grant we'll have the track back in operation in no time."

A few minutes later, Will trotted along the pathway between the railroad tracks and St. Mary's Creek, the same path he'd ridden earlier in the day on his way to the tunnel. He glanced to the south, where Elk Mountain dominated the horizon. Had Lone Eagle gotten back to his cabin? Had Jenny reached North Platte Crossing?

He'd have to think about when he'd get to see his friends again another time. Right now, he had to concentrate on how to get the engineer on General Grant's train to heed his signal to stop. He wanted to get as far down the track as possible in order to give the engineer plenty of time to bring the locomotive to a halt, after he signaled the train to stop—if he could get the engineer to heed his signal.

A whistle echoed from the distance. The train would be coming on fast. Conductor Johnson had said it would take some distance to stop, since it was highballing downhill toward the North Platte River.

Will knew he didn't have much time left. He climbed the embankment to get onto the tracks. He quickened his pace, staying between the rails, stepping on every other crosstie as he ran.

General Jack's workers, in their haste to lay as much track as fast as possible, hadn't wasted time ensuring the crossties were squarely trimmed. Each step Will took landed his foot on a different, uneven surface. He ought to slow down to keep from tripping or twisting an ankle—but he couldn't afford the delay such caution would require.

In the distance he saw the approaching train. It'd already cleared the tunnel. Black smoke belched in rhythmic, balloon-shaped puffs from the smokestack with each surge of the pistons. The engineer had the throttle wide open. General Grant was in a hurry to reach Benton.

Will had taken his eyes off the crossties too long. He stubbed a boot toe against a roughly hewn tie and pitched forward. He threw his hands out to catch his fall, dropping the flag.

"Umph!" He bounced onto the crossties and the intervening ballast with a thud, knocking the breath out of his lungs.

He turned his hands up and looked at them. Splinters protruded from his palms where they'd skidded across the rough wood of the tie. He rolled sideways and his head bumped against one of the iron rails. Through his skull he felt the vibrations from the oncoming train.

He had to get up. He pushed himself onto his knees.

Where was the flag? How was he going to signal the engineer without the flag?

Down there. The red cloth fluttered in the ditch. He'd

dropped the flag when he fell.

He forced himself to his feet, stepped off the tracks, and slid down the steep gravel embankment, pulling splinters out of his hands as he went. He lost his footing again, tumbled over, and rolled into the bottom of the ditch, losing his hat.

The chuffing of the locomotive grew louder with every passing second.

He grabbed the flag, stumbled back to his feet, and retrieved his hat. He scrambled up the embankment, slipping backward in the loose gravel with each step.

When he reached the tracks he crossed over them to the north side. Placing his right foot on the rail, as Conductor Johnson had instructed him, he stood directly in line with the engineer's view out of the right side of the oncoming locomotive's cab. He felt the rail shake beneath his boot as the train hurtled toward him.

He unfurled the red flag and raised it above his head in his right hand. He drew his revolver with his left, cocked it twice, then lifted it high overhead.

He concentrated on the window of the cab, hoping to see the face of the engineer—but the engineer wasn't looking. Where was the engineer?

He couldn't wait any longer. The locomotive was only two hundred yards away. Surely the engineer would appear in the cab window soon.

Will dropped the flag down to a horizontal position across the center of the tracks, then brought it back up vertically. Conductor Johnson had told him that was the signal to the engineer that the track ahead was blocked. He continued to wave the red flag up and down across the tracks with deliberately precise motions.

The conductor had said if the train didn't slow right away, fire two shots into the air. The engineer wouldn't be able to hear the shots over the noise of the engine, but he should see the black powder smoke shoot up from the pistol's barrel. This was a signal to the engineer that he should heed the warning of the red flag.

The engine was only one hundred yards away.

Finally, the engineer appeared, leaned forward in the window, and reached above his head to pull on the whistle cord. He sounded a succession of short, rapid blasts—the signal to clear the tracks.

Will fired two shots and waved the flag up and down rapidly. The locomotive bore down on him. The engine was less than twenty yards away. Why didn't the engineer obey his signal? Had he done it wrong? Had he misunderstood Conductor Johnson's instructions?

He stepped off the track, but continued to wave the flag. He shouted, "Stop! Stop!" He knew the engineer couldn't hear him, but maybe he could read his lips.

Suddenly the locomotive's driving wheels screeched on the rails and ceased turning. Sparks flew from between the wheels and the iron rails. The engine slowed and slid past him, steam from the cylinders engulfing him in a white mist. The engineer hung out the side window of the cab staring down at him as he rolled by.

The tender glided past Will, and then the single passenger car came to a halt beside him.

"Drop that pistol!" A soldier on the rear platform pointed a carbine at him. "Hands up!"

Will dropped his revolver into the dirt and raised his hands. He still held the red flag above his head.

"Shoot him, soldier!" The shouted order came from an open window in the passenger car. "He's trying to assassinate General Grant. Shoot him!"

Chapter 36

"Wait! I know that fellow."

Will recognized the Italian accent. He lowered the flag and let out the breath he'd been holding while staring into the barrel of the soldier's carbine.

Lieutenant Luigi Moretti's head emerged from one of the passenger car's windows. "He works for the railroad. Put your weapon down, soldier."

The soldier lowered his carbine. Will grinned up at the familiar face with its long, waxed mustache points. "Thanks, Luey."

The engineer had alighted from the locomotive and had run back to where Will stood. "What's the meaning of this!" he shouted. "Don't you know this is General Grant's express train?"

"The bridge is out up ahead, sir. Grady Shaughnessy and his crew are hurrying to rebuild it. But it's not finished yet. You don't want to crash into the gulch."

The engineer took off his hat and brushed a hand back through his hair. "Boy, you sure took a chance standing out there trying to flag me down at the speed we were making. But you probably saved General Grant's life . . . and my life, too . . . not to mention the dozen other generals riding in that coach."

Luey stepped down from the rear of the passenger car and joined Will and the engineer. "What's happening, Will? What are you doing out here?"

Will told him about the demolished trestle and the nitroglycerin bombs he'd disarmed in the tunnel.

"Come onboard, Will," Luey said. "General Grant will want to thank you personally for what you've done."

Will picked up his father's old Army Colt .44 revolver and rubbed his thumb over a nick in the handle—a souvenir of its fall onto the ballast rock. He brushed the dust off the pistol, rechecked that each cylinder still held its percussion cap, and returned the revolver to his holster.

A moment later, clutching his slouch hat with both hands in front of his belt, he stood before the great general, who was now the Republican Party's nominee for President of the United States.

"Nice work, son." Ulysses S. Grant blew a cloud of cigar smoke from his bearded face. He reached out and shook Will's hand. "These gentlemen and I all owe you a debt of thanks."

Will recognized some of the dozen men from engravings he'd seen in *Harper's Weekly* and *Leslie's Illustrated News* during the war. Until his father was killed at the Battle of Atlanta, his mother had borrowed the weekly newsmagazines from Judge Sampson, who subscribed to them. After his father's death, she'd lost interest in the war.

If he didn't know who they were, it would be hard for Will to tell they were all senior general officers of the Army. Except for two of them, they wore civilian suits.

General William Tecumseh Sherman, who'd made Georgia howl, and with whom Will's father had served at the Battle of Atlanta, stood taller than all but one of his companions. General Philip Sheridan, known to his soldiers as "Little Phil," had to look up to all his fellow officers, but he still wasn't as short as General Jack Casement.

After receiving the thanks of the officers, Will joined Luey on the rear seat of the passenger car. The train proceeded slowly toward the damaged trestle. When they reached the site of the bridge construction, all of the passengers descended from the coach and gathered in front of the locomotive to watch Grady and his crew complete the construction of the new bridge.

They only had to wait another hour before proceeding the short distance to the end of tracks at Benton.

On the western edge of Hell on Wheels, General Dodge provided General Grant and his entourage with an explanation of what lay ahead for the Union Pacific. "Beyond here, we face a hundred miles of the Red Desert," he said. "There's no suitable water in that great basin for our locomotives, our workers, or our cattle herd. We'll have to haul water from the North Platte. Maybe we can drill some decent wells, but so far we haven't found anything other than brackish swill. We have discovered coal in the surrounding hills, and the UP plans to convert our locomotives from wood burning to coal. Much more efficient."

Will stood beside his uncle, a short distance from the distinguished visitors, and plainly heard Dodge describe the interference he was experiencing from Doc Durant and "Colonel" Silas Seymour.

Grant puffed on his ever-present cigar and nodded. "Well, you're doing a fine job pressing the rails westward, Grenville." Grant called Dodge by his first name. "Keep up the good work. Don't want anything to interfere with joining the eastern states with California."

While Dodge briefed Grant and his party, the express train had reversed position, using the temporary wye track at Benton. The locomotive engineer's two short blasts on his whistle signaled he was ready for the return trip to Laramie.

After Grant and the generals climbed back aboard the passenger coach, Dodge reached for the handrail, placed a foot on the lower step at the rear of the car, then paused. He turned back to Will and his uncle. "Come with us. We're headed for a big meeting tomorrow between General Grant and Doc Durant. The outcome may very well determine the future of your survey inspection team."

Chapter 37

Will stood between his uncle and Lieutenant Moretti along the back wall of the small, log bungalow that served as the Officers' Club at Fort Sanders. His view of the central table, where Generals Grant and Dodge sat opposite Doc Durant, was partially obscured by a dozen general officers and railroad officials who encircled it. The stocky form of "Colonel" Silas Seymour stood directly behind Durant.

General Dodge cleared his throat and raised a hand. The murmurings in the room ceased in anticipation of the commencement of the meeting. "Welcome, General Grant," Dodge said. "Thank you for inspecting the construction of the Union Pacific Railroad. And especially thank you for meeting here today with Doctor Thomas Durant, Vice President and General Manager of our company."

Grant inclined his head briefly toward Durant, in a greeting. "My pleasure." He pulled a cigar from his suit pocket and clipped the end off with a guillotine cutter. An aide reached over his shoulder with a lighted lucifer match and the general puffed the cigar to life. This served as a signal to the others in the room that smoking would be tolerated, and half of the men fired up cigars and pipes. A cloud of tobacco smoke gathered in the open rafters above the heads of the men. Will rubbed his nose with the back of his hand to suppress a sneeze. At least one of the group smoked a particularly pungent cigar. Was it Grant?

Durant rested his forearms against the edge of the table, tapped the fingertips of one hand against the other a couple of times, then held his hands steepled together before him. "General Grant, I want to make it quite clear that I believe General Dodge is taking entirely too many shortcuts with the construction of the railroad. My consulting engineer, Colonel Seymour, has discovered a far better route for the tracks."

Will saw Seymour's chin rise and his chest expand at the recognition bestowed on him by his boss.

Grant looked over Durant's head at Seymour. *"Colonel* Seymour, is it? I don't seem to recall which regiment you commanded during the war, *Colonel.*"

Will heard several chuckles from the surrounding observers.

"It's a . . . an honorary title," Seymour stammered.

"Umm-hmm." Durant cleared his throat. "That's beside the point, General Grant. The fact of the matter is that General Dodge refuses to acknowledge the superior engineering suggestions Colonel Seymour has presented to him."

"Well, General Dodge." Grant turned to face the man seated beside him, removed the cigar from his mouth, and slowly blew out a stream of smoke. "During the war I could always count on you giving me good advice. What do you have to say about this matter?"

"Seymour's route will add time and expense to the construction of the railroad, in my opinion," Dodge said. "My survey inspection team has confirmed that we have laid out the best route. If we are forced to follow the one proposed by Seymour . . . I will resign."

The room had remained quiet since the meeting had been called to order, except for the muffled puffing on cigars and pipes. Even that sound ceased when Dodge uttered his threat.

Grant turned back to face Durant and jammed the cigar back into his mouth. He dragged deeply, then withdrew the cigar and expelled a flow of smoke directly across the table into Durant's face.

"Doctor Durant," Grant said, "let me make my position abundantly clear. The government expects this railroad to be built rapidly and economically. The Army needs to be able to move troops quickly all across the West to confront the increasing threat from the Indians, and to safeguard the lives and property of the citizens of this great country as they expand across the continent, not to mention protecting your railroad."

Grant paused and puffed on his cigar. "You are aware that the Republican Party has selected me to be their candidate for President of the United States. I assure you that I will be elected, notwithstanding that my opponent from the Democratic Party is your consulting engineer's cousin, Governor Horatio Seymour of New York. You can forget about any support you might hope to receive from that party, because they are going to lose. Therefore, since I will soon be the one making the decisions about whether or not the Union Pacific receives government bonds to finance your construction effort, I insist that General Grenville Dodge remain as chief engineer until the work is done."

Durant collapsed his fingers together and squeezed his hands tightly.

Grant clamped the cigar between his teeth. "Do you understand, Doctor?"

"Yes, I understand."

Will knew that the loss of government financing would far outweigh the small financial gains Doc Durant might pick up by routing the Union Pacific in a more circuitous fashion.

"Now that that's settled," Grant said, "it's time we got organized for the trip back East. Campaign responsibilities await." He pushed back from the table and stood.

"General Grant." Dodge stood also. "If you don't mind, the

Union Pacific's official photographer, Andrew Russell, has set up a camera outside, in front of the Officers' Club. We would like a photograph of you, all of our visitors, and of course the railroad officials present today, for our historical records."

"Certainly."

The group vacated the smoky interior and arranged themselves in front of and behind a white, picket fence that ran across the front of the building. The wives and children of some of the officers stationed at the fort were summoned to join the photo shoot.

"Are you ready, Mr. Russell?" Dodge called from where he stood in the open doorway of the bungalow, directly behind Grant.

The photographer stuck his head out from beneath the hood that covered the bulky camera perched on its wooden tripod. "I could use a little help with the wet plates, sir."

Dodge motioned to Will and pointed toward the photographer.

Will moved away from his uncle and Luey, where they were standing on the far left of the assembled dignitaries, and hustled over to the camera tripod.

"Mr. Russell, I'm Will Braddock. Can I be of assistance?"

"Yes, you can, Will. I have a wet plate already loaded in the camera for the first shot, but I want to take a second one right away to be sure I get a good picture. After the first shot, I'll remove the exposed plate and hand it to you. I want you to run it over to my portable darkroom mounted on the back of that wagon." He pointed to a small buggy, on the back of which sat a large, black box about the size of an outhouse. "Lift the back cover, and on the floor you'll see an identical container in which I have already coated the second plate with chemicals. Simply exchange the two and rush the unexposed one back here as fast as you can. Can you handle that?"

"Yes, sir."

"Gentlemen . . . and ladies," Russell said, "take your positions and remain perfectly still while I slip under the hood to adjust the focus."

Russell flipped the heavy, black drape over his head, and Will watched the camera bellows move back and forth until the photographer had the focus he desired. Then Russell stepped out from under the cloth hood.

"All right, folks. We're ready. I'm going to remove the lens cover and count to three, while I expose the plate to sunlight. After three seconds, I'll replace the lens cap, and the picture will have been taken. Do not move while the lens cap is off! That's important."

A final shuffling of the group took place. General Grant stood in the center, leaning both hands on the picket fence. Dodge remained in the club's doorway. Doc Durant slouched against the open gate of the fence, sulking like a three-year-old. To the far left, Will saw Luey twist the ends of his mustache to straighten them, then stick one hand into the front of his uniform coat. Will couldn't suppress his grin. Luey was imitating the famous pose of Napoleon Bonaparte.

"Here we go," Russell said. He removed the lens cover and counted. "One. Two. Three!" He replaced the lens cap and slid a wooden holder out of the side of the camera, handing it to Will.

Will ran to the back of the wagon and exchanged the container for the one that he found, just as Russell had told him. He raced back to the photographer, who inserted the new plate into the side of the camera.

"One more shot, please," Russell said. "Ready now. One. Two. Three!"

Russell stood and held up a hand. "Thank you, ladies and gentlemen. All finished." He shook Will's hand. "Thank you, young man. You were a big help. Everything went fine except I couldn't get those two gentlemen on the far left into the picture. The lens is not that wide."

Will chuckled. So much for Luey's imitation of Napoleon making it into the history books. Unfortunately, his Uncle Sean would be left out, too.

General Grant and his fellow officers shook hands all around and headed across the parade ground toward the fort's headquarters to prepare for their departure. Durant, Seymour, and the other railroad officials walked in the opposite direction. Only Will and his uncle remained in front of the club with General Dodge.

"That's settled then," Dodge said. "My route stands. There's no more need for a survey inspection team. Sean, I'm disbanding your unit effective immediately."

CHAPTER 38

What had General Dodge just said? No more survey inspection team? Will had counted on following his uncle across Wyoming and into Utah—until the completion of the transcontinental railroad. What was he going to do now?

"Sean," Dodge said, "I've got three problems facing me. First, Doc Durant is returning to New York, but he's leaving Seymour out west . . . sending him to Green River to supposedly oversee the development of the UP's new properties there. Second, I have to accompany General Grant back to Omaha, so I can't stay with Seymour and keep him from making a mess out of things. And third, Durant brought along Count Wolfgang von Schroeder, a German aristocrat, who happens to be a major bond holder in the Union Pacific. Durant wants me to escort the count on a hunting expedition beyond the end of track. But, obviously, I can't do that myself."

"How can I help, sir?" Will's uncle asked.

"You can stay close to Seymour at Green River and keep the 'insulting engineer' from creating problems we can't fix."

"All right," his uncle said.

"I also understand," Dodge continued, "that Mort Kavanagh, that so-called mayor of Hell on Wheels, has sent a crony of his to Green River to start buying up land. Between Seymour and Kavanagh, they could create all sorts of havoc for the UP. It's most important to keep Seymour from creating trouble. But if you can head off Kavanagh's land-grab, so much the better."

"I'll do my best," his uncle said. "What about my crew?"

"You can leave your rodman and chainman with Sam Reed in Utah. He can use their help in surveying our route around the Great Salt Lake. As for your cook, Jack Casement can probably put him to work in the construction train's mess hall."

Will stood to one side. His name hadn't been mentioned.

"That will take care of two of the problems. I'm not sure what to do about the third one. If that old mountain man Bullfrog Charlie Munro were still alive, I'd ask him to serve as a guide for the count's hunting expedition."

Will looked at his uncle, then at General Dodge, and cleared his throat. "I can do it," he said.

Dodge stared at him a moment. "You? How?"

"I'm a hunter for the railroad. At least, that's my unofficial job." Will glanced at his uncle. "Officially, I'm on the payroll as an assistant cook to Homer. But I've been hunting this area for the survey inspection team for almost a year, and I've tracked and shot all kinds of game."

Will drew himself up to full height and continued to look Dodge in the eye. Dodge cocked his head to one side and looked at Will's uncle, who nodded his head slightly.

"Well," Dodge said, "maybe that is the solution to my third problem."

"General Dodge," Conductor Hobart Johnson called out as he strode across Fort Sanders' parade ground and joined them at the picket fence in front of the Officers' Club. "The train is ready to depart for Benton. 'Colonel' Seymour is already onboard and demanding we get underway."

"All right, Mr. Johnson. Sean, you go along and try to appease Seymour. I'll talk over this hunting problem with Will and send him along shortly to join you."

Will's uncle followed Johnson across the parade ground, leaving Will alone with General Dodge.

"Come inside a moment." Dodge led the way back into the Officers' Club and approached a wall on which hung a large map of the Dakota Territory. Hand-drawn lines indicated the route of the railroad from the Nebraska border to where it ended now at Benton.

"We'll have to change the label on this map." Dodge tapped the legend. "I've received a telegram from Washington informing me Congress has separated this part of the country from the Dakota Territory and created a new one. We're now standing in the Wyoming Territory."

Dodge placed a finger on the map where the railroad crossed the North Platte River. "Here's where you need to start."

Will followed along as the bearded chief engineer's finger traced the course of the river northward, then westward along the route of the old Oregon Trail. "Guide the count's hunting party up the North Platte, then west along the base of the Wind River Range until you come to the Green River. From there lead the party south to where the railroad will intersect the river at the new town site we're calling Green River."

Will checked the legend on the map, then spaced off the distance with his fingers. "That's over three-hundred miles, General."

"I know. That's what Count von Schroeder wants to do. He plans to gather specimens of our native wildlife for his private museum in Germany. He particularly wants to bag a white buffalo he's heard about that roams with a small herd up the North Platte Valley."

"A white buffalo? An albino?"

"I guess. I understand they're considered sacred to the Indians. After the count gets the white buffalo, he wants to hunt elk and mountain sheep in the Wind River Mountains, then visit the sites of some of the early trappers' historic rendezvous that occurred along the Green River thirty . . . forty years ago.

What do you think, Will? Can you do this?"

Will smiled broadly. "Yes, sir."

"The count has already proceeded to Benton. Report to him there. I'll give you a letter informing him I've assigned you as his guide."

Dodge sat at a desk in one corner of the club and quickly scribbled out a note on a piece of paper. He placed the note in an envelope, addressed it, and handed it to Will. "You'll find Count von Schroeder and his entourage at the only hotel in Benton."

"Entourage, sir?"

"You wouldn't expect a count to travel all the way from Europe alone, would you?"

Will didn't really know anything about royalty. He'd read about them in books, but that was all. "I guess not."

"Count von Schroeder brought a gunsmith and a valet with him."

"Gunsmith and valet?"

"The gunsmith, of course, maintains his assortment of hunting weapons. The valet dresses him . . . I suppose." Dodge laughed.

Will smiled. This was going to be a new experience, for sure. But he'd never been through the part of the country General Dodge had pointed out on the map. "General, if the count has people accompanying him, could I ask someone to accompany me?"

Dodge looked at Will, his eyebrows arching upward. "How's that? I thought you said you could do this."

"I'm a hunter, true. But, I'm not familiar with that part of the territory. I know someone who is."

"And who might that be?"

"Lone Eagle."

"Who?"

"Lone Eagle Munro. Bullfrog's son. He was born and raised along the North Platte. I'd like to take him along as a scout."

"Well, I guess my budget can afford that. Tell Lone Eagle I'll pay him the same wages as the Army pays the Pawnee Scouts."

"Thank you, sir."

"And if you're successful with this hunting expedition, I might be able to arrange a slight raise for you. Say to pay equal to that of a full cook." Dodge grinned.

"I'd appreciate that, sir. Thank you, again."

"Now get along with you. You need to catch Conductor Johnson's train before it leaves the station."

Will sat in the rear of the passenger car beside his uncle and Hobart Johnson as the train pulled away from the Laramie train station and headed west. Will explained to them what General Dodge had asked him to do. Conductor Johnson agreed to stop the train at the North Platte River long enough for Will to disembark so he could head for Lone Eagle's cabin.

When the train passed through Rattlesnake Tunnel, Will pointed out where he and Lone Eagle had dismantled the nitroglycerin bombs Paddy O'Hannigan had planted. A few minutes later, the train slowed and came to a stop before it crossed the long bridge over the river.

"Why are we stopping here, Conductor?" Seymour demanded. He had turned in his seat at the front of the car and looked back to Conductor Johnson. "Savages could attack us here at any moment. Didn't you see that rattlesnake pinned with an arrow to the crossbeams when we came out of the tunnel?"

Conductor Johnson opened the rear passenger door and smiled at Will when he exited. Will had already told his uncle and the conductor the story about the rattlesnake.

It was only an hour's walk along the east bank of the river

until Will came to the clearing for Bullfrog's old cabin. He stopped and cupped his hands around his mouth. "Hallo, the cabin! Will Braddock, here." He didn't want Lone Eagle to think someone was sneaking up on him.

Lone Eagle appeared in the open door of the cabin and waved. "Hello, Will. Come on in."

They sat before the stone hearth on three-legged stools while Will explained the reason for his visit. "I know you don't want to scout for the Army," he said, "because you think they'll be chasing your Cheyenne relatives, but this is different."

"I don't want to scout for anybody. I just want to be left alone."

"But you need money."

"What for? I am a hunter and trapper now. I can find everything I need right out there." He waved a hand toward the outdoors.

"You have to buy ammunition, don't you, to keep hunting? Or are you going to steal it?"

Lone Eagle shrugged his shoulders.

"I need your help, Lone Eagle. I'm a pretty good hunter, but I don't know the territory. Besides, you can probably lead us right to this white buffalo the count wants to shoot."

"White buffalo?"

"Yes, the count's been told there's a white buffalo in a herd that roams along the North Platte."

"True. There is a white buffalo. It is sacred to all Indians. I cannot allow this count to kill the white buffalo."

Lone Eagle stood and lifted a bow and quiver of arrows off a peg beside the door. "Let's go," he said.

Chapter 39

Will rode double on the spotted pony behind Lone Eagle up the single, dusty street of Benton. They stopped in front of a one-story structure whose crudely painted sign proclaimed it to be the Grand Hotel. Will had been in the hotel, before the fancy name had been affixed, and knew that the tent that extended beyond the false-front simply held two rows of bunks—enough for two-dozen sleepers, more if they shared a bed. General Dodge had told him the count would be staying in the only hotel in town. Had to be this one—there weren't any others.

Will slid off the back of Lone Eagle's pony and stepped across the narrow wooden walkway. He paused for a moment to brush his hands down over his buckskin jacket to dislodge the trail dust, straightened his haversack on his shoulder, then turned the knob of the front door. Locked. He jiggled the knob, and when it still didn't open, he knocked.

A moment later a clean-shaven, middle-aged man opened the door a crack. "Ja?" the man asked. The stiff white collar of his heavily starched shirt held his neck rigidly straight above his black suit.

"I have come to see Count Wolfgang von Schroeder."

"Und who are you?" The German accent was unmistakable.

"Will Braddock. General Dodge sent me."

"Ja. Come in." The man opened the door fully and motioned for Will to enter what used to be the small lobby of the hotel.

The opulent furnishings and thick draperies so startled Will he jerked off his old slouch hat and pressed it against his stomach with both hands. "I thought this was a hotel." He'd walked into an elaborate sitting room.

The man closed the door behind Will and snorted. "The count has rented the entire hotel, so he can be somewhat comfortable in this wild country. Please to wait here. I will inform his Excellency of your presence."

The man disappeared through a canvas flap separating the former lobby from what used to be the bunkroom. Will could only imagine how that larger, second room must look now.

Since the man who answered the door hadn't acknowledged he was Count von Schroeder, Will assumed he must be the valet General Dodge had mentioned. He'd read about butlers in Dickens' novels, but he'd never seen one in person.

Will, still clasping his hat in front of him, glanced around the room, admiring the overstuffed chairs and sofas. The count must be very rich to afford such luxury.

The flap to the adjoining room opened and the man whom Will assumed was the valet returned, followed by a taller man who wore a dark green uniform, embellished with rows of gold braid. The waxed ends of his mustache extended the width of his face, ending in spear points. Even Lieutenant Moretti's mustache wasn't that long. How'd he sleep with that thing?

"Goot day. Count Wolfgang von Schroeder, at your service." The uniformed man clicked the heels of his boots together sharply and bowed slightly.

"You have met Rupert Ostermann, my personal servant." The count indicated the man Will had decided was the valet. Rupert hadn't actually introduced himself, but Will decided not to mention that fact.

"Rupert tells me General Dodge sent you. Are you a member of the guide's team?"

"I am the guide, sir."

"Humph! You are very young, no?"

"I'm old enough. But I will be assisted by Lone Eagle Munro, a Cheyenne scout."

The count raised his eyebrows, jutted his head forward, and stared at Will. "An Indian? And where is this one you call Lone Eagle?"

"Outside, sir. He doesn't like buildings. He prefers the freedom of the outdoors."

Will withdrew an envelope from his haversack and handed it to the count. "General Dodge asked me to give you this."

The count studied the envelope, which was addressed to Count von Schroeder and bore a return address of General Grenville Dodge, Chief Engineer, UPRR. "UPRR?" the count asked.

"Union Pacific Rail Road, sir," Will said.

"Ah, but of course." The count handed the envelope to Rupert without saying anything. The servant stepped to a writing desk, slid a letter opener deftly under the envelope's flap, and handed the envelope back.

The count extracted a single sheet from the envelope and unfolded it. He read it slowly, then looked at Will. "General Dodge writes you are well qualified to be my guide. He also mentions that this Lone Eagle is a half-breed. Can he be trusted? Can I understand him?"

"Lone Eagle is very trustworthy, sir. He speaks excellent English. I don't know about his German."

"English is fine," the count said. "So, then, we prepare for a wonderful hunt. No?"

"Yes, sir."

"Goot. In the party will be my Austrian gunsmith, Herr Conrad Eichhorn. He is the hunting master from my estates in Germany. Herr Eichhorn is out gathering supplies for the hunt at the moment."

Will nodded.

"And Rupert, of course," the count said, "goes with me everywhere. He will manage the camp. Rupert had engaged a Mexican to cook for us, but he got drunk last night and was beaten in a fight so badly he can't work. Rupert will have to find another cook. I wish we had a real chef."

"I have a friend who's a cook," Will said. "I guess Homer's not a chef, but I can vouch for his ability to turn wild game into a pretty good meal. I might be able to get him to come along . . . but you'd have to pay him more than the railroad does now."

"Hmn, interesting."

Will thought Homer would prefer serving the count more than shoveling grub at the gandy dancers. "My friend's also good with pack animals."

"Send your friend to Rupert, who will interview him and determine an appropriate wage, if he engages him." The count motioned to his servant, who snapped his heels and bobbed his head to acknowledge his instructions.

The count stepped to the doorway behind him, lifted the flap, and extended a hand in invitation to someone in the back room. "Herr Braddock, there is another member of our hunting party. May I present Miss Elspeth McNabb."

Will's mouth fell open. In the doorway stood Jenny's sister, Elspeth.

The count handed Elspeth into the sitting room, and when he turned to face Will, Elspeth shook her head and held a finger to her pursed lips.

"Rupert," the count said, "step into the back room with me. I want to give money to you and Herr Braddock for hiring the horses and mules."

"Ja, mein Count."

"Elspeth, my dear," the count said, "please be so kind as to entertain Herr Braddock for a moment."

"Of course." Elspeth stepped forward to allow the count and Rupert to pass into the room behind her. Her skirt rustled as she glided over to stand in front of Will.

"Herr Braddock, so nice to meet you." She spoke loudly enough for her voice to carry into the other room. "Sh." She mouthed the caution silently and extended both hands with her palms up, inviting Will to give her his hands.

Will closed his mouth, which had remained open since Elspeth's appearance. He complied with Elspeth's request, placing his hands in hers. The low-cut neckline of her dress revealed bare shoulders, across which spread her golden hair in tight ringlets. Elspeth looked directly into his eyes with her deep blue ones—eyes that shone with a brilliance matching her smile.

She squeezed Will's hands, then spoke in a whispered drawl. "Will, please don't give me away. This is my ticket out of here. My chance to get out from under the grasp of Mort Kavanagh."

"I . . ." Will could think of nothing to say. Elspeth's closeness mesmerized him. Her perfume accosted his nostrils with a flowery scent he couldn't identify. Her allure hypnotized him. He shook his head. What would Jenny think if she saw him standing tongue-tied before Elspeth?

"Will, Mort Kavanagh convinced Count von Schroeder I should accompany him as his traveling companion." Elspeth kept her voice low. "I offer the count a greater challenge playing chess than can Rupert or Conrad."

Will's eyes remained fixed on Elspeth's lips while she spoke. "Chess?"

"Yes, I play quite well. Papa taught me."

"And you're going alone? With all these men?"

"Mort told the count I was his niece and if anything happened to me he would pay dearly."

"You're going with us to play chess?"

"I'll entertain everybody in the evenings with my singing, also."

"Jenny told me she couldn't get you to leave the Lucky Dollar Saloon, why would Mort agree to let you leave?"

"Mort plans to have Paddy O'Hannigan rob the count while we are on the hunt. The count carries a large amount of cash in a money belt that Mort claims exceeds fifty thousand dollars. Mort wants that money and his real reason for positioning me with the count is so I can help Paddy with the robbery from inside. I will not do it, though. I'll explain more later, when we have some privacy. But, please don't indicate you know who I really am. And, please don't object to me going along, Will. Promise me! Please, Will."

Will nodded. Elspeth sighed and squeezed his hands.

The count cleared his throat behind her. "So, I see you are on intimate terms already."

"Oh, Wolfgang, I was just admiring Herr Braddock's strong hands." Elspeth lifted Will's hands for the count to see. "He will truly be a capable horse wrangler with such strong, callused hands, don't you think?"

"Ja. Sure."

Elspeth dropped Will's hands and stepped back beside the count, linking her arm through his. She winked at Will.

"So," the count said. "Rupert and you can decide how many horses and mules we need. I was hoping perhaps we could take a wagon?"

"I don't think so, sir. Pack mules and horses will be better where we're going."

"I bow to your judgment, Herr Braddock." The count clicked his heels, offering a quick, short bow.

"When can we expect this cook of yours to join us?"

"Homer can be ready tomorrow, I'm sure."

"Goot. If he is acceptable to Rupert, we can commence the

hunting trip the next day."

A few minutes later, Will and Rupert walked toward the livery stable. Lone Eagle trailed behind them on his pony. When they passed the Lucky Dollar, Will caught a glimpse of movement behind the saloon's single window. A curtain dropped across the glass before he could see if it might be Mort Kavanagh.

Elspeth said Kavanagh planned to have Paddy O'Hannigan rob Count von Schroeder. Even if she didn't help Paddy, Will would have to keep alert. That conniving O'Hannigan could turn up anywhere, anytime. Will clenched his fists. He was tempted to dash across the street and confront the so-called mayor of Hell on Wheels right now and put an end to this. But, he had to help Rupert select the horses and mules, check on Buck, and alert Homer to the possibility of a new job.

CHAPTER 40

Paddy O'Hannigan held aside the drape and peered out the window of Mort Kavanagh's office. Across the street, in the corral of the livery stable, he observed the assembly of Count Wolfgang von Schroeder's hunting party.

"Sure, and that be Will Braddock loading them horses," Paddy said. "And that no account nigger Homer's packing up that mule of his. And over yonder, leaning against the rail beside that spotted pony, is that half-breed Lone Eagle. Sure, and I'm gonna get them all!"

"Forget that," Kavanagh said. "I've got more important things for you to do right now."

"Someday I'll get them. Sure, and I will, if it's the last thing I do."

"Fine. Someday you can do that. Right now, pay attention to what I'm telling you. This job will mean a big paycheck for you . . . and me, of course." Mort flipped opened the lid of a humidor on his desk and pulled out a long, black cigar. He bit the end off of it and spit the chunk into the spittoon beside his desk.

Paddy watched Will continue with the saddling of six horses, including the black Morgan, and the loading of a dozen pack horses. Some of the pack horses were loaded with tents, folding tables, and collapsible chairs. Homer stowed boxes and sacks of food, crates of cooking utensils, and cases of wine and champagne, in the packsaddles. A tall, slender man dressed in green European hunting clothes loaded an armful of rifles and boxes of ammunition onto one pack horse.

"Who'd be that fancy dude in the green outfit?" Paddy asked.

Kavanagh swung his swivel chair around, pulled the drapes farther apart, and looked to where Paddy pointed. "He's the count's Austrian gunsmith."

"The whole bunch looks more like a carnival sideshow, than a hunting party, if you ask me," Paddy said. He shook his head from side to side. "And what's Braddock doing, anyway?"

Kavanagh turned his chair back, struck a match across the top of the desk, and held the flame to the end of his cigar. He puffed vigorously for a moment, checked the growing white ash on the cigar's end, and tossed the match into the spittoon. "Well." He paused to draw deeply on the cigar. "Will Braddock's the count's guide."

"Guide? Sure, and what's he knowing about being a guide?"

"General Dodge thinks he knows enough. He recommended him to the count. Seems Braddock's a pretty good shot, and we know he's good with horses."

"Humph!" Paddy grunted.

"But the count's going to be in for a surprise." Kavanagh blew out a lazy smoke ring. "And that's where you come in, O'Hannigan."

Kavanagh pushed his swivel chair back and stepped to the window beside Paddy. The two of them stood there watching as preparations for the departure of the count's hunting party neared its conclusion.

"The count wears a money belt stuffed with hundred dollar bills," Kavanagh said. "He's done a considerable amount of gambling in the Lucky Dollar and he always settles his account with crisp, new paper bills. A maid, that I conveniently provided to take care of the count's quarters, has seen him hide the money belt in the bottom of a leather traveling trunk he keeps under his bed. Apparently the only two persons allowed access to it are the valet and the count himself."

"Cash, huh? And a lot of it, you think, Mort?"

"I do. And I intend to make the count's money, my money. You are going to steal that money belt."

A sly grin crossed Paddy's face. Stealing. Now that was something he really enjoyed doing. He'd never failed to steal whatever he wanted, when he put his mind to it. Of course, there'd been that delay in stealing the Morgan horse last year, but he'd eventually pulled off the job.

"Hire yourself a good riding horse," Kavanagh said. "Get enough grub to take along for a week or two. I want you to follow the count's party. And do it alone. No companions. I don't want to share that cash with anybody else. Understand?"

"Sure, and I can be doing that."

"Wait until they're far enough away from Benton so they can't easily send for help. Find a way to distract the count and his entourage."

"Entourage?" Paddy asked.

"Yeah. It's a big word, I know, Paddy. Entourage means the group of people traveling in the count's hunting party."

"Humph."

"You can't go busting into the count's camp shooting up the place. There's too many of them. They'd gun you down. That Bowie knife of yours should make short work of cutting through the straps of the count's leather traveling trunk. But you'll need to distract all of them long enough for you to get into the traveling trunk and find the money belt."

Paddy nodded. Yeah, he had an idea how to distract them. He'd been fooling around with rattlesnakes. Teasing them until they'd strike. He was quick enough to jump aside without getting struck. But that was because he watched the snake's every move. If there were a whole lot of snakes he could create a real distraction, all right.

"But, how am I gonna know for sure where this traveling trunk is kept?" Paddy asked. "I won't have much time to open it and grab the money belt."

"I've got a secret weapon for that, and here it comes." Kavanagh pointed out the window.

Count Wolfgang von Schroeder and a woman strolled arm in arm, up the boardwalk on the opposite side of the street, heading toward the stable. The brim of a large hat concealed the woman's face. Both were dressed in riding clothes.

The count's waxed mustaches bounced with each step. His dark brown hunting jacket sported leather inserts at the shoulders, to provide a cushion for the recoil of a rifle. Beneath the jacket he wore a red waistcoat over a white shirt. His fawn-colored breeches were tucked into calf-length brown leather boots sporting black turned-down tops. He swished a riding crop against his boot as he walked. When he passed others on the boardwalk he tapped the crop against the wide brim of a jaunty hat that covered long, curly brown hair.

Paddy thought the count made a striking figure as he strode confidently along with the woman on his arm. As the couple drew abreast of the Lucky Dollar Saloon, the woman raised her head from beneath her wide-brimmed hat and looked directly at Paddy. A long feather in the band of her hunter green hat shook as she laughed at something the count had said to her.

Paddy gasped. "That's Elspeth McNabb!"

"That's the secret weapon." Kavanagh blew a cloud of smoke into Paddy's face.

Paddy looked back at Elspeth, but she'd dropped her head. Her blond locks flowed in ringlets beneath the big hat. Her riding costume was the same dark green as her hat. The formfitting jacket enhanced rather than concealed her figure. The ground-length skirt brushed along the boards of the walk.

"Elspeth attracted his attention when she frequently beat him at chess."

"Chess?"

"Yes, when the count came into the Lucky Dollar on his first night in Benton looking for someone to play chess Elspeth said she knew how. The count immediately challenged her to a game. When I heard the count exclaim after one of their games that none of his entourage played as well as Elspeth, I suggested she go along on the count's hunt. He liked that idea immediately."

"Sure, and how's the secret weapon going to be helping me?"

"Elspeth will locate the traveling trunk for you and assist in whatever you decide for a diversion."

Chapter 41

"Whoa." Paddy pulled up on the reins and brought the mare to a halt on the west bank of the North Platte, directly across the river from Lone Eagle's cabin. He raised up in the saddle, the leather creaking softly when he stood in the stirrups, and surveyed the clearing to ensure no one was around.

He smiled to himself when he spotted the reason for visiting the cabin. He patted the horse's neck and settled back onto the saddle. "Aye. Sure, and the travois is still there. That'll make it easier for ye, and for me, too. I was pretty sure this one would be here for the taking."

An hour earlier he'd selected the roan mare from an assortment of horses available at Benton's livery stable. Ezekiel Thomas, the stable owner, had told him the mare was strong, not easily spooked, and capable of running for long distances. She fit Paddy's requirements exactly.

Bullfrog Charlie's old raft rested against the far bank. Lone Eagle had ferried Paddy across the river on the raft a few weeks ago when he was on his way to California. He would return to use the ferry again later this same day—if he had good luck. He'd need it to haul his intended cargo back across the river.

Paddy dismounted and grasped the tow rope that was tied to either end of the raft. The rope passed overhead through hand-carved wooden pulleys fastened to the trunks of sturdy cottonwood trees on opposite banks. Without the old mountain man's ingenious towing system, the river's current would simply sweep the raft downstream.

By the time Paddy had hauled the raft across the river by pulling on the rope and beaching it against the west bank where he stood, sweat drenched his shirt and dripped off his nose. He sank to his knees, gasping for breath. That was hard work just to keep from getting his feet wet.

He led the horse down to the river's edge and coaxed her into the water. He tied her bridle to the rear of the raft, then he clambered aboard the log deck. "Now, girl. Let's see how good ye are at swimming. Sure, and it'll be hard enough dragging meself across without having to pull ye along, too."

Paddy grasped the rope above his head and heaved on it, edging the raft into the stream. The mare didn't hesitate, swimming easily beside the small craft. The current swept them swiftly to the middle of the river, then Paddy had to haul more vigorously on the rope to drag the weight of the raft against the current to complete the traverse to the far side.

It only took a few minutes to cross over to the east bank. Paddy led the mare up to the cabin's door and looped the reins around the protruding end of one of the logs that formed the walls of the hut.

"Good girl." He patted the horse and stepped over to where the travois leaned against the wall. "Aye, sure and this'll do. Just need to tighten her bindings a wee bit."

Paddy pushed open the door and entered the dim interior. The only light came from the open door, but he didn't plan to stay long enough to light a fire to enhance the illumination in the one-room structure.

"Ah, sure and that's convenient." He picked up an axe he found leaning against the fireplace and went back outside. "This will make an easier job of it than using my knife."

He stepped into the grove of cottonwoods. The scaffold bearing the remains of the mountain man hung prominently in the center of the grove. He steered clear of it, finding what he needed on the fringe of the small growth of trees. He chopped down a straight sapling and trimmed the branches away with a few swings of the axe, then cut the ends off to create a slender pole, six feet long.

Returning to the cabin, he removed an iron cooking pot from where it hung suspended over the center of the stone fireplace. He used the axe to break away the mud chinking that held an iron bar in place where it stretched across the width of the fireplace, pried the end of the bar away from the stone, and slid the pot hook off.

Next, he dumped the husk-filled mattress off the single cot and hacked away at the rawhide support thongs with his Bowie knife. He sat on one of the three-legged stools and lashed the pot hook to one end of the pole with several turns of a leather thong. He extended the pole and rapped it sharply on the hard-packed dirt floor. The hook didn't twist or turn. He smiled to himself. His newly crafted tool would do the job nicely.

He went back outside with the remaining lengths of rawhide and wove them back and forth across the body of the travois, strengthening its center. He would use the travois to transport his surprise to the count's hunting camp. He felt pleased that he'd remembered seeing the travois earlier. So far, his plan was going well.

He untied four burlap sacks from behind his saddle. He'd stolen them from the rear of the Chinaman's café last night, dumping the rice they contained into the alley. He lashed the bags and his new tool to the travois, then dragged the lightweight sled up behind the mare. The travois still had the strapping necessary to fasten it behind his saddle, so he didn't have to make any modifications before slipping the ends in place over the rump of the horse and attaching the two poles.

Paddy mounted and rode the horse away from the cabin. He

headed north, up the east bank of the river in the direction of the railroad tracks. He looked back at the cabin just before he left the clearing and saw he hadn't closed the door. He shrugged. Too bad. Custom dictated that someone using an empty cabin should have the courtesy to leave it as they'd found it. Since he'd trashed the interior, it wouldn't make much difference. "Sorry, Lone Eagle." He laughed.

A quarter of an hour later, he turned the old mare to the east, and rode alongside the tracks heading toward the Rattlesnake Hills. This took him away from his ultimate destination, that of following the count's hunting party up the west bank of the North Platte. But he needed to get the snakes first. He might have found some along the North Platte, but he knew for certain he'd find them in the Rattlesnake Hills.

In the distance he could see the entrance to the railroad tunnel. It was near this spot where he'd found that four-foot rattlesnake he'd placed on the tunnel entrance's timber bracing when he'd planted the bottles of nitroglycerin. That big rattler undoubtedly came from a den in this vicinity. Now all he had to do was find the den.

The mare whinnied and pranced—more anxiousness than she'd displayed previously. Maybe she sensed the snakes. Nothing else seemed to have upset her easy disposition since he'd ridden her out of Benton.

A whistle signaled a train approaching the far entrance to the tunnel. He didn't want to be spotted, so he turned the horse off the roadbed he'd been following and rode down into a small stand of brushy trees along the dry creek bed that paralleled the railroad tracks. A couple of minutes later, a 4-4-0 locomotive pulled a string of freight cars past at a modest clip. The engineer and fireman looked straight ahead, up the tracks toward the west. They didn't see him.

While waiting for the train to disappear, he surveyed the cliff that rose on the opposite side of the tracks from where he sat concealed in the brush. He decided the snake den must be in that rocky slope. Right here was a good place to conceal his horse while he conducted his search.

He tied the mare to a scrawny tree and unpacked his sacks and the new tool. He climbed back up the embankment and walked along the rails, studying the sandy soil until he spotted a wriggly track left by a snake. The snake's path disappeared into the rocks at the base of the cliff that rose a hundred feet above him.

He'd bet that was where he'd find the den. But he didn't want to approach it from directly below. That's the way the snakes would come and go. He walked down the roadbed a ways until he found a more gentle slope up which to climb.

Fifteen minutes later he was on top of the ridge, looking back down at the railroad tracks. He could see his horse in the copse along the creek. But, unless a passerby studied the terrain carefully, he wouldn't spot the mare's hiding place.

He eased along the ridgeline until he came to the spot above where he'd seen the snake's track turn up the slope. He studied the cliff that fell away beneath him.

Aha! Found it.

Directly below he watched brown-speckled, scaly bodies glide in and out of an opening in the hillside. He checked the ground around him, rustling the bushes with his hooked tool. Not likely the snakes would approach the den from above, but best to be sure. Nothing stirred in the brush or among the rocks where he stood.

He laid out the burlap bags one atop the other, then took the pole and stretched out on his belly on the edge of the cliff. He eased forward to get a good view below. He counted at least a dozen rattlers moving around in the open end of the den. He didn't want a four-footer this time. That'd be too big. Three feet would be better.

He studied the den, estimating the length of each of the intertwined snakes. He extended his pole down. The distance was perfect. The hook reached into the center of the twisting reptiles. He held it steady for a minute to let the snakes settle. They weren't coiled, so they would be easy to grasp. He selected a likely one and guided the hook beneath the center of the snake's belly, then lifted it. So far, so good.

He rose to his knees as he pulled the pole upward. The snake's long body draped downward on either side of the hook. The snake would be helpless in this position—or at least he hoped so.

He took a deep breath, breathed out, and stood up. He kept the hooked end of the pole extended away from him. He glanced down to assure himself the burlap bags were within easy reach.

Slowly he hoisted the pole and brought the hook end back toward himself. The snake writhed, twisted, and turned, trying to get off the hook. Paddy carefully eased the creature closer. He waited until the snake lifted its head, and when the head swayed in the direction away from him, he grasped its tail and lifted it free of the hook. He dropped the pole and held the snake up and away from him, allowing its weight to straighten and neutralize it. The right size for what he wanted—three feet long.

Keeping a close watch on the thrashing serpent, he picked up a burlap sack and eased the head of the snake into it. When he had more than half the length of the reptile into the sack he let go of the squirming creature. He clasped the top closed and tied the neck of the bag with one of four pre-cut strips of rawhide he'd looped through his belt.

One down. Three to go. More than once, a snake slipped off the hook, and he had to start his maneuvering all over. After an hour, he had a three-footer secured in each burlap bag.

Now all that remained was to load the bags onto the travois without spooking his horse, get back to Lone Eagle's cabin, use Bullfrog's old ferry to cross the river without drowning his snakes, and pursue the count's hunting party.

CHAPTER 42

By the second night away from Benton, setting up the count's camp had become routine. Lone Eagle, scouting ahead, would locate a suitable campsite near where the North Platte flowed and Will would organize the layout of the facilities. To spare Lone Eagle from the embarrassment of performing manual labor, something that might be considered unsuitable for an Indian warrior, Will assigned Lone Eagle the responsibility of standing guard on a nearby rise. He'd decided not to mention to his mixed-blood friend the potential threat from Paddy O'Hannigan until he could find a time to discuss with Elspeth what the actual danger might be.

Once the site had been selected, Will, Homer, and Rupert tackled the job of raising the count's large tent, pitching a smaller tent for Elspeth, and erecting the cooking fly. Herr Eichhorn busied himself unloading and tending to the count's array of weaponry, conveniently avoiding any physical labor required in preparing for the evening's meal and the night's rest.

"Will," Homer said, "it be downright wasteful, to my way of thinking." He shook his head and waved a hand toward Rupert, who prepared to light the cook fire.

Rupert extracted a wooden lucifer from a paper packet, struck the match against the side of the box, then held the flame beneath a pile of kindling.

"Flint and steel would start that fire jest fine," Homer said. "They's got a whole case of them lucifer matches. Never saw so much waste in my entire life."

"Don't worry about it, Homer," Will said. "The count has an excess of everything, it appears. Doesn't seem to bother him any."

"An excess of everything about says it all," Homer said. "Including cases of champagne. Can you imagine? And two cases of cognac, too!"

"Homer," Rupert said. "Take three bottles of the champagne down to the river and chill them. Then come back and prepare the count's supper. We'll roast that antelope he shot this afternoon."

"Yas, suh," Homer said. He gathered three bottles from one of the many cases of champagne and tied their necks together with a cord, which he'd dangle into the swiftly moving stream that flowed beside the campsite.

"I've got to water and picket the horses, Homer," Will said. "I'll be back later for some of that antelope. Save me a steak."

"Sure thing, Will."

As Will gathered the halter ropes of four horses in preparation for leading them to water, he could see Rupert setting the folding dining table with a linen cloth and china dishes. The protocol for the evening supper had been established the first night they'd camped, and it was evident to Will that it would be continued throughout the hunt. Count von Schroeder, Conrad Eichhorn, and Elspeth McNabb would sit around the table on folding chairs, waited on by Rupert. Following the meal, the count and Elspeth would engage in a game of chess. Eichhorn would polish and clean the arsenal of weapons while observing the game.

The smell of the roasting antelope taunted Will's taste buds as he tended the horses. With a dozen pack horses and the six saddle horses, it took an hour to see that all of the animals were watered, then staked out with picket pins to allow them to graze.

Homer cared for Ruby and Lone Eagle took care of his own pony. Will was reminded of his first job as a wrangler with the Union Pacific the year before. That was when he'd first proved his worth to General Dodge.

By the time Will finished with the animals, Rupert was commencing to serve supper to the three seated at the folding dining table in front of the count's sleeping tent. Will, Homer, and Lone Eagle ate with Rupert using tin plates under the kitchen fly.

After the evening meal drew to a close, the count lit his meerschaum pipe with one of the lucifer matches. Conrad Eichhorn puffed on a briar pipe, while Rupert cleared the dishes from the table.

"Miss Elspeth," the count said, "before we start this evening's game, would you favor us with a song?"

"Why, I'd love to, Wolfgang." She pushed back from the table and stood. She brushed her hands down her dress, smoothing out the wrinkles. "What would you like to hear?"

"How about that Stephen Foster song? Something about Jeannie."

Will added his tin plate to the pile of dishes Rupert was accumulating next to the wash pan where Homer did the clean-up following the meal. Will stepped out from under the cooking fly and slipped closer to the count's table, finding a secluded spot beneath a cottonwood tree from where he could listen to Elspeth sing.

Elspeth folded her hands beneath her breasts, shook her hair gently to settle the blonde curls loosely across her bare shoulders, raised her head, and opened her mouth.

I dream of Jeannie with the light brown hair
Borne, like a vapor, on the summer air
I see her tripping where the bright streams play
Happy as the daisies that dance on her way

Elspeth did have a lovely voice. Her southern accent caressed the words a special way. Will smiled to himself as the words unfolded. The song had been one his mother had sung—a song his father had been partial to. That seemed a long time ago, but it had just been a year since his mother had died. His father had been gone the past four years, since losing his life at the Battle of Atlanta in 1864. Will was alone in the world, except for his uncle and his friends.

Will brushed a tear from his eye. No time to get sentimental. He had to concentrate on keeping his job with the railroad. He knew General Dodge expected him to help the count collect the white buffalo as a specimen for his museum, but he also felt an obligation to Lone Eagle to not allow the count to desecrate the Indians' sacred animal.

Chapter 43

As they neared the end of the third day after leaving Benton, Will guided the hunting party north, downstream along the west bank of the North Platte River. The hunting had been sparse so far, just a few antelope.

Will rode at the head of the column of riders, leading one string of four pack horses. Each of the horses was tied to the packsaddle of the horse preceding it. Count von Schroeder, Conrad Eichhorn, and Elspeth usually followed in line behind him. Rupert came next with four more pack horses. Homer brought up the rear with the final string of four horses. He'd inserted Ruby into his string in front of the horses, because the cantankerous mule refused to budge if she were not right next to Homer. Lone Eagle ranged a mile or more ahead of the party, scouting for signs of buffalo and other game.

Will sensed the count's restlessness when the German aristocrat trotted his big stallion down from having ridden to the top of another of the numerous hills, seeking a better view as he searched for the elusive herd that reputedly included the rare white buffalo. He reined in beside Will. "When are we going to find them?" he demanded. "I thought that herd was grazing along this part of the river."

"Sir," Will said, "we only have secondhand reports of recent sightings. Neither Lone Eagle nor I have seen the herd personally. If they're out here . . . he'll find them."

The count snorted and jerked the reins of his horse, turning back toward the rear of the party to rejoin Elspeth.

Will led the way through a defile where a sweeping bend in the river had carved its way through a high ridge. The group emerged from the narrow passage onto a broad plain spread out around a smaller river that flowed out of the west and joined the North Platte a half-dozen miles ahead. Racing his pony back toward him, Lone Eagle circled a hand above his head and pointed behind him with his thumb, signaling he'd located the herd.

Will halted and turned back in his saddle. "Count von Schroeder! We've found them."

The count spurred his mount forward to join Will. The two then walked their horses forward while they studied the valley ahead of them.

The count reached out and slapped Will on the shoulder. "Ja! Goot job. Is the white buffalo with them?"

"I don't see it from here, sir. Lone Eagle can tell us."

In a few minutes Lone Eagle pulled up before them. "Not a very big herd," he said. "That's the Sweetwater River joining the North Platte down there. Provides good water and grass."

Lone Eagle, Will, and the count studied the buffalo herd grazing the lush grass along the stream. The rest of the hunting party rode up, and the entire party of seven halted, while they studied the shaggy beasts. The animals stretched for almost a mile along the near side of the small river.

"How many?" the count asked.

"Maybe a thousand," Lone Eagle answered.

"Is the white one with the herd?"

Lone Eagle glanced sideways at Will before answering. "I do not see it."

"Come, Herr Eichhorn," the count said. "Time to gather some specimens."

Conrad Eichhorn handed his employer a lever-action

Winchester rifle, the successor to the Henry. The gun had been on the market for less than a year. Will admired the design of the new repeating firearm, with its side-loading cartridge receiver. He wondered if a single shot from the Winchester's .44-caliber bullet could drop a one-ton bull.

"Rupert," the count said. "Find a shady place down by the river to set up camp while we shoot some of these beasts. Elspeth stay with Rupert, where you will be safe."

Elspeth guided her horse aside to join the count's personal servant.

"Come, Homer," Rupert said, "let us prepare for a feast of buffalo tongue tonight."

Will and Lone Eagle accompanied Count von Schroeder and Eichhorn down the gentle slope into the valley, where they rode slowly along the outer edge of the herd. The animals grew restless and moved as one mass down the south bank of the Sweetwater toward its junction with the North Platte.

The count selected one of the bigger bulls, which jogged ahead when the horseman and his stallion nudged nearer. The German's leg brushed against the side of the buffalo. The big horse shied from the buffalo's swinging horns, but the count held him tightly in line with the reins he grasped in his left hand. The bull picked up its pace, its shaggy beard bouncing as the large head careened up and down in time with its stride. Soon the entire herd joined in the race.

The count leaned forward over the stallion's withers, pulled the rifle against his shoulder, and shot the beast in the chest. The Winchester proved it had the necessary stopping power. The count only had to fire once and the big bull stumbled and dropped.

Will and Lone Eagle rode some distance behind the count and the gunsmith, their presence forcing the herd to travel close to the river's edge. Neither shot at a buffalo. The roar of the pounding hooves of a thousand animals made talking impossible.

Will guided Buck closer to Lone Eagle. "Did you see the white one?" he shouted.

Lone Eagle jerked his head back over his shoulder in the direction of the ridge they had ridden around. "It's with a dozen others over there, in a small box canyon. It will be safe if it stays there."

The count continued to select the larger animals as his target, rode in close to them, and blasted them in the chest. When he emptied his rifle he handed it to Eichhorn, who replaced it with a loaded one. The hunting master didn't shoot anything himself.

From time to time Will glanced at Lone Eagle, whose clenched jaw mirrored his own frustration. The slaughter continued for over an hour.

Then the herd slammed into the confluence of the two rivers. The pressure from the following animals forced the leaders to plow into the water. Their momentum broken, the buffalos milled about as they tried to find room to join their companions in crossing the North Platte.

The count pulled up and ceased firing. "No sport in shooting sitting ducks, Herr Eichhorn. Let's select the best specimens from those that are down."

The count rode back up the stream studying each of the bulls he'd shot. Will shook his head. Their small hunting party certainly couldn't use all of the meat from the two dozen dead buffalos.

The count reined his horse to a halt, turned to Will, and pointed at one of the dead bulls. "I'll take that one back to Germany for mounting in the museum. I want the entire hide and head. Oh, and the hooves, too."

"And the others?" Will asked.

The count shrugged. "Not handsome enough. Select the next

best one and remove its head. I'll mount that head on my library wall. Cut out as many tongues as you think we can eat and take them to Rupert. Let us test Homer's cooking ability. We will have a feast tonight to celebrate a most successful hunt. Ja?"

The count handed his empty rifle to Eichhorn. He and the Austrian turned their horses back toward the camp Rupert had established, visible a half-mile away at the river's edge.

The count reined in abruptly.

Emerging from the box canyon a hundred yards away trotted the white buffalo.

Chapter 44

"Give me a rifle, Herr Eichhorn!" Count von Schroeder shouted.

Beside him, Will saw the count wheel his stallion closer to the gunsmith and reach out a hand. On the other side of him, Lone Eagle kicked his pony hard and raced toward the white buffalo and the dozen or so brown ones in the small herd that had emerged from the box canyon.

"They are not loaded, mein Count!" Eichhorn replied. He swung one of the Winchesters off his shoulder and pulled a handful of cartridges from his vest pocket. He quickly fed the shells into the receiver on the side of the rifle.

"Will!" Lone Eagle called back over his shoulder. "Help me drive the white buffalo across the river."

Will jabbed his heels into Buck's flanks and flicked the reins. "Let's go, Buck!"

The black Morgan's speed closed the gap with Lone Eagle's pony and the two youths soon raced side by side to head off the white buffalo.

"Check the ridge above us," Lone Eagle shouted. His quick glance guided Will's eyes to a spot along the ridgeline. Eight mounted men sat motionless on the crest.

"Who are they?" Will asked.

"Shoshones. This is their land."

Lone Eagle shouted and waved an arm in the air as he rode full speed at the white buffalo. The big animal stopped and pawed the ground. Will jerked off his slouch hat and waved it overhead. He kicked Buck in the sides to keep pace with Lone Eagle, joining in shouting.

The white buffalo tossed its head, then turned away from the advancing horsemen and led its shaggy, brown companions at a gallop toward the Sweetwater River. The small herd did not slow down at the narrow stream, but plunged down the near bank, splashed straight through the shallow water, and surged up the opposite bank.

Lone Eagle halted his pony when he reached the river. Will reined in Buck beside him. The white buffalo's herd disappeared into the scrub brush, their progress visible only by the cloud of dust that rose around the bushes and stunted trees as they raced away.

Count von Schroeder galloped his stallion up, brandishing his Winchester. He pulled up beside Will and Lone Eagle and leveled the gun at Lone Eagle. "What did you do that for? I could have shot that beast easily once I had a loaded weapon."

Eichhorn galloped up on his slower mount and shook his fist at Will and Lone Eagle. "Ja! Count von Schroeder is an excellent shot. He would not have missed, if I had not been late loading the rifle."

Lone Eagle stared at the count. He raised a finger and pointed to the ridge behind them.

The count looked in the direction indicated and slowly lowered the Winchester. He looked back at Lone Eagle. "Who are they?"

"Shoshone warriors. This is their hunting ground. A white buffalo is sacred to all Indians, but this one is particularly sacred to the Shoshones. If you had killed the white buffalo, you would now be dead . . . we would all be dead."

"Why didn't they stop us from shooting the other buffalo, if they consider this to be their private hunting ground?" the count asked.

Lone Eagle shrugged. "They are probably respectful of the firepower you have with your new rifles. I see only two guns among the eight braves . . . and they are single-shot, muzzle-loaders. The others have bows and arrows."

"So? If they are afraid, I could have shot the white buffalo and had a magnificent, rare specimen for my museum."

"If you had shot the white one," Lone Eagle said, "they would have attacked us no matter the odds. The shame of not avenging the death of the white buffalo would not be tolerated by the tribe. All eight warriors would be willing to die, if necessary."

Lone Eagle unslung his bow from his shoulder, raised it above his head, and waved it back and forth. One of the Shoshones returned the gesture. The eight Indians swung their ponies in unison and trotted away, along the crest of the ridge.

The count handed the rifle back to his gunsmith. "Come along, Herr Eichhorn. Let us return to camp. I feel the need for a glass of champagne. We will drink a toast to a successful hunt, even though I did not shoot the white one."

Will sat beside Lone Eagle and watched the count and the gamekeeper trot back toward the camp, the white tents of which were visible along the North Platte River. Were it not for the carcasses scattered in the grass around them, Will thought the scene would be idyllic.

"I have some butchering to do, Lone Eagle." Will tugged on Buck's reins and walked the Morgan toward the two big buffalo the count had designated earlier.

"I will assist you," Lone Eagle said. "We will take the tongues and humps from those two back to Homer for preparing our supper. That will provide enough meat for our group for several days. The Shoshones will return after dark and take the meat and hides from the others."

"At least the count's slaughter won't go to waste," Will said.

Chapter 45

Paddy stood beside his horse and peered through the branches of the cottonwood trees. He patted her neck. "Aye, ye're a good girl," he whispered. "Sure, and ye are."

The mare had been a good selection. She went where he guided her without hesitation and seldom whinnied or snorted. She possessed a steady gait that chewed up the ground at a rapid pace, even when dragging the travois. He wished she weren't so tall. He had a hard time climbing into the saddle when he couldn't lead her next to a rock to stand on.

The sun hung low in the sky on this warm day in early August. He'd sneaked up on the count's camp from the downwind side. He felt confident the hunting party's horses could not pick up either his or his horse's scent from where he now hid.

Paddy studied the campsite spread out before him. A large wall tent evidently provided the sleeping quarters for the count. A smaller tent to the right probably housed Elspeth. To the left of the big tent, Homer Garcon and another man cleaned dishes under a kitchen fly. Farther to the left, the party's string of horses, a spotted pony, and Homer's mule stood hitched to a picket line strung between some cottonwoods. Between the big tent and the smaller one, he saw Lone Eagle sitting under a tree alongside Will Braddock, who was occupied cleaning a rifle.

"Wolfgang, I'm going down to the river to wash up." Paddy recognized Elspeth's southern drawl.

He saw her step around the side of the small tent carrying a towel. What good fortune. She was headed in his direction. He wouldn't have to find a way to sneak in close to the camp to get her attention.

"Miss Elspeth, are you sure you should go alone?"

From the German accent, that had to be Count von Schroeder who'd spoken, even though Paddy couldn't see him, nor had he ever heard the man speak before. The final member of the hunting party had to be with the count.

"A lady needs some privacy in these matters, Wolfgang. I'll be fine."

"Lone Eagle?" Paddy heard the count's voice again. "What about those Indians we saw earlier? Do you think they are near?"

"They are near," Lone Eagle answered. "They are more interested in butchering those buffalo you shot than spying on a white woman."

"All right, Elspeth," the count said. "Don't be gone long."

"Just a few minutes, Wolfgang." Elspeth swung the towel beside her and hummed as she strolled toward the riverbank.

Paddy stepped back into the trees and rubbed his hand over the mare's muzzle to keep her quiet. He patted the horse's forehead and tied the reins around a branch.

He watched Elspeth kneel at the river's edge, loosen her hair, and shake the long, blonde curls out over her shoulders. She leaned forward and splashed water onto her face with her hands, then patted her cheeks dry with the towel.

Paddy slipped up behind her. A twig snapped under his boots.

Elspeth's head jerked around. "Paddy!"

"Ah, me darlin'. 'Tis nice ye've found a way to meet with me in private, so it is."

She stood and faced him. "What are you doing here?"

"What am I doing here? Well, sure and I thought we were in this together. Mort told me ye were going to help me with rob-bing the count."

"I've changed my mind!" Elspeth's voice spat the words out.

Paddy grasped her throat, ripped his Bowie knife from its boot sheath, and stuck the point of the blade against her neck.

"Ah!" Elspeth groaned.

"Keep yer voice down! Do not cry out, me pretty, or I'll silence ye right now."

"Miss Elspeth, are you all right?" The count's voice called from beyond the tent.

"Answer him," Paddy said. He pressed the blade harder against Elspeth's throat.

"Fine, Wolfgang. I just stubbed my toe on a rock."

"Good job, darlin'," Paddy said. "Now, about this not wanting to help. Ye're supposed to make a scene when I release the snakes. Ye're job's to create panic in the camp."

"I'm not going to do it," she whispered. "The count likes me. He treats me well. I'm planning on going with him to Sacramento. This is my chance to get away from Mort."

"Sure, and that makes no never mind to me, darlin'. I'll do the job meself." Paddy pressed the knife blade into her throat, knowing he'd drawn blood. He wanted her full attention. "Where is it the count keeps his money belt?"

"In a leather traveling trunk, under the bed in the back half of the large tent. A drape separates the sleeping chamber from a lounge area in the front."

"I see Braddock and Lone Eagle under that tree. Homer and somebody are under that kitchen fly. Where be the count and that other fellow . . . and what be they doing?"

"Wolfgang and Conrad are sitting at the dining table in front of the main tent, sipping cognac and smoking their pipes."

"Elspeth, me darlin'," Paddy said. "It's sorry I am that ye'll not be helping me steal the count's money. I don't think Mort's going to like it when I tell him ye backed out on yer arrangement with him."

"It wasn't an arrangement. I never told Mort I'd help. I only listened to what he told me."

"So ye've planned this all along. Well, sure, and I don't care what happens to ye in the long run, but I'll not have ye interfering with what I have to do. Ye'll have to settle up with Mort yer own self . . . later."

Paddy spun Elspeth around and pushed her deeper into the trees, holding the knife against her back.

"Don't kill me, Paddy. I've never done anything to hurt you."

"Aye, and ye've never done anything to show ye cared for me, even though I be the one what got Mort interested in ye in the first place."

When he got her back beside the mare, he shoved her against a tree.

"Stand there! I'm going to tie ye to the tree. If ye cry out, I'll kill ye for sure. Understand?"

She nodded.

"Give me yer towel," Paddy said. "And don't ye move."

Paddy retrieved a length of rope from the travois and wrapped three turns around Elspeth and the tree, knotting the line behind the trunk. He twisted the towel into a tight roll and tied it around her head, forcing a portion of it between her lips to form a gag.

"Too bad, Elspeth, Mort might have shared some of the count's money with ye if ye'd cooperated."

He had counted on Elspeth to help keep the count and the others away from the tent while he located the traveling trunk. This was going to be a little tougher now that he had to do it all himself, but Mort would have his hide if he didn't try.

He untied the travois from the mare, dropping the sled to the ground behind the horse. He grasped the four sacks by their tied ends and lifted them off the travois. He crept closer to the camp, holding two sacks in each hand, away from his body.

The sun had dropped behind the mountains to the west and a full moon rose in the eastern sky. There would be enough daylight left for him to finish his task before darkness set in. He looked back to the clump of trees. Elspeth and the mare were hidden from sight. Now to create some panic with his four rattlesnakes.

CHAPTER 46

Will leaned back against the tree and ran his fingers along the golden frame of the Winchester. He'd offered to clean one of the count's rifles because he wanted to get a better look at the new firearm.

Conrad Eichhorn sat on a camp chair beside the count at the folding dining table in front of the spacious tent, smoking his briar pipe and working on the other rifle. "What do you think of the 'Yellow Boy'?" he asked.

" 'Yellow Boy'?" Will responded.

"That's what hunters are calling it," Eichhorn said, "because the bronze frame has such a yellow cast."

Will weighed the firearm in his hand, lifting it up and down. "It has a nice balance."

"You may load it, now that it is clean," Eichhorn said. He tossed a box of cartridges to Will.

Will dropped the rifle into his lap to catch the box. He fed one .44-caliber cartridge after another into the gate on the side of the rifle's frame. When he'd finished loading all fifteen rounds, he tossed the box of shells back to the gunsmith.

"I believe you and Lone Eagle are not happy with my shooting so many buffalo today," Count von Schroeder said. He removed the meerschaum pipe from his teeth and raised a large snifter to his nose. He inhaled the aroma of the cognac, sipped from the glass, and smacked his lips. "Am I right?"

"Sir, it's your hunt." Will sighed. "I'm just the guide."

"I do regret not getting that white buffalo," the count said, "but I admit it is wiser to keep my scalp." He chuckled.

"Not to mention our scalps," Will said, under his breath.

Hee-haw! Ruby's bray caused Will and the others to look beyond the kitchen fly to the picket line.

Neighing, snorting, and the pounding of hooves, added to repeated brays from Ruby.

Will jumped to his feet. "Something's wrong at the picket line," he said. He snapped the lever down and back up on the Winchester, feeding a shell into the chamber.

Lone Eagle rose, quickly strung his bow, and nocked an arrow.

The count set his brandy snifter on the table and stood. He took the second Winchester out of the hands of his gunsmith. "Come along," he said.

Will, the count, Eichhorn, and Lone Eagle reached the picket line to find the horses crashing their way through the small thicket of cottonwoods and scattering out across the adjacent prairie. The picket line lay on the ground.

"What's happening?" asked Homer. He and Rupert had joined the others.

Will held up an end of rope still tied to one of the tree trunks. "Someone cut the picket line." He fingered the cleanly severed strands of the remaining piece.

"But why did all the horses bolt?" the count asked.

Zzzzz.

"Rattlesnake," Lone Eagle said. He loosed an arrow at the feet of the count, pinning a three-foot snake to the ground beside the German aristocrat.

Will raised the Winchester and fired. Blood spewed from the severed head of a second snake that lay coiled next to Eichhorn.

"Where did they come from?" the count asked.

Eichhorn pointed to a pile of brown sacks. "There," he said.

He'd barely spoken the words, when another snake crawled out of one of the bags. Will dispatched it quickly with another rifle shot.

The fourth sack wriggled. Lone Eagle stepped over, grasped the top of the sack, closing it, and tossed the bundle deep into the underbrush.

"Mein Gott!" the count exclaimed. "Four rattlesnakes. What is going on here? Und where is Elspeth?"

The count ran back to the main tent. "Elspeth!" he called. "Where are you?"

Will and Lone Eagle joined the count as he ran between the two tents and headed for the river. Eichhorn, Homer, and Rupert followed.

"Elspeth!" The count shouted. "Answer me."

Lone Eagle soon found where Elspeth had washed at the river's edge, then been led back into the thicket. All of them halted as one when they discovered Elspeth tied to a tree.

The count pulled the gag from her mouth, while Lone Eagle sliced the binding rope.

Elspeth fell into the count's arms, tears flowing down her cheeks. "Oh, Wolfgang. It was awful. Paddy O'Hannigan almost killed me."

"Paddy O'Hannigan?" said Will. "Is he still here?"

"No," Elspeth answered. She caught her breath, then spilled out her story in a continuous rush. "Paddy came to steal your money, Wolfgang. Mort Kavanagh sent him to do it. I was supposed to help him . . . but I refused. He had a horse, with a travois . . . to carry rattlesnakes. The travois is over there. He left it behind when he rode away."

The count turned to his valet. "Rupert. Check the money belt."

Rupert ran back to the tent.

"You said this man almost killed you," the count said. "Why didn't he?"

"He said he would leave me to face Mort's wrath," she answered. "Oh, Wolfgang, I'm so frightened."

"There, there, Elspeth. Everything will be all right." The count held her closer.

"Wolfgang, I have deceived you." Elspeth sobbed. "It was Mort's idea for you to bring me along so I could help Paddy steal your money. I never intended to help him, Wolfgang. You have to believe me."

"Why did you come if not to aid in stealing my money?"

"I've been searching for a way to get away from Mort's domineering. I saw this as a way to escape his clutches. I'm sorry, Wolfgang. You've been so kind to me. Please forgive me."

The count wiped the tears from her cheeks with his thumb. "I forgive you, Elspeth, because I enjoy your company. I'm glad this Paddy fellow didn't hurt you. Come, a brandy will calm your nerves."

Rupert came racing back. "It's gone, your Excellency. The money belt is gone."

Lone Eagle headed for the rear of the tent, and Will joined him. Lone Eagle pulled aside a slit in the rear tent wall where Paddy had made his entrance. Lanterns hanging in the sleeping area revealed a large, traveling trunk with an open lid. Lone Eagle raised a severed leather strap for Will to see.

Will followed Lone Eagle away from the tent and back into the trees to where they'd untied Elspeth.

Lone Eagle pointed to the disturbed ground near the abandoned travois. Deep hoof prints in the soft soil revealed that a horse had dug in deeply when its rider urged it to race away. "He rode south," Lone Eagle said.

"I'm going after him," Will said.

"I'll go with you."

"No. You help the count round up the horses. And, we don't know for sure what those Shoshones might do. Stay here and protect the others. Paddy's trail will be easy to follow. He'll most likely stay on the river trail."

Will puckered his lips and whistled. *"Tseeeee, Tse, Tse, Tse."*

He still held the Winchester, and as he returned to the dining table in front of the count's tent, he whistled again. *"Tseeeee, Tse, Tse, Tse."*

This time a whinny answered and Buck trotted into the clearing and up to the tent.

"Good boy," Will said. He held out a hand and the Morgan came to him.

Will reloaded the weapon from the box of shells Eichhorn had left there, then he led Buck back to the picket line where he retrieved his saddle.

The full moon aided Will in following the trail by the river. He held Buck back, not wanting to blunder into an ambush. He had no doubt he could overtake the Irishman, but he wanted the contact to be of his choosing.

It was almost an hour later when he caught sight of Paddy, his silhouette appearing like a shadow before the moon when he rode over the crest of a ridge.

"Let's go, Buck. We've got him now." Will tapped his heels against the horse's flanks and picked up the pace.

A few minutes later, Will topped the ridge where he'd spotted Paddy. Several yards ahead, the Irishman slapped his reins back and forth across his horse's neck, trying to urge the animal to run faster.

Will halted Buck and raised the Winchester. The Morgan continued to step skittishly. "Steady, boy, steady."

Will took a deep breath, blew it out, drew the stock firmly back against his shoulder, aimed, and fired. Buck moved again at the moment Will pulled the trigger. The shot whined high over Paddy's head.

Paddy glanced back, then dug his heels hard into his horse. "Hie, hie!" he shouted.

Will tapped Buck with his heels. It was as if the big Morgan sensed they were pursuing revenge for the snake attack. He leaped forward and gained easily on Paddy.

Paddy kept looking back, whipping and kicking his horse, and shouting encouragements.

"Stop, Paddy!" Will shouted. "This is a Winchester. I have fourteen more shots."

Will watched Paddy reach down to his boot. The moonlight glinted off the blade of a huge knife. Paddy cut the leather thongs tying his saddlebags to the rump of his horse and pushed them off his mount.

A few yards farther along, Will reined Buck in beside the saddlebags and dismounted. He gathered up the bags and rummaged through them, finding a thick money belt among the contents. He opened the belt and whistled softly. He held more money in his hand than he would probably earn for years to come.

In the distance, Will saw Paddy disappear over the next ridge. Will had confidence that Buck could catch the other horse, but the risk at night of Buck steeping into a hole was too great.

"We'd better get the count's money back to him, Buck. We'll find Paddy O'Hannigan another day."

CHAPTER 47

Paddy returned the mare to the livery stable in Benton, after two days of hard riding from the count's hunting camp along the Sweetwater River.

"What'd you do to her?" Ezekiel Thomas, the stable owner, ran a hand along the sweating flank of the horse. "Look at her tremble. She's wore out. Didn't you water or feed her?"

"Sure, Zeke, and I didn't have time to stop." Paddy slapped dust from his vest and pants. "Had to ride hard to get here."

"That's the last time I rent one of my horses to you, O'Hannigan. I don't cotton to mistreating an animal this way."

Paddy shrugged. "Suit yerself, old timer. Sure, and there's other folks what have horses for hire." He waved a hand, as if to push Ezekial away, and left the stable.

Up and down the street, men worked to dismantle buildings and tents and load their components onto a string of flatcars parked along the rail siding. The time had arrived for moving Hell on Wheels again. The UP's construction train was gone. How far west had the rails stretched since Paddy had left here over a week ago?

The Lucky Dollar Saloon still stood intact. Mort Kavanagh always kept it open until the last minute in order to sell whiskey to the workers when they took a break from disassembling the ramshackle elements of Hell on Wheels.

Paddy slipped around to the rear of the saloon and entered the tent area through its back door. He raised his bowler hat in salute to Randy Tremble, the bartender, who just shook his head and grimaced. Paddy didn't care for Tremble either, but he pretended to be nice because the bartender doubled as Kavanagh's bouncer.

Sally Whitworth rose from a table where she'd been entertaining some card players. "Mort's been wondering where you were," she said. She flipped her red curls off both shoulders with a sweep of her hands.

"Where're we moving to now, me beauty?" Paddy asked.

He kept walking and Sally hurried to keep pace. "Green River . . . tomorrow."

He'd usually stop to ogle the beauty, but he didn't have time for that now. He wanted to get this business over with. He stepped up onto the false-front's wooden floor and rapped on the door that led to Kavanagh's corner office. Sally stepped up behind him.

"Come in." The brusque summons was unmistakable.

Paddy took a deep breath and opened the door. This meeting with his boss wasn't going to be a pretty one. He entered the office, but before he could push the door closed, Sally slipped in too. Paddy closed the door behind him.

Sally sidled over to Kavanagh's desk and sat on the edge of it. She crossed her legs and dangled one high-buttoned shoe in front of her, swinging her foot back and forth—knowingly teasing Paddy.

"Ah, Paddy, my lad. Welcome home." Kavanagh pushed a stack of papers away and leaned back in his swivel chair. "You've returned with the count's money?"

Paddy remained standing in front of the door, shuffling from one foot to the other. He removed his bowler hat and looked down at the floor. "Well, now, Mort. There was a bit of a problem, don't ye see."

Kavanagh leaned forward in his chair. "What do you mean . . . problem?"

"Sure, and I had the money for a wee bit. But, sure, and it got away from me."

"It got away from you? It just up and ran away from you."

"Well, not exactly."

"And just *exactly* what happened?" Kavanagh stood and rested his knuckles on the desktop. "You'd better be explaining yourself . . . and it better be good."

Paddy described what happened at the count's hunting camp and how he had to cut the saddlebags loose when Will Braddock threatened to shoot him.

Kavanagh's fingers clutched into tight fists. Paddy watched the big man's jaws clench and unclench. He felt as if his godfather's eyes would burn a hole through him.

"Can't I trust you to do anything!" Kavanagh slammed a fist on the desk.

Sally jumped at the force of the blow, slipped off her perch, and stepped to the side of the room.

"Sure, and it's Elspeth McNabb who's to blame." Paddy clutched his bowler hat closer to his chest, trying to use it as a shield. "If she'd done her part, like ye told her, I'd have had plenty of time to get away with the money."

"I'll take care of Miss McNabb as soon as the count's hunting party reaches Green River. But for now, I want you out of my sight. You're on half-pay effective immediately."

"What?" Paddy surely hadn't heard correctly.

"You don't know how many times I've regretted promising your mother I'd look after you. You've brought me nothing but grief. Stay out of my way until I send for you."

Paddy's mouth dropped open. He blinked hard, staring at Kavanagh. "Half-pay? What about my ma and my sister? How am I going to support them?"

"I don't care. That's not my problem. Now, get out! And don't come back until I say you can."

"Mort, please."

Kavanagh reached into a desk drawer and pulled out a revolver. He pointed it at Paddy and cocked the hammer. "Out!"

Paddy glanced sideways at Sally, whose smirk only added to his frustration and humiliation. He returned his gaze to the pistol in Kavanagh's hand and backed up to the door. He reached behind him, turned the knob, and stepped outside the office without turning his back on his godfather.

He jammed his bowler hat on and slipped out the front door of the saloon into the bright sunlight. He didn't want to have to walk past Randy Tremble by going out through the back. If it hadn't been for Will Braddock this wouldn't be happening.

"I'll be getting ye for this, Braddock. Just see if I don't. And ye too, Elspeth McNabb."

CHAPTER 48

"Wapiti." Lone Eagle pointed with his bow up the slope into the trees.

"Elk?" asked Count von Schroeder. "I don't see any. How can you tell?"

"They are up there," Lone Eagle said. "I saw a big buck moving on the ridge top."

"If he says there are elk up there," Will said, "I believe him. I suggest we split up, sir."

Conrad Eichhorn jacked the lever down on his Winchester Yellow Boy and drove a cartridge into the breech. "Ja. That is what I advise as well, mein Count."

"It's too steep for the horses," Will said. "We'll have to leave them here. And it's too warm to wear a coat on such a climb. You may want to leave yours behind too, sir."

Will dismounted from Buck and removed his buckskin jacket. He rolled it neatly and tied it behind his saddle. The other members of the hunting party shed their coats as well.

"All right," the count said, "Herr Eichhorn, you and Lone Eagle head up to the right. Herr Braddock and I will go off to the left. When we reach the crest turn inward and come back together. Hopefully we can drive the elk between us. Careful. Don't shoot each other."

For the past three weeks, after the count's party had left the North Platte River, they had slowly made their way up the Sweetwater following the old Oregon Trail, then crossed the Continental Divide at South Pass, before continuing along the southern base of the Wind River Mountains. Will knew they should be approaching Green River, which the count's map showed flowing around the western end of the mountain range.

Elspeth, Rupert, and Homer had set up camp a mile from the base of the ridge the four hunters now climbed and would be preparing for the meal at the end of the day. At least Rupert and Homer would—Elspeth might set the table if she were in a good mood. Ever since Paddy's attack, she'd withdrawn into herself. Will stopped beside the count as they paused to gasp for breath on the steep climb through the pine, fir, and spruce trees. His eyes searched for the elk that Lone Eagle had spotted, but he could see neither movement of the thick brush nor antler racks appearing above the greenery.

"Still a ways to go to the top, sir." Will spoke softly, so his voice would not carry and spook the elk. He bent forward, using the butt of his carbine as a brace against the steep hill, and took in several deep breaths.

"Ja. Let us continue."

The count pressed on, and Will fell in behind him. The count carried his Winchester and Will his Spencer. The Winchester could definitely bring down a big elk at a distance, but Will would have to get close to make a kill with a single shot from his smaller caliber carbine.

The count had shot several elk, as well as a mule deer and a couple of mountain sheep, over the past several days. But he was still not satisfied with the size of the elk they'd found. He was determined to find a more impressive specimen to add to his museum collection.

They topped the ridge and stepped out into a large meadow devoid of heavy brush, its floor covered in a panoply of wildflowers scattered over dozens of yards.

"Whew! Some climb," the count said quietly. "But the view is spectacular."

Will joined him in admiring the high, snow-capped mountains that stretched far beyond the ridgeline where they stood.

A rustling in the trees on the far side of the clearing caught Will's attention. A magnificent elk stepped out of the woods and froze. Will doubted he could span the spread of the elk's antler rack with both his arms extended full width. This elk would certainly meet the count's requirement for a superb specimen.

The count raised his Winchester and settled it against his shoulder. Will could see that the elk's attention was riveted on something, but it didn't seem to be the count or him. The elk's eyes stared off beyond them. At what? That didn't seem right.

The count fired. The elk reared upward and leaped, but fell immediately.

The explosive crack of the rifle was joined by a loud roar.

Will spun around.

Standing on its hind legs not twenty yards away stood a huge grizzly, its claws extended toward him. This bear towered higher than the one that had killed Bullfrog Charlie.

"Mein Gott in Himmel!" The count seemed to freeze, dropping the rifle from his shoulder.

Will stepped in front of the count, raised his carbine, and fired. Dust flew from the bear's shoulder, but the animal swiped at the wound as if it were a bee sting. Will levered another round into the breech and raised the gun.

The bear dropped onto all fours and charged.

"Shoot, Count! Shoot!" Will shouted and fired the Spencer again, the shot smashing into the bear's face.

The sting of the bullet caused the bear to rear onto its hind legs, swatting at its snout with a paw.

The roar of the Winchester beside Will's ear let him know the count had regained his composure. The power of the rifle's bullet jolted the bear, causing it to drop to all fours again. But the shot did not stop the bear. It kept coming.

Before Will could chamber another round into the Spencer, the bear closed the gap between them and reared onto its hind legs. The massive head lunged forward.

Will almost gagged when he smelled the strong breath accompanying the deafening roar that blasted him in the face. He raised his carbine to fend off the blow he knew was coming. The bear's powerful swat swiped the Spencer out of his grasp. Will threw both hands up to protect his face.

Sharp claws slashed across Will's chest muscles. Excruciating pain engulfed his left side. Was this what Bullfrog Charlie had felt when the grizzly attacked him?

Will dropped to his knees, looking at the bear as it raised a paw for another strike. Suddenly, in rapid succession, through eyes filled with tears, Will watched three arrows plunge into the bear. The bear's paw swatted at the arrows buried deep into its massive chest. Lone Eagle had fired the arrows faster than a rifleman could reload, even with lever action.

Then both Winchesters blasted another time. The count and Conrad Eichhorn had each fired.

The bear bellowed, staggered, and dropped. A final groan escaped from the wide open jaws. Then silence.

Will fell forward onto his hands, gasping for breath.

Lone Eagle stepped up to the bear and paced off the length of the carcass. "It is the biggest grizzly I have seen," he said.

"Two magnificent trophies to add to your collection, mein Count," Eichhorn said. "A mammoth bear and a beautiful elk."

Lone Eagle reached down to help Will stand.

"Oh!" Will groaned. He sank back to his knees, grasping his left side.

"What's wrong?" Lone Eagle asked.

Will stared up at his friend and pulled his sticky hand away. Four bloody gashes appeared through rents in his wool shirt.

Chapter 49

Jenny McNabb had just wiped her hands on her apron and slipped it off over her head, when her father entered the front door of the Green River home station.

The McNabb family had transferred from their old assignment when the Union Pacific completed its tracklaying across the Red Desert from Benton and the railroad no longer needed the interchange with Wells Fargo at the North Platte River Crossing. Each westward leap of the railroad caused the stage line to contract. Once the UP joined up with the Central Pacific, probably someplace in Utah next year, Wells Fargo would be out of the cross-country stage business.

"Papa," she said, "I've got to run over to Abrams' store to buy some flour, some spices, and other things. I can't prepare a decent meal with what I've got here in the kitchen. The passengers will expect better."

"All right," her father said. "Don't be gone too long. As soon as you return, Duncan and I are heading out to Fort Bridger. Those new horses Wells Fargo promised are ready for us to pick up over there. It may take us several days to get there and back, moving a small herd."

"It won't take long to get what I need. I'll be gone less than an hour."

"Jenny?" her father asked. "Are you sure you can handle things here?"

"Yes, Papa. Don't worry. Franz and the drivers can change

the teams for the few days you'll be gone. I'll lend a hand. We just won't be setting any speed records, without you here." She grinned at her father.

Franz Iversen, the elderly stockman, had moved with the McNabbs from North Platte Crossing. He routinely complained of his rheumatism, but he never let it slow him down.

"I'm not worried about speed records," her father said. "I've asked Sean Corcoran to keep an eye on you."

Corcoran had the task of establishing the Union Pacific's switching yards and maintenance facilities at Green River. Jenny frequently saw him, since the depot was close by the stage station.

Jenny pulled on her bonnet and opened the door. "Be back soon," she said. Closing the door behind her, she walked down the dirt street that led toward the center of the new town that had sprung up almost overnight along the banks of the Green River. A temporary railroad bridge stretched across the river and workers were busy constructing a more permanent one with stone buttresses. Interspersed among a few more substantial structures were the ramshackle huts and tents that comprised Hell on Wheels, which had transferred from Benton along with the railroad.

One of those transplanted shacks was Abrams General Store. Jenny opened the door to the tinkling of a bell suspended overhead and stepped up onto the board floor of the canvas-covered store. "Morning, Mr. Abrams," she said.

"Good morning, Miss McNabb." Benjamin Abrams wiped his hands down the front of his apron and leaned forward on the glass top of a counter. "Nice to see you. What can I do for you today?"

"Need flour, salt, assorted spices, maybe some bacon, if you have any."

"That I do. Follow me."

Jenny followed Abrams through strands of swinging beads that served as a curtain separating the front of his store from the back. Hanging from a beam that supported the side wall of the tent were half a dozen slabs of bacon.

"Choose whichever one you want," Abrams said.

The door bell tinkled again, and Abrams returned to the front.

"Afternoon, Mr. Abrams." Jenny moved away from the row of meat and peeked through the curtain to see who had come into the store.

"Afternoon, Miss Whitworth," Abrams said. "How can I help you?"

"Mort sent me to pick up that shipment of playing cards he ordered. He sent O'Hannigan to carry the box."

"That shipment arrived this morning, but I haven't had a chance to unpack it. It's still in a crate out back. I'll get it, if you have time?"

"Certainly," Sally said. "I'll look around a bit to see if you have anything new that catches my fancy."

When Abrams passed through the curtain, Jenny held her finger to her lips. She didn't want Paddy to see her.

Abrams nodded, picked up a crowbar, and went out the back of the store into the alley.

Jenny stepped to the side of the doorway, where she could remain concealed while still able to see into the front part of the store.

"Mort's been in a foul mood ever since you told him Elspeth McNabb double-crossed him," Sally said. "It's good to have an excuse to stay away from him for a few minutes."

Jenny leaned closer to the edge of the doorway. What was Sally saying about Elspeth?

"Sure, and ye've got that right, Sally, me love," Paddy said.

"I'm not your love, and don't you forget it!"

Paddy cackled. From Jenny's viewpoint she had a view of his broken, rotten teeth.

"If you and that prissy lass had pulled off stealing the count's money, like you should have, we'd all be better off. Will Braddock should be leading the count's hunting party into Green River soon. It'll be something to see when Mort gets his hands on Elspeth."

Abrams came through the back door from the alley with a medium-sized wooden box in his arms. He glanced sideways at Jenny, then brushed on through the curtains into the front of the store. "Here it is, Miss Whitworth."

"Well," Sally said. "Don't just stand there, Paddy. Take the box."

Jenny watched Abrams pass the box to the skinny Irishman.

"Oomph!" Paddy groaned. He almost dropped the box when the weight was transferred into his arms.

"Thank you, Mr. Abrams," Sally said.

"Good day, Miss Whitworth," Abrams replied.

The door bell jingled, followed by the slamming of the door, causing the false, wooden front to shake.

Jenny selected a ham and stepped out through the curtain, shaking her head. What has Elspeth gotten herself into now?

Chapter 50

The sunlight above him seemed to flicker, diffused as through a white sheen. The rhythmic sound of fluttering canvas enhanced the shifting rays of light that he saw dimly through half-opened eyes. Muffled voices surrounded him. Will forced his eyes to widen. He lay stretched out beneath the protection of a tent.

"He's coming around." Will identified Homer's voice.

A hand pressed a cool, damp cloth against his forehead. "Will? Can you hear me?" That was Elspeth's voice. It must be her hand that held the soothing cloth.

"Yes," Will croaked. "What happened?"

He raised up, but a gentle hand pushed him flat again.

"You mustn't move," Elspeth said. "You've lost blood and need to rest."

"Where am I?"

"You're in the count's bed, in his tent," Elspeth said.

"How'd I get here?"

He struggled to recall the moments after the death of the big grizzly. He vaguely remembered Lone Eagle and Conrad Eichhorn struggling to carry him down the steep slope. The count had carried all of the weapons. The three men had hoisted him up onto Buck and Lone Eagle had ridden behind him to keep him in the saddle.

"They brung you back here after that bear took a swipe at you," Homer said.

Those words concentrated Will's mind and he felt the throbbing in his chest. He looked down and saw a white, frilly cloth bound around his ribs. Stains of red showed where he'd bled through the bandage.

"It's one of my petticoats," Elspeth said. "We didn't have any regular bandages big enough to wrap you with."

Will gazed into Elspeth's blue eyes. He hadn't noticed before how much darker they were than Jenny's. The light shining through the roof of the tent shown off Elspeth's blonde curls, forming a halo effect. She looked like an angel.

"Thank you," he said.

"Are you hungry?" Elspeth asked.

"A little."

Homer stepped closer to the bed and handed Elspeth a cup. "I made you some broth. Be good for you. Help get your strength back."

Will recalled trying to get Bullfrog Charlie to drink some broth after the bear had mauled the mountain man. Will knew he must drink some of the liquid to start the healing process.

Homer raised Will's head and Elspeth added another pillow behind him. Then she sat on the edge of the bed beside him and held the cup to his lips. Will sipped a little of the warm brew.

"Where's everybody else?" Will asked.

"They went back to get the bear and the elk," Homer said. "Rupert is outside setting the supper table. And I'se got to get back to cooking, cause those three hunters are going to be mighty hungry when they gets back. You lets me know, Miss Elspeth, if you needs more of that broth."

Homer left the tent and Elspeth helped Will take another sip.

"I can't stay here . . . in the count's bed," he said.

"You most certainly can," Elspeth said. "Wolfgang insisted that you be brought in here. You saved his life."

"Saved his life?"

"Yes, Wolfgang told me how you stepped in front of him and shielded him when the bear attacked."

Will forced his thoughts back to that moment. He'd instinctively moved between the bear and Count von Schroeder when the count had frozen upon hearing the roar of the attacking beast.

"Halloo the camp!" The sound of hooves announced the return of the hunting party.

A moment later the count entered the sleeping portion of the tent. "How's the patient?" he asked.

"He's awake now," Elspeth answered, "and taking some nourishment."

"How do you feel, Herr Braddock?" he asked.

"All right, sir, unless I breathe. Then it hurts." He chuckled and wished he hadn't.

"Thank you, Herr Braddock, for saving my life."

Will did not know how to respond, so he just nodded his head. "Sir," he said, "I can't stay in your bed."

"Oh, but of course you can. I'll sleep in the sitting portion of the tent. There will be no argument about this."

"Sorry you had to make the extra trip to recover the bear and the elk, sir," Will said.

"I certainly was not going to abandon those magnificent specimens. Not after all the trouble we went through to bag them. That bear will be mounted in the entryway to my castle. I can see it now rearing on its hind legs, threatening with outstretched forelegs ending in those ferocious claws, its jaws wide exposing fearsome teeth. The only thing missing will be the roar. But I will remember that sound every time I see that grizzly. Most frightening noise I ever heard. Yes, I will remember it."

Will raised up and tried to swing his feet off the bed. Elspeth and the count both pushed him down.

"And just what do you think you are doing?" the count asked. "I have already decided you are staying here in this bed."

"We have to get ready to travel on tomorrow, sir," Will said.

"Not tomorrow. Not for a couple of days, most likely. You need rest to stop the bleeding. We will hunt the mountains around here while we wait. Maybe I can find a better example of a bighorn sheep."

"Wolfgang's right, Will," Elspeth said. "If you move too much now, the bleeding will start again. You have four big gashes across your side where those claws dug in. We don't have anything to stitch the wounds together, so my petticoat will have to do."

Will remembered the difficulty he'd had trying to stop Bullfrog Charlie's wounds from bleeding. Elspeth spoke the truth. He needed rest. He closed his eyes.

Chapter 51

"There it is!" Count von Schroeder halted his horse on the crest of a hill and surveyed the broad valley that spread out before him. "Just like the painting."

Elspeth reined in beside the German aristocrat. "What painting, Wolfgang?" she asked.

"Your great American artist Alfred Jacob Miller painted this scene thirty-one years ago. In fact, he may have been working from this very spot with his canvas and paints. In the painting, the valley was entirely covered with tepees and horses and Indians and fur trappers." The count pointed toward the valley. "Right there, where Horse Creek flows into Green River, is the site of the mountain men's 1837 rendezvous."

The other members of the hunting party drifted up to join the count and Elspeth. All seven sat their mounts side by side, admiring the green expanse that lined the banks of the two streams. A little to the south of where the creek joined the broader river, a small cluster of tepees hugged the far bank. In the distance, the snow-capped peaks of a mountain range formed an impressive backdrop.

"That would be Fremont Peak," the count said, "the tallest peak in the center of that range. It is as if we had stepped into the painting."

Will leaned forward and patted Buck's neck, immediately wishing he'd done so more slowly. This was the first time he'd ridden the horse. The four previous days, he'd been towed on the travois Paddy had stolen from Lone Eagle's cabin. The day following Paddy's attempt at stealing the count's money, both Lone Eagle and Will had recognized the abandoned travois as the one Bullfrog Charlie had built when he rescued Will from the freezing water of the North Platte River. The count's party had kept the travois to help haul specimens as the hunt progressed. They'd been able to transfer those specimens to a pack horse after several days of consuming foodstuffs originally hauled by a horse, and Will had then ridden aboard the crude sled as a passenger for the second time this year.

Will gritted his teeth to keep from groaning from the stab of pain Buck's movement brought to his chest muscles. The petticoat bandage around his rib cage helped control the discomfort as long as he sat upright. It was difficult enough to keep the deep gashes from reopening without his twisting unnecessarily. He blew out his breath to compose himself. "You sound like you've been here before, Count," he said.

"This is one of the reasons I came to America, Herr Braddock. Oh, I wanted to get specimens for my museum, of course, but seeing this place has been a dream of mine since I was a boy. I accompanied my father on a visit to Lord William Stewart's estate in Scotland when I was about ten. The castle's walls were covered with the magnificent paintings Miller had created to commemorate Lord Stewart's participation in that 1837 rendezvous. I promised myself someday I would see it in person. And so I am. Isn't it spectacular, Herr Eichhorn?"

The Austrian gunsmith guided his horse closer to the count's. "Ja, it is, mein Count."

"Are those friendly Indians?" asked Rupert, whose mount stood next to Eichhorn's.

The count looked beyond Will to Lone Eagle. "Who are they, scout?" he asked.

"Shoshones. They may be the band our constant companions belong to."

The half-dozen warriors who had observed the count's attempt to shoot the white buffalo had made repeated appearances throughout the hunting party's journey.

"I will ride down to talk with them," Lone Eagle said. "Where is your bear claw necklace, Will?"

"In my haversack. Why?"

"Put it on. The Shoshones will be impressed that we have a great hunter with us who has slaughtered a grizzly." He grinned.

"You're serious?" asked Will.

"Yes. The Shoshones will probably remember my father. I will tell them you tried to save his life, and the claws you wear are from the bear that killed the great Bullfrog Charlie Munro."

Will shrugged, reached into his haversack, and took out the bear claw necklace.

Lone Eagle kicked his pony and descended the slope toward Green River.

"Stay close to me, Elspeth," the count said. "Herr Eichhorn, you bring up the rear."

Eichhorn handed the count one of the Winchesters, then turned his string of horses back and took up a position behind the group. He led four pack horses loaded with museum specimens, as well as ammunition and assorted weapons. It was an assignment with which the Austrian was not particularly happy, but Will's injury prohibited him from being able to struggle against the tug of the animals that had been his normal responsibility.

Elspeth rode beside the count as he led the party slowly toward the riverbank. Will wheeled in beside them. Homer followed leading Ruby, the mule loaded with the kitchen supplies and the last few bottles of champagne, and four pack horses burdened with the count's tent and folding furniture. Rupert preceded Eichhorn at the rear of the procession with his string of horses, the last of which bore a freshly killed elk carcass. The other horses hauled the rest of the museum collection.

Far ahead, Lone Eagle trotted toward a ford that showed years of repeated crossings by mountain men, Indians, and the soldiers who had been battling the Shoshones for the past dozen years.

Will watched Lone Eagle cross the river with his hand raised in peaceful greeting to an increasing crowd of Indians who emerged from the two dozen tepees. The count halted his group fifty yards from the ford. There they waited and observed the animated discussion Lone Eagle conducted with an elderly Indian, evidently the band's chief.

A few minutes later, Lone Eagle turned his pony and rode back to the shallow river crossing, splashed through, and trotted to the count's party. "They are Shoshones," he reported. "Their chief is White Shadow. I met him when my father brought me to Green River on a hunting trip when I was young. They are the band of our recent observers, who have already reported to the chief that you did not kill their sacred white buffalo. Hunting has been poor this year, but the chief says you are welcome to come in and share what they have."

"What if we gave them the elk we shot this morning?" The count pointed to the pack horse burdened with the kill.

"That will please them," Lone Eagle said.

"Homer," the count said, "follow Lone Eagle with that elk carcass. Give Ruby and your horses to Rupert."

"But, your Excellency," Rupert said, "that mule does not like me."

"Just for a short time. The Indians will probably keep the pack horse, as well as the elk. I do not want the Shoshones to think they can have Homer's mule and the other horses, too."

Homer followed Lone Eagle back to the camp, leading the

single pack horse. After handing the reins to the chief, Lone Eagle motioned for the others to cross the ford.

The count directed Rupert and Homer to pitch the tent and kitchen fly along the riverbank, not far from the cluster of tepees. Once the camp was established, the count told Rupert to unpack their remaining four bottles of champagne and display them prominently on the folding dining table.

"Lone Eagle," said the count, "invite the chief and his braves to have a drink."

"Are you sure?" Lone Eagle said. "Things could get out of hand if they have too much to drink."

"Little chance of that. This is the last of the liquor. I am honored to share it with them. They cannot get drunk on what little we have." The count checked his Winchester and propped it in a conspicuous position in a camp chair, which he positioned at his side.

Conrad Eichhorn stood behind the count, cradling his rifle in his arms. Will, Homer, and Elspeth remained under the shade of the sleeping tent's front fly, Will's carbine within reach against the tent wall.

Lone Eagle gathered the camp's two dozen warriors and led them to the count. The chief stepped directly up to the table, while the others spread out behind him.

"Count von Schroeder," Lone Eagle said, "This is Chief White Shadow."

"Honorable Chief White Shadow of the Shoshones," the count said, "Welcome." He nodded, clicked his heels, and withdrew a hunting knife from his belt sheath.

The chief's head jerked back, his brows furrowed as his eyes concentrated on the knife blade. A low growl emanated from the warriors, who closed in tightly behind their chief.

"We thank you for your hospitality in allowing us to join your encampment. Allow me to reciprocate by offering you some refreshment." He picked up one of the bottles and deftly whacked the stopper with the knife blade. The cork shot out of the neck with a bang, followed by a spray of warm champagne.

The braves laughed and grunted their approval, pushing toward the table with extended tin cups and gourds. Rupert poured, as the count lopped the corks off the remaining bottles.

The bubbly wine disappeared in minutes and several of the warriors became vocal in demanding more. The count spread his hands wide. "Sorry, that is all."

Lone Eagle translated for the gathering, then turned back to the count. "Show them the packs," he said, "so they can see for themselves that you speak the truth."

Rupert invited the men to inspect the bundles he'd taken from the pack horses. Some of the more belligerent warriors tossed pots and pans on the ground and managed to break several dishes and cups as they rummaged through the stores. Finally satisfied, they dispersed.

Rupert shook his head. "What a mess. Maybe we should not have done this?"

"They might have taken the liquor with force had we not given it to them," the count said. "Better that we control the situation."

"Ja, you are probably right. Homer, help me clean this up."

Homer joined him in gathering up the scattered supplies. Elspeth pitched in and assembled the unbroken dishes and cups. Conrad Eichhorn moved back beside Will beneath the tent fly where the two of them maintained a vigilant position until the last of the warriors returned to camp.

CHAPTER 52

Later that afternoon, Lone Eagle brought an older Shoshone woman up to Will, who sat beneath a cottonwood tree alongside Elspeth.

"Will," said Lone Eagle, "this is Moon Woman. I have asked her to look at your bear claw wounds."

"Why? Elspeth keeps checking the bandage."

"The wounds need to be stitched."

Will looked from Lone Eagle to the woman and back again. "Stitched? Is she a doctor?"

"She is a shaman . . . a medicine woman."

The woman, the top of whose head only reached to Lone Eagle's shoulder, looked up at him and spoke in Shoshone for a couple of minutes.

"She said to tell you she is the grandniece of Sacajawea. She learned her medicine from that famous Shoshone lady, who treated injuries for the members of the Lewis and Clark expedition. I can assure you she knows what she is doing. She treated me for a hunting injury when my father brought me here as a boy." Lone Eagle lifted his buckskin shirt and pointed at a scar on his side.

Will looked at Elspeth, who shrugged. "I thought about using some sewing thread," she said, "but I didn't think it would stand up to twisting and pulling. I agree with Lone Eagle. You need stitches."

"And what will she use?" Will asked Lone Eagle.

"Buffalo sinew."

Will blew out his breath. He looked back to Elspeth again, who nodded.

"All right," he said. "Where do we do this?"

"Moon Woman will take you to her tepee. Elspeth can accompany you."

A few minutes later, Will sat shirtless in the tepee. Moon Woman lifted the bear claw necklace off Will's neck and laid it reverently in his lap. She handed Will a piece of rawhide and motioned for him to bite on it. Moon Woman unwrapped the scrap of petticoat that had adhered to his wounds, causing them to open and seep blood. She positioned a curved, bone needle, threaded with a long, thin piece of sinew, below the first of the four eight-inch-long claw marks the bear had gouged around his side.

Moon Woman looked into Will's eyes and pushed with the bone needle.

Will winced when the needle pierced his skin. He closed his eyes and clamped down on the leather mouthpiece. He could not suppress the tears that formed in his eyes, but he managed to contain the scream that desperately wanted to leap from his throat.

After sunset, the count's party joined Chief White Shadow and his band in feasting on the elk meat. Following the sharing of the meal, several young girls danced around a large fire to the accompaniment of drums.

Lone Eagle sat cross-legged on the ground next to Will, who perched on a log.

"I notice you keep your eyes on that one dancer," Will said.

"I had not noticed," Lone Eagle replied.

"You haven't *noticed* anything else, all evening." Will chuckled. He forced himself not to laugh out loud. He wasn't sure how the new stitches would take to a more boisterous show of emotion.

"Humph!" Lone Eagle grunted.

A few moments later Moon Woman took the hand of the girl and led her around the fire to stand in front of Lone Eagle. The girl kept her head bowed. Moon Woman spoke at length to Lone Eagle in Shoshone.

"What'd she say?" Will asked.

"Moon Woman says the girl is her daughter, Butterfly Morning. Moon Woman tells me that when she was younger, she had her eyes on my father when he brought me here on our hunting trip. But he was already married to my mother and was not interested in taking another wife."

"And now her daughter has eyes for you," Will said.

"I guess."

"You guess?" Will laughed and winced at the same time. "There's no guessing about it. Look how she grins."

"Humph!"

Everyone gathered around the fire grew silent as they eavesdropped on the conversation between Lone Eagle and Moon Woman. Elspeth, who was observing from where she sat beside the count, spoke. "Take Butterfly Morning for a walk, Lone Eagle. Don't be shy."

"Do not offend our hosts, Lone Eagle," the count said. "It is obvious to all of us that the girl has her eyes on you . . . just as you do on her."

"Humph!" Lone Eagle rose and walked away from the fire. Butterfly Morning followed.

CHAPTER 53

"Mayor wants to see you, Paddy." Randy Tremble swiped a rag back and forth across the top of the bar.

Paddy had entered the Lucky Dollar through the back door flap and paused opposite Kavanagh's bartender. "Sure, and what's he want?"

"Well now, the mayor don't confide in me. You'll just have to be finding that out for yourself." Tremble turned his back on Paddy and busied himself straightening the bottles on the shelf behind the bar.

Paddy took a quick look around the saloon's dance floor seeking Sally Whitworth. Maybe she could give him a heads-up on what his godfather wanted. Since Kavanagh had told him to stay out of his sight following the abortive attempt at stealing the count's money, Paddy had avoided further confrontation with his boss. Sally was not to be seen, however.

He reached down and drew his Bowie knife from its sheath inside his right boot and used the big blade to slice an end off a twist of tobacco he'd taken from his vest pocket. With the tip of the blade he slipped the chaw into his jaw, then returned the knife to his boot. Staring at the office door behind which the self-appointed mayor of Hell on Wheels conducted his business, he bit down on the tobacco, releasing the bitter taste onto his tongue. He swished the wad around in his mouth until the bite of the tobacco stimulated his senses, then walked to the door.

In response to his knock, Kavanagh's voice called for Paddy to come in.

Sally sat on the arm of Kavanagh's swivel chair, running her fingers through the big man's curly, black hair.

"O'Hannigan," Kavanagh said, "you've been avoiding me. What have you been up to since we moved from Benton to Green River?"

"Well, now don't ye know, I've just been doing like ye said to stay out of yer way, so to speak." Paddy took off his bowler hat and held it before him with both hands.

"Just staying out of my way, huh? Well, you've done a pretty good job of that. I wish you could do everything that well."

Paddy stared back, took shallow breaths, and forced himself to stand still. He felt his face flush, the scar on his cheek twitch. He resisted the urge to reach up and massage it.

Kavanagh leaned forward in his chair, forcing Sally to slide off the arm. She stepped to the side of the desk.

"It's time you start earning your pay again," Kavanagh said. "The count's hunting party can't be too far from here, I suspect. He'll be riding in with Elspeth in tow and I want to know as soon as they are near. I don't want to wait until they're in town and she can slip away. She's got some explaining to do and I intend to make her pay for double-crossing me."

Paddy glanced sideways at Sally. He didn't like the broad smirk she wore on her face. He returned his eyes to Kavanagh and shifted his feet.

"And just what is it ye're wanting me to do, Mort?"

"Go out a day's ride beyond town to the north and keep a lookout for the count's return. Hightail it back here when you see them, without you being seen of course, and give me plenty of notice so I can set up the proper reception for the returning Miss McNabb."

"Sure thing, Mort. Ye can count on me, and that's the truth."

"I don't care what you think is the truth. I want action this time. If you do this right, I'll restore you to full salary. And I don't want you distracted trying to pull off your vendetta against Braddock or that colored fellow. Concentrate on what you're being told to do. If you don't deliver this time, you're fired."

Fired? What would he do if he lost this job? He couldn't work for the railroad. They had fired him a year ago for thievery. He needed the meager salary his godfather paid him in order to satisfy the demands from his mother and sister for support money. He would have to find a way to get this job done right.

"Sure, and Zeke at the livery stable won't rent me a horse no more, Mort."

"Tell Randy to rent a horse and put it on my tab. He can bring it back here for you. Zeke won't know the difference, if you don't ride past the livery stable."

"I'll need some spending cash, too, don't ye know."

"No more cash for you until this thing is over."

"And what about food to eat while I'm waiting out there?"

"That's your problem. Now get out of here and get to work."

Paddy stopped to give Randy the instructions from Kavanagh about renting a horse, then he settled his hat on his head and went out through the back door. With the couple of dollars in his pocket he could only buy some jerky and hardtack—couldn't afford anything else. What a disgusting mess this was turning out to be.

"Will Braddock," Paddy hissed, "this is all yer doing. I'll get ye. And that nigger, too. I don't care what Mort says."

He kicked at a rock in the dusty path and missed it. "Bloody hell!" That's the way everything had been going lately.

Chapter 54

On the morning of the fourth day following the arrival of the count's party at the Green River rendezvous site, the Shoshones struck their camp. The band's women knocked the tepees down in less time than it took Count von Schroeder and Elspeth to complete the breakfast Rupert served them at the folding table where they sat in front of their tent. While the count enjoyed his second cup of coffee, the tepee poles were strapped to the backs of the ponies, the trappings of the band's shelters secured to the newly constituted travois, and the small band aligned itself in an organized marching order.

Chief White Shadow walked his spotted pony over to the count's table and nodded his head. "Goodbye," he said, in English.

The chief had informed Count von Schroeder the evening before, while they'd relaxed around the campfire, that he intended to lead his band north in the morning. White Shadow's band had been summoned to join other bands who were gathering on the Shoshones' newly established reservation north of the Wind River Range.

"Lone Eagle?" the count called.

Lone Eagle, who had been eating breakfast with Will beside the cooking lean-to, stepped over to the count's table.

"Please convey my thanks to Chief White Shadow. Tell him how much I have enjoyed meeting him and sharing these few days with him and his people."

Lone Eagle spoke a few words to the chief, who nodded again, raised a hand in salute, turned his pony, and trotted away. The band stepped into motion without spoken command as soon as he reached the head of the column. Women led their ponies pulling travois laden with the tepees, older children herded dogs dragging miniature travois loaded with utensils and other possessions, while the younger children skipped alongside the procession. The same group of warriors who had earlier kept a close eye on the count's party now sped ahead of the chief to serve as scouts. Other men spread out on either side of the band to provide security.

Will sipped his coffee from a tin cup. He felt uncomfortable drinking from the china that the count and Elspeth used. Lone Eagle returned and stood beside him. No one in the count's party said anything while they watched the Shoshones depart.

Butterfly Morning rode by on a small pony dragging a loaded travois behind her. She glanced quickly at Lone Eagle and Will, then turned her gaze steadily forward.

"I recognize that travois," Will said.

"I gave it to her," Lone Eagle said.

Will smiled and nudged his friend.

Fifteen minutes after the goodbyes had been spoken, the trailing elements of the Indians disappeared over a ridge.

The count stood and poured the last of his coffee from his cup onto the ground. "Time for us to leave, too. It has been a most interesting end to a successful hunt. Rupert, pack it up."

Rupert and Homer dismantled the hunting camp, stowing the gear onto pack horses and Ruby. Conrad Eichhorn checked the collection of weapons and assembled the small arsenal and the remaining ammunition for packing. He kept out the two Winchester rifles.

While they had rested in the camp, the skins of the specimens bound for the count's museum had been staked out to speed their drying. Lone Eagle assisted Will in folding up the hides and binding them with rawhide thongs into compact bundles. Will noticed that his companion frequently looked to the north, where the Shoshone caravan had disappeared.

"Are we ready?" asked the count. He looked around at each of his party who nodded that their share of the preparations was complete. "Then let us find the railroad."

They mounted and sorted out the pack animals. Will checked his Spencer carbine to ensure a round was chambered, then guided Buck to the front of the party. Lone Eagle did not join him.

"I am not going with you," Lone Eagle called out.

Will turned Buck around and rode back to the rear of the column where Lone Eagle sat his pony. "Butterfly Morning has captured your heart, I see."

Lone Eagle blushed and nodded his head once.

Will grinned. It was the first time he'd seen his friend turn such a dark shade of red.

"What will you do?" Will asked.

"Go with them to their reservation. Maybe Butterfly Morning will agree to leave and join me at my father's cabin on the North Platte."

"And how do you propose to support a family there?"

Lone Eagle shrugged. "I have been thinking that maybe the Army at Fort Fred Steele could use a scout."

"I think you could do a lot of good for the Cheyenne, as well as the Shoshones, by helping guide the Army."

"Perhaps. If the Shoshones have agreed to go to a reservation, it may not be long before the Cheyenne . . . and the Sioux . . . and all the others, will be forced to do the same."

Will cradled his carbine under one arm, took his hat off and held it in one hand, while with the other he lifted the bear claw necklace from around his neck. He held the necklace out to

Lone Eagle.

"Take this with you, Lone Eagle. You will soon be taking your father's bones to join your mother's in the cave on Elk Mountain. I would like you to bury this with Bullfrog Charlie. I've seen all the bear claws I want to." He gently touched his side.

Lone Eagle took the necklace and tied it to his saddle. "Thank you, Will."

"General Dodge owes you wages for serving as the scout for the count's hunting party. I'll ask him to send them to the commanding officer at Fort Steele. You can collect the money there. You will need a nest egg for you and Butterfly Morning to start your family."

Lone Eagle nodded and extended a hand. "Goodbye, Will Braddock."

Will shook Lone Eagle's hand. "Good luck, Lone Eagle Munro. I hope we meet again . . . someday soon."

Lone Eagle kicked his pony and raced after the Shoshones.

After he could no longer see Lone Eagle, Will tugged on Buck's reins and headed back to the head of the column. He paused beside the count and Elspeth. "I'd be willing to bet that Hell on Wheels has reached Green River right along with the railroad. If so, we'll have to sneak Elspeth in to avoid running into Paddy O'Hannigan and Mortimer Kavanagh."

CHAPTER 55

Jenny poured another cup of coffee for Butch Cartwright, plunked the pot on the table, and sat down on the bench across from the female stagecoach driver.

"Sorry the replacement teams are in such bad shape, Butch," Jenny said. "Franz has been working to get meat back on the horses, but it's slow business. Papa and Duncan are bringing in new teams from Fort Bridger. Once they get back, we'll have a better selection."

"Can't be helped. Not your fault. Solomon Tucker weren't much good as a station manager. Drunk most of the time. Soon's he got word Wells Fargo was bringing your dad in to replace him, he quit taking care of the animals."

The back door to the Green River Station opened and Jenny turned to see what had caused it.

"Will!" He'd really surprised her, even though she knew he would eventually return from the hunting trip.

Will stepped into the room, pulling the door closed behind him.

"Hello, Jenny. Hello, Butch."

"Welcome back," Jenny said.

"Got any more coffee in that pot?" Will laid his slouch hat on the end of the table and sat on the bench beside Jenny.

Jenny rose and retrieved a cup from a cupboard along the side wall. She returned and poured coffee for Will. "What brings you here alone?" she asked. "Where's the rest of the count's party?"

Will blew his breath across the steaming cup and took a sip. "Hmm, good." He set the cup on the table. "Elspeth needs your help, Jenny."

"Elspeth? I heard something about her being in trouble with Mort Kavanagh. Is that what this is all about?"

"Yes, it is."

Will told Jenny and Butch how Elspeth had double-crossed Paddy O'Hannigan and her fear of retribution from Kavanagh when she arrived in Green River. "The count's party is halted a couple of hours north of here," he said. "I came on ahead, hoping to find you. If I can sneak Elspeth into the station, maybe you can hide her."

"What good's it going to do to hide her?" Jenny asked. "She can't stay here forever. Kavanagh and Paddy are both in town. Hell on Wheels is well established here, and they're not going anywhere real soon."

"I didn't mean for her to stay here. Just keep her hidden until you can sneak her out of here on the stage."

"How do you propose we do this?" Jenny looked at Will.

"It'll be dark soon. I'll bring her in the back door. When are you leaving, Butch?"

"First light. Waiting for the teams to rest. They're short good replacements here, and I prefer the horses I came in with to any they've got in the corral."

"The count and his two companions want to take the stage. How many passengers do you have?"

"Six, right now. There's room for nine inside. I can reserve the remaining three seats. That'll give us a full coach. One will have to ride topside."

"I don't have a shotgun messenger this run," Butch said. "Any of them any good with a shotgun?"

"I'd bet Conrad Eichhorn can handle one. He's the count's gunsmith."

"Then we can accommodate everybody," Jenny said. "What else?"

"We've got a string of pack horses laden with the count's specimens," Will said. "I'll have to find a way to take care of shipping them."

"Oh, didn't you know?" Jenny said. "Your uncle is here. He's managing the UP's business in Green River."

"He is? Great. He can arrange the shipment of the count's smelly hides back East. Get them off my hands, finally." Will laughed.

"I'll ask him to be here first thing in the morning," Jenny said.

"Sounds like we've got a plan. I'll bring Elspeth. You can get her into the coach before the count and the main hunting party arrive. Once that string of pack horses comes into view, Kavanagh will know Count von Schroeder is back. You'll need to get moving quickly once the count's onboard." Will grunted when he stood.

"What was that groan?" Jenny ask. "You that worn out?"

"Just a bear scratch."

"What do you mean, just a bear scratch?"

Will told her about the run-in with the grizzly and the buffalo sinew stitching the Shoshone woman had done. He pulled his buckskin jacket open and pointed out the rips in his wool shirt, which Elspeth had repaired for him.

"Let me see that bandage," Jenny said.

"Elspeth's been nursing me. She rewrapped me before we left the Shoshone camp." Will unbuttoned his shirt and revealed the bandage that encircled his rib cage. Steaks of dried blood showed through the faded white cloth.

"Take that shirt off and sit down. I'm going to change that bandage."

Jenny took the shirt from Will and laid it on the table. She slowly peeled the stained cloth off the wounds, causing only minor bleeding in a few places. She leaned forward to study the wounds and touched one of the sinew stitches.

"Ow," he said. "That hurts."

"That's some neat stitching. That Shoshone woman probably makes fine clothing too." Jenny looked up at Will and grinned.

"Very funny," he said.

"You're getting so full of holes," she said, "I'll soon be able to look right through you. First an arrow, then a knife, and now a bear's claws." She poked one of the old wounds in his left arm with her finger.

"Humph." He pulled his arm away from her prodding.

"Now stand still while I wash that dried blood off." She cleaned the wound and replaced the bandage, then handed him back his shirt. "That ought to hold you together for a while longer. Now off with you."

Four hours later the back door opened again, and Will escorted Jenny's sister inside.

"Jenny," said Elspeth, "I'm sorry to put you in this position."

"Oh, forget it, Elspeth. What are sisters for?" Jenny held out her arms and smiled.

Elspeth cuddled into her embrace. "Thank you, Jenny. I've been such a fool."

"Dear Elspeth. We all make mistakes. But what are you planning to do once we get you away from here?"

"Wolfgang . . . I mean, Count von Schroeder has agreed to set me up as a milliner in Sacramento. But first I have to get there in one piece. Mort's going to want to kill me."

"Well," said Jenny. "Let's see what we can do about getting

you away from his clutches. You ready, Butch?"

Jenny watched her sister look at Butch, then back to her. "Who's Butch? And what's he got to do with it?"

"Well, first of all, Butch is the stagecoach driver that's going to take you away from here in the morning. And secondly, Butch is a woman."

Jenny laughed when Elspeth's mouth fell open.

"Butch will sneak you into the coach before the others get on board," Jenny said, "but you'd better wear my old bonnet to hide those blonde curls."

"I'll leave you ladies to it," Will said. "I've got to get back and bring the count's party in. See you again at first light." He slipped out the back door.

Chapter 56

The sun's first rays streaked over the barren hills that rose above Green River. Will led the count's party into the outskirts of the town that had grown up along the banks of the muddy stream and halted at the Wells Fargo station. "Hello, Jenny!" he called.

Jenny McNabb stepped out of the front door of the station with a grin on her face. Following her out the door was Will's uncle and the six passengers Jenny had mentioned last night.

"Good morning, Jenny. Morning, Uncle Sean." Will stepped out of the saddle.

"Welcome back, Will," his uncle said.

Count von Schroeder, Conrad Eichhorn, and Rupert Ostermann dismounted. Homer climbed down from his horse and took the reins from the three Europeans. By the time he'd gathered up the lead ropes for all the pack horses and Ruby, he had his hands full.

"Don't believe I've had the pleasure, Count von Schroeder." Will's uncle extended a hand. "I'm Sean Corcoran, station manager here in Green River for the Union Pacific."

"Ah, the pleasure is mine." The count clicked his heels and shook the proffered hand.

"I understand you have some specimens to ship," Will's uncle said. "Inasmuch as you are a major investor in the UP, I know General Dodge would want the railroad to make the necessary arrangements for you. Where do you want them sent?"

"To my museum in Germany. Rupert will give you the address of my shipping agent in New York and provide you with a letter of credit." The count waved a hand in the direction of his manservant. "I and my two associates wish to travel on to Sacramento right away."

"I have tickets reserved for you, sir," Jenny said. "Butch has just finished harnessing the teams and is bringing the coach forward now."

"Hiyah. Up." The Concord rumbled out from behind the station.

Will noticed a grin cross the count's face when Elspeth, already seated inside the coach, turned her head and smiled from beneath the confines of a bonnet. "I see you have thought of everything, Herr Braddock," the count said.

Butch climbed down from the driver's seat. "If you folks will be giving me your luggage, I'll stow it in the boot." The passengers lined up and handed their bags to Butch.

"Herr Eichhorn," the count said, "give me one of the Winchesters . . . and a box of ammunition."

Conrad Eichhorn, who had been handing luggage to Butch, paused to pass the rifle and shells to the count.

"Herr Braddock. I present you with this Yellow Boy in appreciation for saving my life, not once but twice. First from the snakes, then from the bear."

Will's mouth fell open as he reached to accept the rifle. "My goodness, sir. Thank you." He ran an appreciative hand down the oiled stock.

"You can sell the pack horses and split the proceeds with Homer, as a bonus."

Will nodded. "Thank you, again. That's very generous, sir."

"It was a most successful hunting trip. I enjoyed myself immensely and accomplished almost everything I had my heart set on. Too bad I could not shoot the white buffalo, but I guess it is better to have kept my scalp." The count laughed.

"We all feel that way, sir," Will said.

"Even though I had my doubts in the beginning," the count said, "I admit now that General Dodge made a wise choice in assigning you as my guide. You did well also in recommending Homer as a cook. He produced wonderful meals from the game we shot. When you see Lone Eagle again, give him my thanks as well. Oh, one other thing. Give this letter to General Dodge." The count took an envelope from a pocket and handed it to Will.

"I will, sir," Will said.

"Homer," Will's uncle said, "how about you help me move these specimens over to the depot and I'll get to work on shipping them. You can take the horses over to the livery stable after we've unloaded them. I'll bet the stable owner will buy the lot."

"Right you is, Mr. Corcoran." Homer gathered up the lead ropes, turned the string of pack horses and Ruby away from the station, and followed Will's uncle toward the railroad depot.

"Luggage is secure," Butch said. She appeared from behind the coach and opened the door on the passenger compartment. "Time to roll, folks. All aboard."

"You are Herr Conrad Eichhorn?" asked Jenny.

"Ja."

"I am sorry, but we don't have a seat inside for all of you. Will suggested you might be willing to ride up top with the driver and serve as shotgun messenger."

"Ja. I would enjoy that." Eichhorn nodded to Butch and climbed up onto the driver's seat.

Count von Schroeder and Rupert boarded and selected the rear facing seat beneath the driver's box, sandwiching Elspeth between them. Jenny helped the other passengers, two couples and two single men, get settled into the remaining seats.

"Looks like a nice day for a ride, ladies and gentlemen," Jenny said. "I realize you folks didn't have any choice, but Wells

Fargo appreciates your business." She folded the steps back beneath the coach's body and pushed the door closed.

"Hold on there!" Mortimer Kavanagh hurried up the street, an arm raised. "I need to speak to the count."

Count von Schroeder leaned out the front window of the coach. "Herr Kavanagh. What a pleasant surprise. You need not have come to see me off."

"Where's my niece, Elspeth?" Kavanagh asked. He stood beneath the window looking up at the count.

"Why, I do not know. Didn't she return to your saloon already?"

"No, she did not. It's imperative that I speak with her immediately."

"There she is!" An Irish-accented brogue shouted the warning.

Will spun around to see Paddy O'Hannigan peering from behind the station, pointing a pistol at the coach.

"She's hiding beneath a bonnet right there beside the count, Mort!" Paddy shouted. "If she doesn't get out, I'll shoot her."

Blam!

A shotgun blast roared from the driver's box. Will watched Paddy duck back out of sight as splinters flew from the roof of the building, just above his head. If Conrad Eichhorn had been a practiced shot with the stagecoach's shotgun, Paddy would be dead.

Will stepped forward and slapped the rear horse on the rump. "Get out of here, Butch."

"Hiyah!" Butch snapped her whip and the Concord coach lurched away.

Chapter 57

"I'm going after him," Will said. He handed the box of rifle shells to Jenny. "Hold this while I load."

Jenny held the box open for him. "I'm going with you."

"No, you're not! You stay here. Get inside. I don't know where he is. He might come back this way."

"What makes you think he'd do that?"

"I don't know." Will fed one shell after another into the loading gate in the side of the Winchester. "I just know Paddy's been giving us trouble for too long. It's time to put an end to it."

"What's the meaning of all this?" Kavanagh stepped between Will and Jenny. "What was Elspeth doing hiding in the coach? Why did that shotgun messenger shoot at O'Hannigan? Why was Count von Schroeder in such a hurry to leave Green River?"

"That's too many questions to answer right now," Will said.

"I demand some explanations." Mort Kavanagh planted his hands firmly on his hips. "What's your sister up to?"

Will grinned when Jenny looked at Kavanagh, raised her eyebrows, and shrugged. Dumping the remaining cartridges from the box into his pants pocket, Will raised a departing hand to Jenny, then trotted down the side of the building.

At the back corner of the station, he knelt and studied the ground. He easily picked up the fresh boot tracks indicating the direction Paddy had headed. He'd get the Irish rascal this time. Will rose and took off at a run.

The footprints leading away from the rear of the station toward the river pressed deeply into the soft soil, making it easy for Will to follow his prey in the early morning light. The trail made an abrupt right turn to the south where the high bank dropped away to the narrow body of water flowing below. Green River had gouged out a miniature canyon at this point, leaving steep bluffs on either side. Will paused and scanned ahead. He spotted the bowler hat a hundred yards away and raced after Paddy.

His side throbbed with each pounding step he took along the cliff's edge. His healing wounds from the bear's clawing grew more painful and he stopped running. Raising the Winchester, he sighted down the barrel and drew a bead on Paddy. He took a deep breath and groaned as his lungs expanded, creating even more discomfort to his rib cage. He forced himself to hold his breath while he adjusted his sighting to compensate for the breeze that blew across his face from the right. He squeezed the trigger. The rifle recoiled sharply against his shoulder when it fired.

The bowler hat sailed off Paddy's head and disappeared down the riverbank. Will chuckled. That's the third time he'd shot the hat off the Irishman's head. He'd done it a year ago in Julesburg and three months ago in California.

Paddy glanced back over his shoulder as he picked up his pace.

"Stop, O'Hannigan! Or the next round goes into your back."

Paddy raised an arm and Will saw the smoke puff from the barrel of the pistol at the same time he heard the sound of the shot his enemy fired at him. A bullet whizzed past his ear, followed quickly by a second one that dug into the dirt at his feet.

Will levered another shell into the chamber of the Winchester and raised the rifle again. He couldn't bring himself to back-shoot the man, but he could certainly wound him. He aimed low and pulled the trigger. When the smoke cleared from the muzzle, Paddy hopped toward the railroad yard that lay ahead of them. Will had hit the Irish thug in the leg.

Paddy snapped two more shots in Will's direction, then disappeared between two boxcars parked along a siding. Will proceeded more cautiously now. Paddy could hide behind or beneath a railcar and ambush him.

When Will approached the spot where Paddy had disappeared, he crouched and peered beneath one of the boxcars to see if he could spot legs. A whistle signaled the approach of a train on the main track. The ground shook gently from the vibrations created by a string of freight cars.

Stepping around the sidetracked boxcars, Will kept his rifle at the ready. He checked the ground alongside the tracks and spotted drops of blood, confirming he'd wounded Paddy. Across the expanse of half-a-dozen tracks comprising Green River's railroad yard, Will watched a freight train gliding slowly by on the main line, heading east toward the temporary bridge that crossed the river. Two quick blasts of the engine's whistle signaled the engineer was clear of the station buildings and planned to increase speed. Puffs of black smoke belched from the locomotive's stack, indicating the engineer had pushed the throttle forward.

Will scanned the width of the yard before him. Paddy had to be hiding someplace close by. There! Just as the last of the cars in the freight train eased past the depot, Paddy jumped from the station platform onto the last car, a flatcar hooked behind a string of a dozen boxcars. Paddy limped down the length of the flatcar and reached to climb the ladder leading to the roof of the next car in line, one of the boxcars.

Will raised his rifle, but a group of workers spreading ballast along one of the intervening tracks appeared in his sights. He couldn't take a chance on hitting them. He jumped when something brushed his shoulder.

Jenny appeared at his side. The sound of her coming up behind him had been masked by the rumbling of the passing freight cars.

"What are you doing here?" he asked.

Jenny held up her Colt pistol.

"I told you to stay back, *Miss* McNabb."

"You don't *tell* me to do anything, *Mr.* Braddock." Her eyes glared at him, their blue irises turning a deep gray. "I'm entitled to a shot at him. He tried to kill me, too."

"Here, keep this." Will extended the Winchester to Jenny. "I'm going after him, but I can't climb onto that train holding a rifle."

Jenny grasped the Winchester.

Will raced across the rail yard at an angle to intercept the end of the train before it reached the bridge over Green River. Paddy continued to hobble forward from one boxcar to the next, pausing momentarily to regain his balance after he'd leaped from the top of one to another.

The engineer whistled his approach to the bridge. Workers constructing the stone pilings of the UP's permanent bridge they were building adjacent to the temporary wooden truss laid down their tools and stepped back to await the passage of the freight.

Will dashed across the open space between the sidings and the main line, catching up to the trailing flatcar before it reached the bridge. He grasped the rungs of the ladder at the rear of the car and pulled himself up.

Wow! His side hurt with the jerk on his rib cage as he heaved himself onto the bed of the empty flatcar. He felt the stitches pull tight where they held the wounds together from the bear's clawing.

The train swayed significantly as it rolled onto the open

trusses of the bridge. Will got to his feet and struggled to maintain his balance. He stumbled down the length of the flatcar and reached across the gap to grab the ladder that led to the top of the boxcar. The pain from extending his arm and stretching his side caused him to grit his teeth, but he stepped forward onto the ladder. He hugged the ladder's steel side rails and remained motionless while he caught his breath.

He climbed the rungs and eased his head above the back edge of the boxcar. Paddy was three cars ahead of him.

Blam!

Splinters plastered his cheek where Paddy's shot blasted the wooden roof next to his head. He ducked as another shot whined off the top of the metal ladder. That was Paddy's sixth shot, by Will's count. He'd have a few seconds to climb onto the top of the car while Paddy reloaded. Or had Paddy already reloaded?

Will took the final steps up the ladder and lunged forward onto his stomach on the top of the car. He withdrew his revolver from its holster and cocked it. Paddy was loading his pistol.

"Drop the gun, O'Hannigan!" Will shouted. "Don't make me kill you." That's what he probably should do, but he didn't like the idea of murdering the Irishman. Now that he had the chance, he wasn't sure he could live with that.

Paddy continued to plunge the rammer into the cylinders of his revolver to complete the reloading.

Will pointed the revolver at Paddy. The rocking of the train made aiming difficult. He pulled the trigger.

Paddy grabbed his leg and sat down, dropping his gun onto the roof of the car. Will had hit him again. Was it the same leg he'd hit with the rifle shot?

"Ye're not going to stop me, Braddock! I'll kill ye, and ye're uncle, and that bloody nigger, if it's the last thing I do." Paddy rolled down the sloping roof and tumbled off the top of the boxcar.

Will scooted to the edge of his car and watched Paddy drop down the depth of the trestle and plunge into the water. Why would he jump? Could Paddy survive hitting the water from this height?

Would Paddy be able to swim his way out of the swiftly flowing river? Will remembered the incident at the beaver dam the previous summer when he'd heard Paddy tell Lone Eagle he didn't know how to swim. And now one of Paddy's legs bore a wound—maybe both legs. How could Paddy O'Hannigan ever make good on his vendetta threat?

Chapter 58

Jenny leaned over Ida's neck and pointed toward the water flowing beneath the railroad bridge. "You mean Paddy fell all the way down there?"

"Yes." Will sat Buck beside Jenny on the cliff above Green River. "I got off the train as soon as I could on the far side and hoofed it back here. I checked the banks for a mile downstream, but didn't find any trace of him. I don't know if he's still alive, or not."

"You shot him, too?"

"Yes, in a leg—maybe both. There was blood on the roof where he rolled off the car."

"I doubt if we'll ever see him again. I don't see how he could survive such a fall. I remember when we were hiding in the beaver lodge, we heard him say he couldn't swim. Even if hitting the water from such a distance didn't kill him, he probably drowned."

"I wouldn't be too sure. That Irish ruffian seems to have more lives than a cat."

Jenny shook her head and looked at Will. "And how are you this morning?"

Will shrugged.

"If you don't have to keep chasing after Paddy O'Hannigan, maybe you can let those bear scratches heal. I'm running out of bandages." Jenny laughed. She had re-bandaged his wounds when he'd returned to the Wells Fargo station after his encounter with Paddy.

"Thanks for patching me up . . . again."

"What I'm looking forward to is the day I can take those buffalo sinew stitches out of you." She grinned.

"Humph! I'm not looking forward to that." The sinew stitches had hurt badly enough when Moon Woman had inserted them. He didn't want to think about what it would feel like to have them pulled out.

A train approached the bridge from the far side of the river, opposite where Will and Jenny sat their horses. Two quick whistles and a clanging bell announced the train's arrival at the Green River depot. The locomotive pulled a short string of three boxcars and a single passenger coach.

"That's General Dodge's private car," Will said. "Let's go see what's going on."

The two of them wheeled their horses away from the river and rode to the platform that stretched down the track side of the depot. The train stopped and General Dodge emerged from the rear of the coach at the same time Will's uncle and Homer stepped out of the station building.

"Well, everybody's here to greet me, I see," Dodge said. He stepped from the railcar onto the platform. "Nice to see you all."

Will raised a hand in greeting. He hadn't seen the chief engineer since he'd been given the assignment to escort the count's hunting party.

"Corcoran," Dodge said, "Now that we're almost across Wyoming it's time to get serious about where we're going to join up with the Central Pacific in Utah. We should effect that joining sometime early next year. You know our competitor's managers better than anyone, since you met with them in California last spring. Silas Seymour's out in Utah messing with the route again. I can't afford to have him deciding where we hook up with the CP. I need you to get out there and help Sam Reed deflect the 'insulting engineer's' meddling."

"We can be on our way in a few hours, General. I'm just wrapping up the shipment of Count von Schroeder's specimens. Soon as that's complete, our work can end here."

"Good. You can take Will and Homer with you. We can probably find something useful for them to do." Dodge turned and motioned for Will to join him.

Will dismounted directly onto the depot's platform, handing Buck's reins to Jenny. He approached Dodge and extended his hand. "Hello, sir."

"Hello, Will," Dodge said.

"Let me introduce Jennifer McNabb, sir." Will indicated Jenny with a wave of his hand in her direction. "She works for Wells Fargo."

"How do you do, young lady." Dodge lifted his hat.

"General Dodge, it's a pleasure." Jenny nodded from Ida's saddle.

"How was the hunting expedition?" Dodge asked. "Your uncle just said he's sending specimens someplace for the count."

Will summarized the expedition's incidents, including Lone Eagle's participation. "Oh," he said, "the count asked me to give you this letter." He extracted the envelope from his haversack and passed it to Dodge.

Dodge quickly read the letter, then looked at Will. "According to this, you did a fine job. Count von Schroeder writes he is so pleased with the results of his expedition that he plans to buy more Union Pacific bonds. That'll please Doc Durant, for sure."

The door at the rear of the passenger car opened and a face familiar to Will appeared, struggling to drag a large box camera and its tripod onto the rear platform. Andrew Russell, the Union Pacific's official photographer, smiled when he saw Will. "Will Braddock, as I recall," Russell said.

"Yes, sir, that's right."

"You helped me once before. At Fort Sanders wasn't it?"

"That's right."

"Perhaps I could impose upon you again."

"What can I do?"

"General Dodge brought me along to document some of the historical points. I want to take some pictures of the construction of the new bridge over Green River. You can help me lug this camera gear out there." He motioned down the tracks to the river's edge.

"Certainly. Be glad to."

"We'll only be here an hour or two, Mr. Russell," Dodge said. "As soon as Sean Corcoran and I finish our business, I plan to head this train back. Be ready."

"I'll be ready."

Will helped Russell haul his camera gear and portable developing station out of the passenger car and down to the bridge abutment. Jenny rode Ida alongside them, leading Buck. She dismounted and let the two horses browse on the scrub brush nearby.

Russell busied himself setting up the heavy tripod and inserting the glass plate for his first exposure. "What's that impressive butte called?" He pointed across the river to a prominent, flat-topped peak that jutted high above the rails.

"The locals call it Citadel Rock," Jenny answered.

"Ah, an appropriate name."

Russell worked for an hour exposing a half-dozen plates. "That will do it. We can pack all the gear back on board the general's car now."

After they had returned the camera gear to the passenger car, Will sat beside Jenny on the edge of the station platform. A short time later, General Dodge, Will's uncle, and Homer stepped out of the depot's waiting room.

"You've got your instructions, Corcoran," Dodge said. "Good luck."

"Thank you, sir. We'll do our best."

"General Dodge," Will said. "I told Lone Eagle I would ask you to deposit his guide's salary with the Army at Fort Fred Steele. I think he plans to seek employment there as a scout."

"I can do that," Dodge said. "The next time I see you we'll probably be someplace out in Utah. Thanks again for a good job as hunting guide." The general re-boarded his private coach.

"Will," his uncle said. "Homer and I will pack up the gear and be ready to head out in about an hour. Jenny, I'll say goodbye for now."

"Goodbye, Mr. Corcoran," she replied. "Soon as the railroad tracks get laid beyond here, Papa will close the Green River Station, and we'll head west ourselves."

"Goodbye, Miss McNabb," Homer said. He touched the brim of his hat.

"Goodbye, Homer. I'll see you all in Utah."

Will's uncle and Homer walked down the platform and disappeared around the far end of the station building.

"Guess it's time for us to say goodbye, Jenny," Will said. "Don't know when we'll see each other. Hope it's not too long."

Jenny caressed Will's arm. "Take care of yourself . . . and keep that wound from splitting open until it heals. You should be able to remove the stitches in a couple of weeks if you do."

"Thanks for patching me up . . . again and again." He grinned. "I'd prefer to have you around to take the stitches out, but I guess I'll have to let Homer do it."

Jenny mounted Ida and reined the horse around. She looked back over her shoulder, a smile on her face. Her blue eyes glittered in the sunlight. "Bye, Will." She tapped her heels into the mare's flank.

Will rubbed his hand over the white star on Buck's forehead as he watched her ride away. "Bye, Jenny."

HISTORICAL NOTES

In *Bear Claws,* Will Braddock encounters the following historical characters:

Grenville M. Dodge, Union Pacific's chief engineer

General Ulysses S. Grant, Republican candidate for President

General William Tecumseh Sherman, Commander, Division of the Missouri

General Philip Sheridan, Commander, Department of the Missouri

Jack Casement, Union Pacific's construction contractor (partners with his brother Dan)

Thomas "Doc" Durant, Union Pacific's vice president & general manager

"Colonel" Silas Seymour, Durant's consulting engineer

Jacob Blickensderfer, former Department of Interior railroad inspector

Samuel B. Reed, Union Pacific's engineer of construction

Brigham Young, Mormon leader

James Strobridge, Central Pacific's construction superintendent

Hanna Marie Strobridge, wife of James Strobridge

Samuel S. Montague, Central Pacific's chief engineer

Charles Crocker, one of the "Big Four" Central Pacific founders

James Howden, Central Pacific's Scottish chemist

Andrew J. Russell, Union Pacific's official photographer

All other characters are fictitious.

Will's adventures in *Bear Claws* take place during 1868, the second year of major construction on the transcontinental railroad. The sequence of events in the building of the Union Pacific and Central Pacific occurred as presented.

Union Pacific, Central Pacific, and Wells Fargo are authentic companies. The *Sacramento Union* was the oldest daily newspaper west of the Mississippi River. It closed its doors in 1994. The other businesses Will encounters are fictional. The towns, mountains, streams, and other geographical locales mentioned in the book are real. Hell on Wheels, the itinerant shack town, relocated more frequently than described.

The nitroglycerin attack on Grant's train is the invention of the author. Grant's meeting with Durant did happen and is included in Dodge's autobiography. The dialogue at the Fort Sanders' meeting is imagined, since it was not documented. The meeting between Sean Corcoran and Charles Crocker is the author's creation.

Count Wolfgang von Schroeder is a fictional character, inspired by various historical personages who hunted wild game in the west in the 1800s. Alfred Jacob Miller did produce several paintings, including the one described, for Sir William Drummond Stewart's 1837 hunting expedition.

ABOUT THE AUTHOR

Robert Lee Murphy introduced Will Braddock in his first novel, *Eagle Talons. Bear Claws,* the second book in *The Iron Horse Chronicles* trilogy, continues Will's quest to determine his own destiny, as he works to help build the first transcontinental railroad. Following graduation from the University of Oklahoma, and a seven-year tour in the Army, Murphy worked for over thirty years with national and international organizations on all seven continents, including Antarctica, where Murphy Peak bears his name. During his career, he wrote various articles for magazines and numerous technical and professional documents.

Murphy is a member of Western Writers of America, The Society of Children's Book Writers & Illustrators, and the Railway & Locomotive Historical Society. Visit the author at his website: http://robertleemurphy.net.